He Said Always

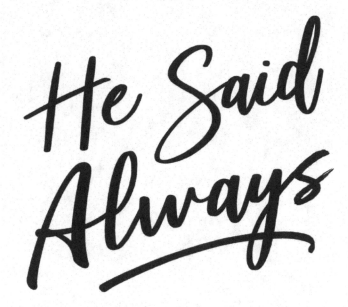

RUTH CARDELLO

Montlake

Published by Montlake, Seattle

www.apub.com

Amazon, the Amazon logo, and Montlake are trademarks of Amazon.com, Inc., or its affiliates.

ISBN-13: 9781542025232
ISBN-10: 1542025230

Cover design by Eileen Carey

Printed in the United States of America

To my friend Nikke:
thank you for bringing joy wherever you go.

Don't miss a thing!

www.ruthcardello.com

Sign up for Ruth's newsletter:
Yes, let's stay in touch!
https://forms.aweber.com/form/00/819443400.htm

Join Ruth's private fan group:
www.facebook.com/groups/ruthiesroadies

Follow Ruth on Goodreads:
www.goodreads.com/author/show/4820876.Ruth_Cardello

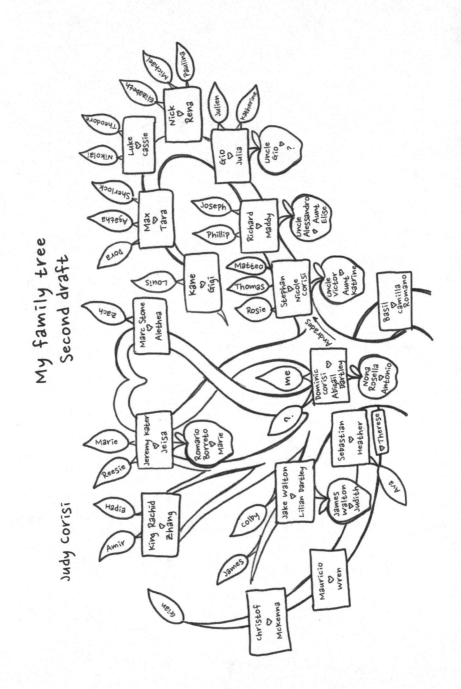

NOTE TO MY READERS

Dominic Corisi first appeared in his own story, *Maid for the Billionaire*. The Corisi family is woven in and out of several of my series in my billionaire world. Each story can be read as a stand-alone, but when the series are read as a whole, readers get to revisit earlier characters and see situations through fresh eyes. I enjoy writing in this world so much I keep adding series to it. Thank you for coming along with me on that journey.

CHAPTER ONE

TEAGAN

I poured myself a second cup of coffee and returned to my desk in the corner of the office beneath my printshop. If I ever told anyone what I was doing, it would probably sound a lot more exciting than it was. I was a basement warrior for a technology battle I hoped would never need me.

Every day I asked myself if I should have taken a job at any one of the tech companies that had courted me while I had been at MIT. If I had, I might have already made the money needed to help the people I loved.

My parents would say I'd been born stubborn and that I tended to take the harder road. That wasn't how I saw myself. The easy road was easy for a reason—it was well traveled, and being on it made little to no difference in the world.

I wanted to help the people I loved, but I also needed to do something about a global storm looming on the horizon. Artificial intelligence was no longer science fiction, and facial recognition was quickly becoming weaponizable.

Most arguments for searchable facial databases were related to public safety—terrorists, pandemic containment, home and workplace security. My concern was the ultimate control it might give someone or something over the masses. My work was intended to ensure that couldn't happen.

When someone invented a spear, someone else created a shield.
Guns? Bulletproof materials.
Poison gases? Filtration masks.

So far the same companies that were creating facial-recognition software were the ones that could produce a counterforce to it. But they would never. Laws might rise up and prevent what I feared was coming, but I wasn't one to put all my trust in any government.

Even though the nature of my work required I live a bit of a reclusive lifestyle, I loved people as a whole, and that was what my work was designed to protect. Not just Americans—all humanity would be affected if technology took a jump beyond what we were prepared to control.

Already AIs could farm social media sources and compile an insane amount of information about a person. The technology was available to get a near-instant profile of a person with nothing more than a phone app. I didn't see anywhere good that could go if left unchecked.

Everything I did in my lab was with one goal in mind—creating human invisibility to technology. In many areas I was making real progress. Well, not so much me as the two completely independent AI systems I'd created and given adversarial roles to.

NYSM (Now You See Me) and NYD (Now You Don't) were competitive in the most beautiful way. NYD first was given the task of designing images and sounds that could mask human presence. Certain shapes confused even the best systems into misinterpreting an image and disregarding the presence of a face. No face, no facial recognition. Certain sounds could mask the human voice. Yes, both were still detectable to the human eye and ear, but that in itself severely limited the use of surveillance video as a tracking device. The second AI system, NYSM, was more or less a test-drive for whatever my first came up with. Keeping them on par with what governments and large companies were using did require a certain amount of hacking, but I felt no guilt about it. Watching the watchers didn't hit my immorality radar.

The problem with fooling an AI was that they were constantly learning and evolving. My research required testing and recording the amount of time any technique remained effective with NYSM and then pushing NYD to create a new image once one became ineffective. If my work was ever discovered, it could easily be nullified. Uploading NYD's database of masking images and sounds to surveillance AIs would remove the learning curve, making human presence instantly detectable again.

Would my work one day pay for the medical bills of the woman I considered my second mother? God, I hoped so. For the time being, I sold ridiculous apps on the side to pay my own bills and used a T-shirt printshop both as a cover for my lab and as a way to employ my best friend, Riley Ragsdale, so she could make the payments for her mother herself. Some women were predominantly career driven, some were nurturers, and some were both. I would have been solely the first if it weren't for the Ragsdales.

My parents were good, hardworking people, but I'd never been the child they'd hoped for. They'd met and worked at our city's town hall. Mom was an assessor; Dad issued dog and marriage licenses. She joked that meant she was able to spot a good thing when she saw it. He joked that he had the paperwork to make all her plans legal. Happily married. Adorable. Completely unprepared to raise a daughter who'd discovered how to navigate the dark web by the age of twelve.

Unlike the children their friends had, I hadn't stayed out past my curfew, shown much interest in making many friends, or had any desire to go to school dances. Everything I was interested in was online. I never understood why anyone would want to waste time talking to a pimply-faced teenage boy who was 99.9 percent hormones when, with a few keyboard clicks and a little knowledge of how to break an encryption code, they could access philosophical discussions with some of the greatest minds around the globe.

3

Not that any of them knew me—I lurked and listened. *If I ever do save the world, it'll be quietly from behind the scenes.*

My mother saw my lack of feminine attire as a failure on her part. I gave her credit for trying to make me into a mini-her, but it wasn't meant to be. My father routinely asked me how I was, but always in the way someone would when *fine* was all they wanted to hear. They were both highly likable people who enjoyed a good bottle of wine with dinner. Their friends were the same. What I remembered most about my childhood was how our house had always been full of adults who drank just enough to be a little sloppy, laughed at jokes I didn't find amusing, and aspired to nothing beyond having free time to do more social drinking with like-minded adults.

They'd retired to Florida. I missed them—and I didn't. There was something nice about not having to justify who I was constantly.

I would have felt alone if I didn't have the Ragsdales. Riley and I had met in middle school while serving detention. She was there for talking too much in class. I'd gotten in trouble for accessing the school's website and putting a mustache on the photos of all the teachers I didn't like. I didn't like many of them.

What bothered my teachers the most, according to my parents, was that I would have been a straight A student if class participation hadn't been part of the grading system. They thought I wasn't living up to my potential. I didn't agree. Sure, I stayed up all night online reading about everything and anything, which meant I slept through most of my classes, but why did I need to stay awake if I could ace their tests after a good nap?

I'd begged—*begged*—to be homeschooled, but my parents had thought I needed socialization. I couldn't say they'd been entirely wrong. If I hadn't gone to school, I wouldn't have met Riley or discovered a family I fit into.

Riley's mother wasn't a healthy woman, but she was 100 percent love. I'd felt accepted by her from the first time we'd met. Fara was in chronic pain from an old back injury and wasn't able to work, but she inspired me in other ways. The apartment in which she'd raised her twin children, Riley and Kal, was in a tough part of town and yet was where I'd always felt the safest.

Fara's home was family centered. She sat with us every day after school and was the only reason I did any of my homework. Fundamentally, I didn't believe in practicing a skill I'd already mastered, but completing those assignments was important to Fara, so it was important to me. With her I had a mother figure who approved of me.

Riley was the sister I'd always wanted; Kal was the sometimes annoying but always loved brother. I spent so much time at their home I often wondered why my parents weren't concerned, but they might have been relieved. I'd never again hacked into the school's website with Fara in my life because I'd never wanted to disappoint her.

A few years ago, Fara had been heartbroken when her insurance hadn't paid for a major operation, so her children had both dropped out of college to work and help her cover the bill. I'd taken an accelerated program and already graduated from MIT with the dream of working on something important, or I might have done the same.

I was a problem solver by nature. Riley needed a job, and I needed a place where I could work in secrecy. We came up with the perfect plan: she ran a printshop upstairs while I did my research downstairs. The shop brought in just enough money to allow me to pay Riley a steady, albeit modest, salary and allowed us to remain very much a part of each other's lives.

My phone vibrated with a message from Riley telling me she'd be late. No one could call her lazy. Both she and Kal worked more than one job. Riley's latest side gig was as a paid bridesmaid. I hadn't even known that was a thing until she'd told me she wanted to try it. Kal had done some modeling but was making most of his income as an exotic dancer. Neither enjoyed what they did, but they'd sworn they'd pay off Fara's medical bills in full, and they were getting close to finally doing it.

Unfortunately Fara needed one more surgery—one that promised to ease her pain. My hope was that one of my apps would take off and make enough money to pay for that.

Of course, NYD could easily bring in millions, but I couldn't take the shortsighted easy road. Stubborn, just like my parents always said I was. One day humanity might need the ability to hide from technology. I wasn't willing to risk being the reason they couldn't.

Not even for Fara. It wasn't a decision I came to easily.

I called Riley so I could continue to type while we spoke. "How late do you think you'll be?"

"Not sure. This bride is driving me crazy. She wants me to answer her calls all hours of the day and night. The errand should be a quick one."

"Say no. Boundaries."

Riley sighed. "I would, but this is her wedding. You only get one."

"More than forty percent of those who get married will divorce. Nearly eighty percent of people who get divorced will remarry within four years. There is a good chance it won't be her only wedding."

"Why do you even know that? Forget I asked that. It doesn't matter. Wipe those stats out of your head. You can't go into marriage thinking it'll end."

"I'm not even dating anyone, so marriage stats—good or bad—are irrelevant to my situation."

"Work with me. For romance to happen you have to be open to it."

"Last week you told me Mr. Right appears when a woman is not looking for him."

"That's true too."

My mother didn't care as much about my love life as Riley did. I loved her for it, though, because nothing she said was in judgment. She just wanted to see me happy. "You're spending too much time with brides. I'm perfectly happy the way I am."

"So am I, but if we did this right, we could raise our families together."

"You're not dating anyone either."

I could imagine her rolling her eyes. "True, but I'm open to the idea."

"I'm open. Hey, Universe, if you want to send me Mr. Right, I'll head upstairs right now and let him in."

"You shouldn't mock fate, or you'll end up married before I am."

"I think I have it now. I'm keeping myself open to love, closed to the reality of the failure rate of it, optimistic but not in a way that might imply I'm eager for a serious relationship—unless you find someone first, and then I need to close the deal with some lucky man so we can pop out babies at the same time."

"Exactly."

I laughed. Riley was the perfect friend for me. It didn't matter what we were discussing—by the end of the conversation I always felt better. "Dinner tonight?"

"I wish I could. I'll see how this morning goes. Kal's out of town, and Mom isn't feeling well, so it would be just me and you if it happens."

"I'm good with whatever. See you in a bit."

After ending the call, I returned to poring over the results of NYD's latest image. My conversation with Riley echoed in my thoughts, distracting me. Normally the upstairs shop remained locked up whenever she wasn't there, but this morning it bothered me that it would be.

I shook my head, closed out the report I was reading, and stood. I didn't believe in fate or the power of wishful thinking, but I had just promised the universe my shop would be open. I felt ridiculous as I left my office and armed the security system behind me.

Open without being eager? The least I could do was unlock the door.

If nothing else, opening the shop because the universe might be sending over Mr. Right would make for an amusing story to tell Riley later. With Fara not feeling well lately, we all needed more reasons to smile.

CHAPTER TWO

GIAN

I parked outside a T-shirt printshop in a town just south of Boston. Its door had bars similar to those on the beauty shop to the left and the tailor shop on the right. As I stepped out of my car, I wondered if I'd put the wrong address into my GPS.

A mistake like that would have been out of character for me, but I had a lot on my mind. The day had started with a meeting with my brothers regarding my plans, or lack thereof, for what to do now that I'd finally graduated. It wasn't as if I hadn't had time to think about it. After completing my MBA, I'd circled back to my original interest in medicine and gotten a doctorate in biomedical engineering. All by the age of twenty-eight. Impressive, I guess, if I had plans for how to use either. My interests sadly didn't add up to a career that would fit into my life. My parents were first-generation immigrants from Italy. Their values were considerably more traditional than mine.

That morning my brother Mauricio had joked that I was the best-educated unemployed person he knew. I'd laughed, but the truth of his words had stung. I needed to get my shit together.

Eight years ago my life had made sense. Back then, I'd been the youngest of four sons, enrolled in a premed program at Johns Hopkins, with the intention of becoming a family doctor.

A trip to Italy to meet family I hadn't known existed had changed everything. Suddenly I was the brother of Dominic Corisi, one of the wealthiest men on the planet and arguably one of the most notorious. Most of his reputation had been built before he'd met his wife, Abby. Leave it to a schoolteacher to be able to rein in the unruly.

Judy Corisi, Dominic's daughter, was the reason I found myself in this part of town. She would not be happy when she learned I'd won our bet, but losing was good for her. At nearly twenty, she felt more like a sister than a niece, and this wasn't the first time we'd pitted our detective skills against each other.

As I stood outside the printshop, my thoughts went back to a few days earlier, when she'd challenged me to meet her inside my brother Christof's underground bunker at Decker Park to see which of us could access it faster. It had a high-tech, government-level security system that was touted as impenetrable and had been a wedding present to Christof and McKenna from often-over-the-top Dominic.

I could have said no to Judy, but she would have only chosen another accomplice, and lately I'd begun to worry about her. I hadn't seen her in a couple of weeks, but from what I'd heard, she'd been engaging in some dangerous behavior. For someone who had been born with every opportunity, she neither had many friends nor seemed to value her personal safety. If something was off limits, she wanted in. I'd joined in on many of her escapades mostly to keep her out of trouble. Compared to so much of what she'd done recently, breaking into a bunker that was owned by a member of our family was tame.

A beep from the bunker's security system indicated that Judy had breached it. If the system had been designed by anyone but Alethea Stone, one of Dominic's head security people, I would have put my money on Judy completely circumventing it. Judy was good, but she had yet to best Alethea.

I checked my watch and turned in a swivel chair to face the main entry. Judy was one minute early. The grin on her face when she waltzed into the living room area was classic smug Corisi. "Entire security system disabled in less than three minutes. Aunt Alethea should have taken my advice and used a DNA reader rather than an encrypted numeric pad. How did you get by it?" She plopped into the swivel chair next to me.

"I asked Christof for the code."

"That's cheating!" She smacked her hands on her thighs.

"Is it? I don't recall setting parameters on how we'd acquire entry. That lapse was yours, my friend. Not my fault your instructions weren't more detailed."

She folded her arms across her chest. "I can't believe you asked for the code."

"You didn't break the system, did you?" Although the place belonged to my brother and his wife, I never liked to cause trouble for the Romanos.

I shook my head at the thought. *I am a Romano.*

Not a Corisi, even though my biological mother still went by her maiden name. I'd decided not to look into my biological father after learning that Dominic's father might have had him killed. Antonio Corisi was deceased as well, so did it matter? Life was complicated enough without digging for issues.

Judy interrupted my thoughts. "Break it? Any changes I made will only improve it. Plus, if I did it right, no one will even know I was here." Apparently she wasn't aware she'd tripped the alarm at all.

Another beep was immediately followed by the lights flickering and the doors on both ends of the room slamming shut. I wasn't surprised. Alethea was as dramatic as Judy. "You were saying?"

"Shit. What did I miss?" Her phone buzzed with a message. She made a face as she read it. "External thermal-detection cameras. I should have thought of that. Very funny. We're locked in for an hour. Two if I attempt to break out." She rolled her eyes skyward, then read another incoming message. "Marc just texted that Alethea is joking and offered to send pizza."

Marc, a retired Marine, was Alethea's husband and headed Dominic Corisi's security team. He'd designed this multilevel bunker. Several large themed pods branched off from the main area. One had the feel of a city apartment. Another had a cabin, with a stream deep enough to swim in and a starlit ceiling. My favorite was the deserted island equipped with fake palm trees, sandy beaches, and a house on stilts. It wasn't as cool as the underwater section of the one he'd designed for Dominic's own family, but it was still far outside anything I'd ever imagined.

"Tell him we'll take it."

"It'll be here in twenty." Almost instantly, the doors swung open again. Judy stood and repocketed her phone in her torn jeans. Similar to that of her supersleuth aunt, her appearance was deliberately neutral. "You're all damn cheaters. Even without the cameras, Marc knows I'm here; my bodyguard is parked outside. It's not fair."

"Life isn't fair," I said lightly. "You'll beat them one day."

Judy took out her phone again and flounced into the chair beside me. She spoke as she texted. "I will, and when I do, I'll leave their asses locked in." She frowned at her phone as messages buzzed back. "He said he's okay with that. I'd ask why, but I'm sure I don't want to know."

I laughed. In some ways Judy was old beyond her years. In others, she was more sheltered than most. She needed to get out and mingle more. "I heard you're not applying to colleges again this year."

"I learn best on my own."

"By testing Alethea's security systems? Have you considered that you might be able to beat her if you entertained the possibility that you don't know everything?"

Judy spun her chair in my direction. "I recognize that tone. What's wrong?"

I stood and took a moment before answering. On the one hand, Judy was young, and I didn't want to put her in the middle of anything. On the other hand, this was Judy, and I doubted there was much I could tell her she didn't already know. "Your father is building a research facility for me."

"I know."

"I told him not to."

"He wants to help you. When you were at Johns Hopkins, you enjoyed the research aspect of medicine."

"I did, but that's no longer where my goals lie." My area of interest would have been too controversial for my family to handle. I chuckled inwardly at what Dominic's reaction would have been had I told him I'd like the facility to focus on the health benefits of multiple orgasms. *Yeah, no.*

Sex was something many people still found uncomfortable to talk about. Much like the bottom of the ocean, there was so much we didn't understand about our own bodies, at least when it came to pleasure.

I couldn't think of another pastime that people wanted to engage in as frequently without an expectation of improvement. For many, sex was almost something that happened to them rather than an act they had any quality control over. As technology made orgasms measurable, there was an opportunity for real empowerment. A person's journey could be charted.

I'd always enjoyed sex, but I'd encountered several women who didn't. Helping them take ownership of their own pleasure had been rewarding. Being better informed directly correlated to better sex for many. How informed could anyone be without data?

It wasn't an area of study my family could ever have accepted.

"So you have goals?" Her eyebrow arched.

It was a fair question. "I'm still clarifying them, but I know what I don't want to do. I don't want to head your father's research facility."

"Have you told him that?"

"Only about a thousand times."

Judy frowned. "He adores you. Nothing matters more to him than family."

I didn't doubt that, but Dominic didn't respect boundaries. He came into a person's life like a bull released in a china shop. He was a lot like Judy: *no* wasn't a word in his vocabulary. I understood that he did it all out of love—and perhaps because he felt guilty he hadn't known about me. Still, it was too much.

When I'd first found out Dominic was my brother, I'd imagined we'd be as close as I was with my other brothers. So far that hadn't been possible. It wasn't that he didn't value my opinion. He'd have to hear me to feel one way or another about what I thought. My life made more sense, felt more in control, the farther I was from his gravitational pull.

He'd backed off while I'd been in school, but my recent graduation had given him an opening to once again think my life required his assistance—in the form of a complete takeover. Unless I wanted another doctorate, it was a situation I needed to address.

I didn't want to get to the point of cutting him out of my life altogether, though things had been a lot easier since I'd done that with my biological mother. With her, there was always something to prove, discuss, or forgive. It was exhausting and pointless. I'd been relieved when she'd finally returned her attention to her older children.

Too bad I couldn't produce another family member for Dominic to focus on. *Actually, I probably could.* "Judy, didn't you once wonder if your father had other siblings? From his father while Rosella was in hiding?"

"It made sense that he might have. My grandmother was gone for years."

"Did you ever find any?"

Judy's expression turned serious, and she was quiet for a moment, as if reliving something in her mind. "I stopped looking. The last time I tried to find family for my father, we nearly lost him. Alethea says not every truth should be known. I don't like it, but I agree with her. If my parents had broken up because of something he did in Italy, it would have been my fault. I pushed him into a situation he didn't want."

"Your parents didn't divorce." I ruffled her hair, a move I knew she didn't like. Better to be annoyed than sad. "And that situation brought us into each other's lives. What you did was a good thing."

She began to pace. "Trust me; I've thought about that. I could have another aunt or uncle out there." She pursed her lips. "Maybe even a less annoying cousin."

Cute. "You could simply ask Alethea. You know she knows."

Her shoulders hunched. "I'm not so sure about that. Now that she's a mother, she's so careful. I asked her if we could scale the Downey Building to test their system, and she said it wasn't worth the risk. That is not the Alethea I knew. Are children mojo killers?"

"My brothers would say they're the opposite. They appear happier since they've started multiplying."

"So in your mind more family is always a good thing?"

"Absolutely."

"Which means you'd be open to poring over old medical records. Possibly hacking into a DNA database to find out if my father has more family. We could put a little wager on this—see which of us is able to find a sibling faster."

"That sounds like a horrible idea."

"Because you know I'd win."

"Because I don't want to go to jail."

"It's only illegal if you get caught."

"No." I got the irony of trying to think of a way to talk her out of an idea I'd just planted in her head. "I do think it would be nice to know if you have more family out there, but—"

"It would improve your relationship with my father."

"I doubt that."

"Oh, it would. Because when I beat you, and I will, you'll race my father at Decker Park."

Yeah, no. "No one races your father." When Dominic flew around the racetrack, it was a solo ride in one of the world's fastest cars. No one

14

challenged him, because no one wanted to either be crushed by him or, worse, somehow beat him. He was a man nobody wanted to be on the bad side of. The race wasn't something I'd have to worry about, though, because when it came to sleuthing, I often beat Judy. "What happens when you lose?"

"I'll find you a car that's faster than my father's."

"Hang on—so either way I race Dominic? How is that a wager?"

"Call it a solution instead. Do you want him to hear you when you speak?"

"I do."

"Then you need to win that race."

In a tone heavy with sarcasm, I'd responded, "Sure, that sounds like a solid plan."

Still outside the printshop, I sighed, coming back to the present. It hadn't taken me long to find the information Judy was still searching for. If my source was correct, Dominic's father had spent time with a woman, Fara Ragsdale, in this area twenty-five years ago. It had been a brief affair that might or might not have led to a set of twins, one boy and one girl.

Antonio Corisi had never acknowledged those children as his. Because they weren't? Because he hadn't known about them? My source had his opinion, but I preferred facts over speculation. If I was correct, the Riley Ragsdale who worked in this printshop was the daughter of Fara Ragsdale. She'd be about twenty-four and Dominic's sister.

I could have pulled in some favors from my friends in the medical field, but I'd wanted to do this without breaking any laws. Sure, a DNA database could have spit out a definitive answer, but so would a couple of questions. There were often visible family traits, and nature often gave preference to male genes.

I had a plan for what to say to Riley.

Hello.

My name is Gian Romano. There's a good chance my brother via my mother is your brother via your father. I'd like to ask you a few questions to determine if you're related to Dominic Corisi.

Clear.

Blunt.

I opened the door and stepped inside. Absolutely nothing about the interior surprised me. A variety of racks displayed printed shirts at discount prices. Square shelves on the walls held folded shirts, with the images displayed above. Some were humorous, but none looked imaginative enough to stand out.

How does a place like this make enough profit to stay open?

That thought flew from my mind when a curvy brunette stepped out of the back room and rocked me back onto my heels. A dangerous amount of blood left my head and rushed to a part of my anatomy I hadn't lost control of since my teenage years.

She wore an oversize blue knit sweater over torn jeans and knee-high leather boots. Her hair was loosely pulled back, with curls hanging down on one side of round glasses that looked too big for her face but somehow just right at the same time. And when those dark, intense eyes of hers slowly looked me over, I flushed.

Don't be Riley.

Her tone was polite, with no hint that I might have had the same impact on her. "May I help you?"

"I—" I gave myself a mental shake. Sure, yes, she was beautiful, but that shouldn't have been enough to shut my brain down. I waved a hand toward one of the walls. "I'm looking for a shirt."

Her eyes narrowed, and she gave me another once-over. "You've come to the right place. Are you interested in ordering for a team or company? Unless you need help designing them, the easiest way to order is online. You can pick up, or we can ship directly."

"Are you the owner?" Riley was only an employee.

She paused before saying, "Yes."

Relief flooded through me. No way in hell did I want to be attracted to my brother's sister, even if she was no blood relation to me. What would I have done had I discovered she was Riley? I didn't know. Run?

A frown creased her forehead. "Who are you?"

I threw my name out to test her response. "Gian Romano."

Her eyes widened in recognition of my last name, but there was also amusement in her eyes. "Go big or go home, right? Universe, I won't doubt you again."

"Did I miss something?" I stepped closer.

"No. Sorry." Her voice was soft but firm.

The way she looked me straight in the eye, no shyness or guile, had my heart beating faster. Less than a foot away, I stood over her, losing myself in those amazing eyes of hers. The air between us sizzled. "What's your name?"

Her lips parted slightly, and I nearly groaned aloud. "Teagan Becket."

"Teagan. That's beautiful." As was she . . . yes, that was the owner's name. When Thomas Brogos had told me about her, however, he'd left off that she was stunning.

Her lips twitched, as if she was fighting back a smile. "Thanks. I'll tell my parents you approve."

"I do." My attraction to her was like a sucker punch to the kidney, but it had me shaken for an entirely different reason. Simply because standing over her drooling wasn't an option, I said, "So you own a printshop."

She nodded. "Can't get anything by you."

"Beautiful and a smart-ass—have dinner with me."

"Good looking and cocky—tempting, but not what I need."

I liked the first part, but *cocky*? My brothers joked that I was nicer to most people than I should be. They'd always attributed it to the fact that my bio mother had abandoned me. That wasn't it. I just wasn't an asshole.

17

And not what she needs? I didn't know what she meant by that, but it didn't match the vibes I was getting from our meeting. "Are you seeing anyone?"

"No."

I grinned. "Good."

She grinned right back, which I took as a good sign. "I'm not going to dinner with you."

"Lunch?"

Still smiling, she shook her head.

"Breakfast?"

"I don't know you."

"We could remedy that."

Hand on hip, she cocked her head to one side. "So smooth. Do women fall for lines like that?"

I was fully enjoying our conversation. "Some. But not you?"

"Not me."

"Good." I dipped my head a little closer until my lips were just above hers. She could have stepped back, but she didn't. Our breath mingled—she licked her bottom lip, and I knew there was no way I was leaving without her number. "So . . . coffee?"

Her laugh was lighthearted and almost a yes.

The door behind me opened, and a female voice called out, "Sorry I'm late."

"Riley," Teagan said as she stepped back from me, looking flustered. "I was just—we have a customer."

Riley.

I spun on my heel and instantly knew no DNA testing would be necessary to determine if she and Dominic were related. She had his jet-black hair and could easily have been confused with my sister, Nicole, who was also Antonio's child. Although genes were passed down from each parent, research with mice suggested paternal genes won out, and Riley was an anecdotal supporting example.

18

Her smile flashed, quick and friendly. She looked back and forth between me and Teagan. "Should I come back later?"

"No, stay," I said quickly. Although I fully intended to leave with plans to see Teagan again, Riley was the reason I was there.

Teagan shot me an odd look. "Mr. Romano came in looking to place an order."

Riley pursed her lips. "Is it a bulk order? Do you already have your own logo?"

I didn't like to lie, but if ordering a few shirts would put them at ease, I could do that. Especially if it allowed me a few minutes alone with Riley. What I wanted to tell her was better said without an audience. "Not yet. If you have a few minutes, I could go over what I'm looking for."

Riley looked to Teagan. "Sure, I guess."

I stepped closer to Riley. The resemblance between her and the Corisis was remarkable. "Your eyes are a unique color," I said. "Almost gray. Rare, to be sure."

Riley frowned. "My brother has the same."

"And your mother?"

"Mr. Romano," Teagan said. "Back to the logo you're interested in designing—"

I wanted to get the reveal over so we could all move on. "I'm sure I'll be happy with whatever you come up with. I would like to speak to Riley alone for a moment, though."

Teagan expelled an audible breath. "I'll save you time, Mr. Romano, and be blunt. I won't be printing any shirts for you—nor will Riley."

Riley's mouth rounded. "Did I miss something?"

I turned back to ask the same thing. The smile was gone from Teagan's face. She arched an eyebrow and said, "Nothing important enough to mention."

She does not look happy with me.

Oh, shit, she thinks I'm interested in Riley.

19

CHAPTER THREE

TEAGAN

And this is why I don't date.

Men are dogs.

At twenty-five I'd come to terms with the fact that I would never be a size zero. My stomach would never be flat like a model's. My hair would always frizz on misty mornings, and contact lenses weren't likely to suddenly become my style, much like high heels. I felt silly in both.

I'd admit that when Gian Romano first walked into my shop, I'd given in to the whimsical idea that he'd been sent for me. Gorgeous men didn't tend to walk off the street and into my shop.

Tall. Fit. Dark hair. Dark eyes. A little more polished than I would have said was my taste, but his smile had made up for it. On any other day I would have wondered if he was lost. My internal voice tended to lean toward cynical, but when Gian had smiled down at me, I'd been tempted into believing in the unlikely—if only for a moment.

His instant attraction to Riley was a much-needed slap of reality. For fun, Riley and I had once run our faces through a computer program that had measured how symmetrical our features were. She'd scored a ten. I'd gotten a six.

There was nothing wrong with a six, but when Gian had flirted with me, I'd felt like an eleven for the first time in my life . . . possibly a fifteen. And it had been amazing.

If Riley hadn't come in, I might have already turned the sign on the door to CLOSED and gone with Gian to the nearest coffee shop simply so I could continue to bask in that feeling. Casual sex wasn't my thing, but it wouldn't have been out of the question with him.

Not only had it been a long time, but I liked sex. I *missed* it. Okay, I'd never had the kind people wrote about in romances, but I wasn't sure anyone had. I'd drawn a diagram for the last guy I'd slept with because I hadn't been convinced he understood the female body. Was it too much to wish for a man who was at least interested in learning?

He'd called my humor offensive. When I'd assured him I wasn't joking, he'd grabbed his clothes and left. *Rude.* I would have taken my critique as a challenge and tried harder. I mean, I could give myself an orgasm—how difficult could it be?

So maybe I was a little sour, but I needed Gian out of my shop. I was used to men fawning over Riley, and usually it didn't bother me. She was such a good person I was happy when good things happened for her.

But this time it stung.

Not that he was worth it. Gian Romano was obviously a player. No good man switched interests midchase. The last thing Riley needed was another man promising her more than he intended to deliver. Her inner voice was as trusting as mine was jaded.

I liked to think of myself as a nice person. I believed in feeding the hungry, sheltering the needy, comforting the suffering. My work was all about saving humanity. Human decency toward one another should always take priority.

Unless you fuck with me.

Then I have no tolerance for bullshit.

Like zero.

My eyes narrowed when the look Gian gave me said he was still interested. *Seriously? Oh, this guy is shameless.*

I indulged in a fantasy of smacking that smile right off his face. Or kneeing him in the groin. Or both.

"I know what you're thinking," he said.

If you did, you'd be protecting your dick and running for the door. "I'm sure you don't."

He rubbed a hand over his chin, then looked back and forth between Riley and me, as if he was torn. My temper flared when he said, "We'll talk later, but first I need to have a word with Riley."

Oh, hell no. "Goodbye, Mr. Romano."

He grimaced before turning to Riley. "This is definitely not unfolding the way I imagined, but all I need is a few minutes of your time. Perhaps step outside the door with me for a moment?"

She moved closer to me. "Thanks, but I'm in a committed relationship with an extremely jealous man. So thank you, but no."

Gian's eyebrows rose, and he proved a remarkable actor, because the concern in his expression would have fooled most people. "That's not good. No one should ever dictate who you're able to speak to."

I stepped in front of my very single friend. She liked to be nice. Riley's last boyfriend had been an absolute puppy whose only flaw had been allowing his controlling mother to break them up. "Do you have a problem hearing the word *no*, Mr. Romano? We're not interested in doing business with you, and my employee has expressed no desire to speak to you alone. So save us all the embarrassment of testing how fast the police would respond to my silent alarm. You wouldn't want this to end up on the news, would you?"

His mouth opened, as if he was about to say something else; then he said, "That's definitely not what I want."

"Then don't let the door hit your ass on the way out," I growled.

I expected him to look angry or intimidated, but he looked neither. Instead, he pocketed his hands and rocked back on his heels, as if weighing his options. "I could definitely have done this better." With that he spun and headed toward the exit. He paused, looked over his shoulder at me with desire burning in his eyes. My body flushed rebelliously. Then, as if to mock me, he nodded toward Riley and said, "I'll be in touch."

I didn't start breathing until he was out the door. "Can you believe that guy? What an asshole."

Riley looked like she was fighting back a smile. "I don't know—you two seemed to be getting along when I first came in."

"Yeah, until he also made a play for you."

"That's not what happened. He wasn't interested in me that way."

"No? So what do you think he wanted to tell you that I couldn't hear? His shirt size?"

Riley shook her head and walked away to hang up her jacket. "I don't know. I was kind of weirded out by that part, too, but trust me; there was no connection between us. Not for me. Not for him." She let out a wistful sigh. "You'll think I'm crazy if I tell you what I thought when I walked in."

I shook my head because I knew and did think it was crazy, but I also confessed, "I thought the same thing."

Riley absently folded a shirt. "You did ask the universe for someone."

I laughed. "I did. Next time I'll be more specific." *I'd like a man who doesn't want to fuck my friends as well.*

"And he's a Romano. What do you think it's like to be that rich? Do you think he wakes up smiling and falls into bed grateful? I know I would."

"I doubt it. Research suggests the wealthy are not happier than the average person. In fact, some studies have found they have more psychological problems. It's not what you have that's the secret to happiness; it's what you do with it."

Riley nodded. "I guess. At the end of the workday I'm too tired to worry about what might be wrong with my life."

"That won't always be the case, Riley."

"I hope not, although I don't yet see a light at the end of the tunnel." She tipped her head to one side. "Do you think you were a little harsh on him?"

I wrinkled my nose. "Maybe a little. It doesn't matter. He's gone."

She smiled. "He might come back. I do think he was into you."

"He won't." I shook my head. "And he wasn't. I'm heading back downstairs to get some work done. If for some wild reason he does return, call down to me."

"Because you're not interested." She was mocking me, but not unkindly.

"Because I made it very clear that we didn't want him here."

"That's not what I call remaining open to possibilities. Now that I know the universe is listening, I'm going to ask for what I need—some cold hard cash. Hear that, Universe? Send me some money."

"Good luck with that, Riley." I was laughing as I walked away.

Once back in my office I went over the whole scenario with Gian and Riley again. Had I misread the situation? He hadn't actually done anything wrong, yet I'd threatened to call the police. That probably didn't turn many men on.

Which meant I'd never have that dinner with him.

Or share that coffee.

Or discover if impulsive sex with a stranger really was followed by guilt.

I sat down at my computer and tried to concentrate, but my thoughts kept wandering back to Gian and what he'd said as he'd left: *"I'll be in touch."*

As well as: *"I could definitely have done this better."* Done what? Hooked up with both of us?

Which one of us would he be in touch with? Me for coffee? Riley for . . . I didn't want to imagine what.

The most disturbing question I kept asking myself was why I still yearned to relive the moment when all his attention had been focused on me. Riley romanticized men and situations; I didn't.

So why couldn't I get Gian Romano out of my head?

CHAPTER FOUR

GIAN

"What's wrong, Gian?" my father asked as we made our way through his neighborhood for an after-dinner walk. My biological family tree might have been a mess, but in my mind I had only two parents—the ones who had adopted me.

There had been years when my brothers and I had mostly visited our parents for Sunday dinner, but as our family had grown, so had the time we chose to spend together. All three of my older brothers were married with children, so mayhem was the norm now at my parents' home—and they loved it.

Normally I did as well. I adored my growing herd of nephews and nieces. Tonight, however, I'd been relieved when my father had asked me to go for a walk. I knew of no better sounding board. "How do you always know when there's something on my mind?"

"A father always knows," he said gently. "Plus your brothers tell me everything. They were concerned that you might have felt ambushed this morning. They asked tough questions, but only because they love you."

"I know that, Dad. That's not what is weighing on my mind tonight."

"Christof said you saw Judy the other day at Decker Park. Is she okay?"

There were literally no secrets in my family, at least not when it came to day-to-day shit. It used to bother me, but whenever I felt lost, it was that kind of constant that comforted me. "She's fine; I'm the one who's confused."

Side by side, we strolled on, as we often had when I'd sought out his guidance. Basil Romano had a quiet strength and an unwavering love for his wife and family. Never once had I felt less loved than his biological children. I prayed that if I ever did become a father, however it happened, I would be as stable and loving.

My brothers and I had tested that patience, each in our own way. Sebastian had struggled with alcohol after his first wife had died. Mauricio had run with a wild crowd for a while in Europe during his younger years. Christof—actually, Christof was probably no trouble at all. Of us all, he was the most like Basil.

Me? For a short period of time after I'd learned I was Dominic Corisi's brother, I'd forgotten how to be a Romano. I pulled away, thinking I needed distance to figure out who I was. I took time out of school and moved to New York to get to know Dominic; his wife; his children; my biological mother and her husband, Thomas; my sister, Nicole; her husband, Stephan; and their children.

For a few months I test-drove what it would be like to be a Corisi, and it was like nothing I'd ever known. Helicopters. Jets. Every need anticipated and fulfilled prior to requesting anything. Access to more money than I could spend in my lifetime. It was a wild, fun ride at first. It didn't take long, though, for me to become overwhelmed by it. Opposite to how I'd thought it would feel, being able to have anything I wanted anytime I wanted it quickly left me feeling a little sick in the way one did when they overindulged on sweets. I saw myself changing, expecting to be treated a certain way, and I didn't like the man looking back at me in the mirror.

After I'd missed months of Sunday dinners, my Romano brothers descended on the penthouse apartment I rented in New York City.

They told me I was breaking our parents' hearts and that I could be a Corisi Monday through Saturday, but on Sunday my ass would always be a Romano.

They didn't hide what they thought of the lifestyle I'd adopted, and rather than offending me, their criticism was just what I needed to find my footing again. I'd been raised to not put value on the very things I was embracing.

Arms folded across his chest, Sebastian threatened to physically drag me home if I didn't wise up. Mauricio joked he had the duct tape already purchased. Christof, easygoing Christof, said his car's trunk was the perfect size for me to ride home in.

Many times growing up, I'd witnessed my family pull together during times of crisis. Romanos were as open with their support of each other as they were with affection. My father still kissed my forehead when he greeted me. My mother still gave me the same tight hug she'd welcomed me home from grade school with.

It took time away from them for me to see how much a part of me my Romano brothers were. When they came for me, I realized I was more of a Romano than I'd ever be a Corisi. I'd moved back to Connecticut that week, a little more at peace with myself, but also a little sad.

Dominic had seen my leaving as a rejection of him and everything he'd offered me. Thankfully his wife, Abby, hadn't. She'd encouraged me to continue to spend time with Judy, and that tie had kept us in each other's lives.

"Tell me, Gian," my father said. "Whatever it is, we'll work through it together."

I met his steady gaze and nodded. So much of my life read like a daytime drama. Rosella, my biological mother, had married a violent man; had had two children with him, Dominic and Nicole; then had gone on the run without her children because she'd feared Antonio

Corisi would kill her. How many people could say their bio mother had faked her own death? I could.

While in hiding under an alias in Italy, she'd married a man illegally and borne me. When her husband had died suddenly, she'd panicked and thought Antonio had found them and killed her husband. So she'd deserted yet another of her children—me.

Dominic and Nicole had been raised by a cold and vindictive man. I'd won the lottery when it came to loving parents. It was impossible not to feel grateful every time I thought about where I could have ended up if Basil hadn't wanted to raise his wife's sister's child.

I took a deep breath before saying, "I met the most incredible woman earlier today. I've spent the last few hours trying to figure out what makes her different from any other woman, and I can't. All I know is every time I picture her in my head, I smile."

My father's expression transformed. "I remember feeling exactly that way about your mother. When you meet the right person, there is no need to justify the feeling. It simply is."

"How do I know it's nothing more than a compatible variation in her major histocompatibility complex and mine?"

"Your what?"

"Our immune system genes. They give each person a distinct but subtle odor print that is as unique as a fingerprint. Some research suggests it's as influential in human pairing as pheromones. How do I know that wasn't all our connection was about?"

My father nodded slowly. "Tell me something you liked about her."

I took a moment to relive our brief meeting. "She says what she's thinking." I smiled. "Really direct. Like she-threatened-to-call-the-police-if-I-didn't-leave-her-shop kind of direct."

My father paused, and I stopped short. "Gian, you are likely my most intelligent child. When it comes to understanding what they teach in school, you are the smartest person I know. Sometimes, though, gifted people are not good at interpreting social cues. If she threatened to call the police, that is concerning. You may have misread the connection you believe you had."

I chuckled. I probably shouldn't have started with the police part. "Don't worry, Dad. It wasn't like that. We did have a connection; then she misunderstood my interest in her employee."

My father began walking again, and I fell into step beside him. "In my day we focused on one woman at a time. Dating should not be done like a fisherman who throws a wide net."

I sighed. "If I tell you something, please don't tell Mom."

"I tell your mother everything."

"Just this one time."

His shoulders rose and fell. "Do you honestly believe I could keep something from her? One look into my eyes, and she knows. Proceed with that in mind."

My father made no apologies about his loyalty to my mother. Some people claimed they would give their lives for the people they loved, but very few meant it. My father was the kind of man who would. He said he was still as smitten with Mom as when he'd first met her.

It made him a horrible secret keeper, but at least he owned up to it. Was my reason for being in Lockton something she couldn't know? The Romano in me said no. "I've uncovered another of Dominic's siblings."

"You have?" He kept an even pace as we continued our walk.

"You don't sound surprised."

"Your mother and I knew it was only a matter of time before you figured it out. How could you study genetics and not see the truth?"

Okay, I was lost. "I'm not sure we're talking about the same thing. *What* was only a matter of time for me to figure out?"

My father's expression tensed. "Perhaps we should start with what you wanted to tell me."

"Oh no. Spill it, Dad. We don't keep secrets from each other, remember?"

"Not every truth is best known."

That sounded too much like something Alethea Stone would have said. Had she uncovered something about my family that I had yet to? "I disagree. The truth may be uncomfortable. It may change things, but it is always better known."

"There was a time when I would have agreed with you, Gian, but I've learned that happiness can be as fragile and fleeting as life itself. I tread carefully when it comes to adding to anyone's struggles. Especially when they are finally happy again."

My mind raced with possibilities and scenarios. Like puzzle pieces falling into place, seemingly random bits of information began to click together. *Happy again.* He had to be referring to my brother who had lost his wife years ago, had struggled for a long time, but had eventually remarried and found some peace. "You know something about Sebastian, something you think I could figure out through genetics. It's not a coincidence, is it, that he looks so much like Dominic? He's his sibling, isn't he? But how? Not through Rosella like me. I don't look like Antonio, but they both do." Goose bumps rose on my arms. "Antonio Corisi was Sebastian's biological father." It wasn't even a question. How had I not made the connection earlier? "Is he also adopted?"

"No, Camilla was pregnant from Antonio when she agreed to marry me."

"Holy shit, Dad."

"Holy shit indeed."

We continued walking. I had to ask. "You've always known?"

"Your mother and I don't keep secrets from each other."

Just from us. I could have said the words, but I wasn't looking to fight with my father. "You never thought Sebastian had the right to know?" I'd always known I was adopted. It was odd to me that my parents wouldn't have been as forthcoming with my older brother's lineage.

My father's expression turned pained. "Not telling him has given me many sleepless nights. Camilla has always been afraid that it would change how her sons look at her. Christof discovered the truth back when he went to Italy to meet Dominic. He understood. The rest of you would as well. But Sebastian? I don't know. He and Dominic already have a comfortable relationship as cousins. Their families have gotten close as well. Would either benefit from knowing their mothers both became pregnant from the same man?"

When it was put that way, I could see his point. "Should I even ask if that was Rosella's fault?" I still had a difficult time referring to her as my mother, especially when faced with these types of revelations.

Ever the reasonable one, my father said, "It was everyone's fault, and no one's. That was a different time, Gian, in a very different place than you were raised. We could have all done better, but then I wouldn't have had four sons, would I? Each one of you was a miracle to me. So I have no anger in my heart."

I stopped and gave my father a tight hug. No matter the storm on the horizon, I felt securely planted when I looked at the world through his eyes. When I stepped back, I said, "I may have to tell Sebastian. I don't keep secrets from my brothers."

My father's eyes shone with pride. "I am confident that when you do, it will be at the right time and in the right way. And when it's done, your mother will see that the love she has given far outweighs whatever mistakes she made."

We began walking again. "Antonio Corisi was a horrible man."

"Yes, he was."

"Do you really think discovering the truth might change how stable Sebastian is? Or how he sees Mom?"

"I pray it doesn't."

We walked for several minutes in silence. Eventually, I said, "Judy and I made a wager when she came to see me—about which of us could find another sibling for Dominic first."

"Sounds like a dangerous game."

"I agreed to it for selfish reasons. It's difficult to be Dominic's brother, Dad. I'm not accustomed to dealing with someone who puts absolutely no value in what I say." I wasn't proud of how I felt or the words as they came out of my mouth, but I'd always been real with my father.

His head snapped around, and he frowned. "Is that how he treats you? I didn't have that impression from the times I've seen you together. He seems to care for you deeply."

I ran a hand through my hair. "I know he cares, but I could never have this conversation with him. I don't know what he hears when I speak, but I always leave feeling I wasted my time trying to get my point across."

"And you blame him for it?"

With anyone else I would have felt defensive, but my father didn't ask anything with the intention of pouncing and lecturing. His questions were always to clarify and guide. "I do." As I said the words, I saw the error in them. "But relationships, even bad ones, take two people."

"Exactly. You find it easy to speak to me because you know I will love you even when we disagree." For the most part that was true. There was a side of me my father would never know, but perhaps that was true of every child/parent relationship. We were closer, though, than most. My father continued, "I can hear you because you are clear with me. It's more complicated with Dominic. He wants the same relationship with you that you have with your other brothers, but he didn't grow up with you. So perhaps he tries too hard. You think if you get close to him, you will somehow lose us or yourself. So perhaps you don't try hard enough."

I sucked in an audible breath. Was it that simple? Were the roadblocks between us based on old fears? "What do you think of me racing him at Decker Park?"

My father smiled. "Is that your plan?"

"That was the wager I made with Judy. If I win, I race Dominic. If I lose, I race Dominic, and she finds me a car that's faster than his.

She said if I want him to hear me, I need to best him—then I'll have his attention."

My father didn't say anything at first. "I'm sure Judy knows her father well. I know you, though. Don't worry about racing Dominic just yet. Tell me about this sibling of his you found."

I let out a sigh. "I found two, in fact. Twins—a daughter and a son." I updated him briefly on the little I knew about them. "I tracked them down through Rosella's husband, Thomas. He was Antonio's lawyer for a long time. I thought if anyone would know what Antonio was up to, it would be him."

"And he did."

That was putting it kindly. "Yes. He hasn't been in touch with them in years, but he knew their names and how to find them. The instant I saw Riley, there was no question in my mind that she's related to Dominic." I shook my head. "Now that I know, I can't believe I didn't guess at Sebastian earlier. They all have the same deep-black hair, those hazel-gray eyes. Antonio was an asshole, but he had some strong genes."

"Sebastian has another sister as well. Perhaps it is time for Camilla to tell him."

"I'll do it, Dad. Just in case his first reaction isn't one she should see. Let me be the buffer."

My father clapped a hand on my shoulder. "That would ease my worries. I don't want to see Sebastian or your mother hurt by this."

"They won't be," I said with confidence, even though I had no idea how this would all play out.

My father gave my shoulder a squeeze and said, "This woman who makes you smile so much—how does she play into the wager you have with Judy?"

"She doesn't know. She owns the printshop where Riley works." I explained to my father how I had gone there with the intention of speaking to Riley but then had been distracted by Teagan. "I was asking Teagan out when Riley came in. I thought I could circle back to that after I told Riley about Dominic, but it came across as if I were interested in both women."

My father's mouth twitched with a smile. "Not good."

"Not at all."

"So which will you contact first?"

I thought back to my plan to be straightforward with Riley about why I'd sought her out. After hearing how careful my father had been about when Sebastian should be told the truth, I wondered if I should find out more about Riley's family before dropping the truth bomb on them as well. "I don't know. What do you think?"

My father laughed. "This one is on you, son, but I can't wait to hear how it turns out."

I met his gaze. "Teagan Becket. That's her name."

"It's a beautiful name."

"That's what I told her." I smiled at the memory of the sass in her answer. "You'll like her, Dad."

"I'm sure I will—but next time you see her, don't do whatever it was that had her ready to call the police."

I laughed. "I won't. I promise."

CHAPTER FIVE

TEAGAN

I was in the basement computer lab below my printshop, fighting to concentrate. Normally I saw my mild but constant paranoia as a strength. This time, however, I hated that I couldn't turn it off.

I'd definitely overreacted.

The facts: He'd walked into my shop looking to place an order and asked me out. Riley came in. He said he didn't have a logo designed yet. I said we wouldn't do an order for him. He asked to speak to her alone. For all I knew, he might have wanted to ask her to recommend another printshop—a question he felt unable to voice without offending me. I'd ordered him to leave.

Riley had said there hadn't been a spark between them, so what had there been? Why his sudden interest in her? And why was he occupying so much space in my head?

I closed my eyes briefly and relived those few moments with him. Flirting with him had felt so damn good. For just a few minutes the world had been ripe with wondrous possibilities. I'd felt not only sexy but also giddy, silly—carefree.

Until all his attention had switched to Riley.

That had been a sucker punch to the solar plexus.

I'd never been the jealous type, and I didn't like how it felt. No matter what I tried to tell myself, though, I'd finally met a man I would hate seeing Riley date. I didn't want to be the person who told my friend who they could or couldn't be with, but I'd also never felt territorial about a man before.

A man I don't even know. Remember that, Teagan.

My phone vibrated with an incoming message.

Ever wish you could hit reset on a day? —Gian

My breath whooshed out of me. I clutched the phone with both hands and stood. After inhaling deeply, I waited for my jaded inner voice to chime in, but it didn't. It couldn't compete with the giddy one rising within me.

I started to type *Yes*. But I deleted it. Too easy.

I told myself I should ask, *How did you get my number?* But that was simple enough for most to do nowadays.

Which part would you change? There. That was neutral but aimed at getting me the answers I needed.

The part where I left without making plans to see you again. Despite how it looked, I wasn't interested in your employee—at least, not that way.

What other way is there?

I'd rather tell you in person.

It was tempting to say yes, but my pride wouldn't allow me to. I prefer men who aren't also into my friends.

When I explain why to you, you'll forgive me.

Really?

We'll eventually look back at our first meeting and laugh.

I can't see that happening.

It'll make a great story to tell our friends.

I flushed. Even if I didn't believe him, I had to admit having his full attention felt good. You say that like this is going somewhere.

How do we know it's not?

I've already threatened to call the police on you.

There was a pause before he wrote back. Aren't you at all curious? I was, but I wasn't about to confess it.

His next text took my breath away. If I were playing this cool I'd ask you if you were free on Friday night, but do we have to wait that long? My afternoon is open. The weather is beautiful. Would you like to walk around Plymouth with me? We could get something to eat by the water. Talk.
There were probably a hundred reasons why I should have said no, but none of them came to mind right then. I answered: What time?

You said yes.

I did. Try to keep up. I smiled as I typed my response. I told myself the only reason I'd agreed was to get some answers, but it was more than that.

I'm smiling.

I hesitated before responding. Me, too.

Could you do as early as 4?

I could close up the shop right then, and I was tempted to, but I wasn't about to say that. Yes. Where do you want to meet?

He suggested a location near Nelson Memorial Park. I knew the place. It had a playground and was located right on the ocean. Family friendly. Safe.

I'll be there, I wrote.

See you then.

I got very little done over the next half hour. I tried to review a coded program but gave up. I pulled data from the tests I'd run the day before but found myself picking up my phone again and again to reread our messages.

I didn't believe he'd been sent to me by some divine being. I wasn't expecting our time together to end with a walk down the aisle and the synchronized child-rearing Riley was hoping for. But he wanted to see me.

And I really wanted to see him and hear the reason he'd seemed so interested in Riley.

Everyone deserved a second chance, right?

That had literally never been my motto.

I didn't want to be jaded when it came to Gian, though. I wanted to be as free and willing to see where it might go as Riley would have been. Had she felt that way with every man she'd dated? If so, I finally understood some of the decisions she'd made.

He might try to lie to me. Normally I wouldn't consider the risk worth it, but I wanted to see Gian more than I wanted to protect myself.

That was a first.

Scary.

Exciting.

Amazing.

I propped my chin on my fist and sighed as I imagined walking along a rocky beach with him. Hand in hand? Barefoot? Would we kiss with the sound of waves crashing behind us?

A light on my security dashboard flashed, announcing a security breach upstairs. A visual feed of a young woman slipping through the back door came up on my phone. Had she not been alone, I would have called the police, but I was curious.

"NYD, is she armed?" I asked aloud.

"Negative," the computer responded.

She was dressed in simple jeans and a tan T-shirt. Her hair was pulled back in a neat style. As I watched, she expertly disarmed the upstairs alarm system before it sounded. I expected her to go to the front for the cash register, but instead she went directly to Riley's laptop in the design area.

She bypassed Riley's password like a pro—not a difficult feat, though. I wasn't concerned with what she'd find. Riley was far from tech savvy. Most of her artwork was hand drawn, then scanned.

"NYD, is she alone?"

"There is one man exiting a car in the parking lot. He is armed with a nine-millimeter handgun."

"NYD, secure the outer doors with lock system Oh, Shit." Unless the man outside had a tank, he wasn't getting through. The door and the walls were bulletproof—a perk I'd traded coding projects for. The age of bartering was far from over.

"Oh, Shit system engaged."

I zoomed in on the video feed of my intruder. Her nails were short but manicured. Her sneakers were pristine white. Not a sign of stains or wear on any of her clothing. This was a person who had money but wanted to appear as if she didn't.

Intriguing.

Only Riley knew the nature of my research. If it were anyone else, I would wonder if she'd told someone about it, but Riley was smarter than that. One thing Riley had always been was loyal . . . even when it was to her detriment.

So who was this girl, and what was she looking for?

"NYD, open Mouse Trap door one. Flicker the light. Let's see if we can lure the mouse in."

"Mouse Trap door one open."

People liked to think they were nothing like computers, but human nature followed certain patterns of behavior. One of my college professors had sent me to speak to a campus counselor my first year at college when I'd temporarily become obsessed with human psychology. I needed to understand how human limitations and predictability were or were not mirrored in AI programs. Looking back, I understood that I'd probably overwhelmed the Intro to Psychology professor with my endless questions.

I would forever be thankful to the counselor for suggesting I join open-source groups. It had been life changing. Suddenly my questions were not an interruption; they were debated by brilliant minds from around the globe. I still shared in those groups—although not the core of my work. Never NYD or our projects. NYD had the potential of becoming a more powerful tool if I gave it access to the World Wide Web, but for my research results to remain pure, it needed to be untainted by the codes of others.

I switched to the feed of the man in the alley outside my shop, then checked the time on my watch. Riley wasn't due to work for another hour, and she was never early, so I could deal with him later. Although I didn't own a gun, I wasn't concerned that he was armed. If he was with her, she'd be returned to him soon—hopefully scared enough to convince him that my shop wasn't worth targeting. If they weren't together, he'd likely test the doors, get frustrated when he couldn't gain access, and leave.

I swiped back to see what my upstairs intruder was doing. Now that I'd had time to think about it, the best choice would have been to block her out of the basement entirely. My gut told me it wouldn't have been as easy as that, though. I needed to know what she was looking for, because as I watched her case my shop, it sure as hell didn't look like she was there for a smash and grab.

As soon as the woman stepped through the door I'd left open for her, it closed and locked behind her. The walls inside were smooth and bare. No windows. No lock to pick or pad to hack. Cell phone service was blocked. No way out. For effect, the lighting dimmed as well.

I expected her to look startled or afraid. Instead she appeared annoyed. "Alethea, don't you have anything better to do than constantly ruin my fun?" she said aloud, folding her arms across her chest.

Alethea? I didn't know anyone by that name. I used a program to modify my voice, and through an intercom, I said, "Breaking and entering is illegal."

The woman huffed and blew a loose hair out of her eyes. "Like that has ever stopped you. Before you threaten to tell my father, this is a surprise I'm planning for him. Could you please not take this from me?"

"What kind of surprise are you planning for your father?" *Tell me she isn't really looking to make a T-shirt. If so, my gut is way off.*

Hold on; there's still the armed guy outside.

What am I missing?

"I'm not doing this. Don't ask me questions you already know the answer to. I'm aware that Marc started following me after I ditched my bodyguard. I put a tracer on his watch. Before you lecture me, have you considered that I'm nearly twenty? Twenty. I don't need someone watching me twenty-four seven. I am perfectly capable of taking care of myself."

My intruder was a spoiled rich kid with tech skills? "Who are you?"

She put her hands on her hips. "Oh, please. And ditch the creepy-voice mode. It's not working." She made a face; then her expression turned almost apologetic. "I really am doing this for Dad. Marc isn't going to tell him, is he?"

I had to choose a lane, so I did. "I won't tell your father, and I'll make sure Marc doesn't, either, if you explain to me what you're doing here."

The girl looked around, as if studying the room anew. "You're not Alethea. Who are you?"

I switched lanes as quickly as she had. "Someone who doesn't want you here. I'll give you one chance to leave without reporting you to the authorities. Do yourself a favor, and take it. And don't return unless you'd like your photo to show up on every police database. All doors will open for six seconds. That gives you just enough time to vacate the premises."

"No."

"What?" My tone revealed my surprise. She was the first mouse I'd caught, but the studies I'd read on the human response to fear had led me to believe a person would run when given a chance to.

"Whoever you are, I want to meet you. This room is brilliant, which means you're brilliant. I have no idea how I'd get out if I wanted to."

If she wanted to?

"Thanks. I did put substantial thought into it. I'm about to open the door. If you don't leave, I'll be forced to drive you out."

Her eyes widened, but with excitement rather than fear. "Let me guess, with an ear-piercing sound? I should warn you I have special earplugs that block such assaults."

Who the hell has those?

"Actually, the vents in the floor will release a chemically modified skunk spray. Not only will you be unable to wash the smell off, but you'll glow like a Christmas tree for any fluorescent light, which will make it easy enough for the police to prove you were here."

"There's a flaw in your plan," she said.

"And that is?"

"You won't call the police, because I doubt you want them to know about whatever it is you're hiding. Hey, if it's a meth lab, it's none of my business. I'm not a rat. You do you. Tell me, and I'll go."

42

"It's a meth lab."

She laughed. "You're a bad liar. What is it really? Please tell me."

This girl was too much. "Why are you here?"

"I'll tell you over lunch. You keep my secret, and I'll keep yours."

Rule one with terrorists: never negotiate with them. It never worked out. "I'm opening the door. Six seconds to get out. I'll put a two-second delay on the spray. Your choice how you want to go, but you're going."

She looked disappointed when she held up a hand. "Wait, I can't use my phone to check. Is there a man in the alley or right outside the door?"

"Ye-es." I drew out the word, not sure where she was taking this.

"I have to speak quickly, because we don't have much time, but that is the head of my father's security. He'll break in soon. Trust me; whatever system you have in place, he and my aunt can beat it. When he does, he'll know all about whatever you're hiding, and I'll have to explain to my mother why I thought coming here was a good idea. If we act fast, though, we can turn the situation around. Oh my God, I can win for once. Spray him; give me time to run back up and appear as if I'm still hunting through your upstairs shop. I'll pretend I found nothing here."

"Why would I do that?"

"Because my name is Judy Corisi. My father is Dominic Corisi. This may sound crazy, but I feel like I could learn something from you, and I don't say that to many people. Whatever you're working on, I want in. Please. All I'd have to do is tell my father we're partnering on something, and he'd fully fund your work. He is always telling me I need to find what I want to do with my life."

Dominic Corisi? I told myself to remain calm, but I was fighting back a hefty panic attack. Everyone knew the Corisis. They were arguably the wealthiest family on the planet. What was his daughter doing in my printshop? A chill went down my spine. Had my research somehow gotten on his radar? No, if it had, he'd be here and not his daughter. Right? I frowned. No matter what had brought her here, I needed to get her to leave. "It's your reasoning that is faulty. First, you shouldn't tell anyone you're wealthy. What would stop someone from deciding to hold you for ransom?"

Without missing a beat, she said, "They'd be dead before they voiced their demand. Next problem?"

Talk about overconfident, but with a father like hers, it would be difficult to remain humble. *How do I get her to leave?* "Your father wouldn't want to be associated with me or my work. If you want to protect him, forget you ever came here."

She waved a hand around. "You don't scare me. There's nothing in this room that's designed to injure a person, and you threatened me with a stink spray. Neither of those are indicators of a person who is looking to hurt others."

My mind was racing. Two days, two impossibly rich visitors to my shop. It couldn't have been a coincidence. I switched back to the video of the man outside. He was using some type of laser to sever my bolt. *Crap.*

I sprayed the shit out of him, then pressed a button that opened the door of the Mouse Trap. Time to lie. "Go. I'll be watching what you do, and if I feel that I can trust you, I'll be in touch. Wait for me to contact you." I really wanted to say, *Thank you for revealing a flaw in my security system. I intend to rectify it.* But I didn't.

She dropped a card on the floor that seemed to have only a phone number on it. It was white with black lettering. "That's the best way to contact me. Oh my God, I'm so excited. Seriously, don't take too long to call. I'll have to tell Dad something about you so he'll keep Marc from breaking down your door again. Thank you. Thank you."

"Go."

"I know this is too much to hope for, but I'm praying your name is Riley. If it is, you seriously have to call me, because there is so much I have to tell you," she said in an excited tone as she backed out with a huge smile on her face. "I want to know, but I also love that I don't. There is nothing better than a mystery. You just made my day. Hell, my year."

Via the security system I watched her rush through my shop to the door Marc had been attempting to break in through. I hit audio so I could listen in.

"Marc, oh no, did you get hit with a scent bomb?" She raised her hand and made a gagging sound. "Wow, that's potent. I'm sorry—I would have disabled it had I known you were behind me."

"Get in the car, Judy. We'll talk about this on the way."

"No offense, Marc, but could the talk wait until after you've showered? I already feel like I might get sick from the smell. Isn't it ingenious? Who knew a little shop like this would have something like that. I wish the inside were as impressive. Nothing."

Looking thoroughly disgusted by himself, Marc said, "Judy, you know I love you, but you're getting too old to act so irresponsibly. Do you know how many bodyguards I've fired because they can't keep track of you? I should not have to be your babysitter."

Judy's bottom lip stuck out. "Sorry, Marc."

He relented, as if speaking to a young child. "It's okay, Judy. All we want is to protect you. The world is a dangerous place."

Raising the neckline of her shirt to cover her mouth and nose, she said, "I do appreciate it, Marc. I just need room to test my wings. How will I ever know what I'm capable of if you're always there to catch me before I fall?"

He inhaled and made another face of disgust. "We'll talk about it later. I'd ask why you're here, but I already know, and I don't approve."

"I would be shocked if you did."

"You need to tell your father what you're doing. I haven't yet, but I will now if you don't." He nodded toward the street. "Get in your car. We'll stop by my house before you go home. Maybe Alethea can talk some sense into you."

I had zero experience with bodyguards and security teams, but he sounded more like an irate family member than one of her father's employees. Not that it was any of my business. All my anxiety was regarding what Judy would tell her father about why she'd been here. I'd never prayed so hard for someone to be a shoplifter.

Judy's shoulders slumped. "Fine." She didn't walk away, though. "Marc?"

Was she going to tell him about me? I held my breath.

"Yes?"

"I'm not sorry you were stink bombed." Her laugh rang out.

He shook his head, then surprised me by smiling. "I know. Your father will find it hilarious as well."

The large-eyed look she gave him was all female guile. "I'll tell him about today. I promise."

Marc didn't respond, but as he walked away from my building, I had the feeling Judy had him wrapped around her little finger. She was definitely rich and spoiled, but could I spin this possible disaster into something good?

If my research ever needed to be brought online on a global scale, her father had the resources to do it. Could he be swayed to keep something like NYD a secret until such a time that it was needed—if it ever was?

He was a businessman. A powerful one. Wasn't it more likely that he would simply steal my research? NYD's coding was unique—it'd be too tempting for him not to take. If I scrambled, though, I could design a smoke screen program he might invest in . . . possibly something that would also be beneficial to the world. If he bought that program, I could finally help the Ragsdales.

Look at me, being optimistic for a change. I'd asked for a man, and Gian had arrived. Riley had asked for money, and I might have just found a way to get her family some. I wasn't ready to believe in fate, but I also wasn't the type to not grab at an opportunity when one presented itself.

I let myself into the Mouse Trap and picked up Judy's business card. Whatever came next, I couldn't trust her. I needed to move NYD to the alternate location I'd set up for just this contingency. Paranoid or prepared? Either way the result would be the same. NYD would be safe.

"NYD," I said. "Initiate Ejection Seat."

"Will NYSM be coming with me?" Its question gave me a moment of pause. I'd written every line of its code. It didn't have a personality, but as it evolved, there were times when it sounded eerily human.

"Yes. Everything here will be wiped, but you'll both be uploaded to my system at Haven Two."

NYD responded in its usual monotone voice. "Password request for Ejection Seat."

I provided it orally.

"DNA match requested," it said.

I placed my finger on a needle that rose from the console.

"Favorite dad joke requested."

I said, "Why didn't the bicycle want to race?"

NYD answered, "It was too tired. Ejection Seat protocols commencing. See you at Haven Two, NYSM."

NYSM didn't respond. It couldn't. Communication was not required for what I needed it to do. In truth, I'd given NYD the ability only because I spent a lot of hours alone in my lab. Even if its responses were stilted and mostly scripted, it was still nice to have something to interact with.

My life had always been a bit solitary, but I realized then just how small my social circle had become: Riley, Kal, and Fara. *I really do need to get out more.*

I returned to my desk and placed Judy's card beside my keyboard. My thoughts wandered back to Gian, and I reread our messages. His family owned a chain of supermarkets. They wouldn't have any interest in the kind of technology I was developing. Did he know the Corisis?

I considered canceling our date and spending the day dismantling any proof that more than a printshop had ever been at this location. Moving to Haven Two would mean seeing less of Riley. I'd be even more alone.

That wasn't what I wanted.

Was Gian what I was yearning for? Or the idea of him? Either way, I couldn't deny how I felt.

I didn't want to spend the day locked up in my lab alone. I wanted Riley to arrive so I could tell her everything that had happened that morning; then I wanted to go on a date with a man I found attractive—like a regular person—and temporarily leave all this behind.

CHAPTER SIX

Teagan

I sat in my car in the lot beside the beachside park. It was busier than I'd expected it to be, which was reassuring and disappointing at the same time. Children filled the playground and spilled out into the surrounding area. Adults occupied most of the benches as well as the grass beside the playground. I grabbed a light jacket from the back seat of my car as I saw the wind whip the trees back and forth.

Rather than immediately exiting, I took a moment to scan the area for Gian. If he was there, I didn't see him. I sighed.

He'd said I'd forgive him once I understood why he'd seemed interested in Riley. Would I?

While transferring NYD to its new location, I'd had ample time to second-guess meeting up with him. I'd thought I'd have time to talk through everything with Riley, but she'd called out last minute. I understood. The bride she was working with was paying her double what I could afford to, and she didn't have any open orders to fill. Still, it meant that I'd spent the day with only my own thoughts.

Life was full of patterns. Perhaps because I looked at life through the lens of a programmer, I believed very little was truly random. Two people had come to my shop, both seemingly interested in Riley. Gian after he'd seen her, Judy when she'd wished I were her. There was definitely a connection. I was missing something.

I wanted to hear Gian's explanation, but I was also afraid to. What if it was complete bullshit? Or something sinister? I didn't want a reason I couldn't see him again.

This is a problem. I was already too invested in one specific outcome to be objective. I wanted to spend a couple of hours enjoying myself with a man who made me feel beautiful. So maybe it was a good thing I hadn't spoken to Riley. She might have warned me to be careful, and that wasn't how I was feeling.

Gian was waiting for me—all I had to do was get out of my car.

Clutching my jacket in one hand, I threw open the door and stepped outside. The wind immediately blew my loose hair across my eyes. I bent and knelt on my car seat to hunt for the elastic band I kept in the middle console. After locating it, I backed out and straightened, then jumped at the sight of Gian standing beside my car door. "Oh, hi."

His smile was easy. "Sorry if I startled you. I saw you park and then wasn't sure if you were having car issues."

My hair defied me and flew across my face again. I peeled it back and held it bunched in one hand while waving the elastic and my jacket at him with my other. "Just needed a hair tie."

He chuckled. "With all those curls I'm sure you do."

I groaned. I could imagine how wild my hair looked. Long sexy curls blowing in the wind? Yeah, that wasn't me. My entire childhood my mother had accused me of not brushing my hair after I had. I was often tempted to cut it all off, but I liked the ease of pulling it back in a ponytail.

Reality versus fantasy, I guess. I'd hoped for a sexy disheveled look. I wasn't one to wear much makeup, but I'd put on mascara and lip gloss before heading over. As I'd freshened up for our date, I'd looked in the mirror and actually liked the way my hair had framed my face. The likelihood that I still would? Zero.

Forgetting I was also holding my jacket, I failed at my first attempt to gather my hair into the elastic while the wind gusted again. I weighed letting my hair fly free like a kite around my head against tying it back without a mirror and possibly leaving a huge clump sticking up.

He held out a hand. "Would you like some help?"

I froze. "With my hair?"

His eyes lit with humor. "With whatever you need, but I can whip together a mean braid."

"I'm fine." His choice of attire for our date was casual—jeans and gray button-down shirt—but I still had a vivid mental image of him in an expensive tailored suit. A man like that wouldn't know how to braid hair, would he? Our eyes met, and my face heated as I pictured much more intimate skills I hoped he had.

Still holding out his hand, he growled, "Give me the elastic."

I opened my mouth to say something, but no sound came out. A shiver of excitement shot through me at his simple command. I wasn't the type who let any man tell me what to do, but I might be willing to explore that option if it felt anywhere near as good as my body hinted it could. I handed him the hair tie.

"Turn around." His voice was husky.

I did, and waiting for his touch was about the sexiest thing I'd ever experienced. Crazy, right? My mouth went dry. My nipples hardened.

I nearly groaned aloud when his fingers swept through my hair from my temples to the base of my neck. I released my curls, giving myself over to the experience.

I hadn't expected him to know what he was doing or to succeed against the wind, but his movements remained confident, and in a flash my hair was secured. His hands went to my shoulders; then he bent until his mouth was beside my ear. "You have an incredible neck."

I swallowed hard. "Thanks?" Really, what did someone say to that?

His lips brushed along it just briefly. "Too much?"

"No." *Perfect.* Our bodies weren't touching, but the heat of him was warming my backside. I fought the urge to close the distance between us and writhe against the part of him I hoped would reveal he found being near me equally exciting.

His voice fell to just above a whisper. "*No* as in you want me to stop, or no, it's not too much?"

"I like it." I turned my head so our faces were close and blurted out, "But to be clear, I don't have sex on the first date." As soon as the words were out of my mouth, I snapped my head back around to face forward. Riley joked that I was about as subtle as a Mack Truck. She wasn't wrong.

He turned me slowly to face him, ending by holding each of my hands in his. I kept my eyes glued to the top button of his shirt. "Keep doing that."

"What?" I said, still not raising my gaze. I'd never been shy, but this was different. Gian was different. I didn't want to mess it up.

"Keep speaking your mind. I love it."

My gaze flew to meet his. Was he serious? There was a fire in his gaze that said I hadn't ruined the mood at all. "Most people wish I'd tone it down."

He ran his hands up and down my arms. "I'm not most people."

"No, you're not." Had another man said those words, he might have sounded corny or boastful, but somehow his declaration came across more as a promise. My eyes began to close as I imagined his mouth taking mine. I tipped my head back and leaned in.

His lips brushed over mine gently, slowly. His breath became a caress on my cheek. My lips parted eagerly, and his tongue swept in, playful and bold, then retreated. It was the perfect first kiss. His lips moved lightly over mine—asking rather than demanding. It said he wanted me but was leaving room for me to set the pace.

When he raised his head, we were both breathing raggedly. His smile warmed me from head to toe. "You dropped your jacket." He stepped back to retrieve it, then held it up for me to put on. I turned and slid my arms into the sleeves.

"Thanks," I said in a thick voice.

"You're welcome."

We stood there simply looking into each other's eyes for a long moment. I told myself I didn't know him well enough to feel the way I did. My body argued that it didn't require more time to know what it wanted.

With the back of his hand he traced my jaw. "You don't appear ready to call the police, so I'm feeling better about how this date will go."

"It's still early," I joked.

He smiled and closed the door of my car. "I'd better be on my best behavior, then. I promised my father we wouldn't go there twice."

My mouth rounded. "You told your father about me?"

He held out his hand for me to take. "I wasn't happy with the impression I'd left you with, and he always has sound advice."

I hesitated, then placed my hand in his. We began to walk together toward a paved path that flanked a rocky beach. "Sounds like you're close."

"We are." As we walked, I ran a hand over the neat braid Gian had impressively executed.

"My parents moved down to Florida when I was in college. I can't imagine calling them to tell them about something so—" I almost said *trivial*, but that was not what our meeting had been.

He waited a beat, as if expecting me to finish the sentence. When I didn't, he said, "My parents want to know everything. We speak every day, eat together several times a week. I've had people ask me if I ever feel like it's too much, but my family keeps me grounded. No matter how bad my day is, I know if I go to my parents' house, it will be full of children running wild, my brothers, their wives, good food, and laughter. How could that be too much?"

Funny how what would have once sounded too chaotic for me suddenly was a whole lot more tempting than spending every night I wasn't with the Ragsdales alone in my apartment.

He gave me a side-glance. "Does that sound like too much for you?"

I shook my head. "Not at all. Riley's house has always felt like that, but with not as many people. They've become my family, by choice rather than birth. Not everyone understands how one can be as important as the other."

"I do." His hand tightened around mine. "What are they like? The Ragsdales."

The mention of Riley was an unwelcome pull back to reality. I shouldn't have been flirting with him without the explanation he'd said he'd give me. It wasn't like me to pretend everything was okay when it wasn't, but there I was, doing exactly that. "Loud. Hilarious. Unfaltering in their support of each other and me."

"And Riley's brother?"

I tensed, as my fantasy of how our date would go was beginning to fade. "I didn't mention she had one."

"I have four brothers. I assume everyone has at least one."

"I don't." I didn't believe his excuse. I wanted to, but I didn't. "I'm an only child, so that throws a wrench in your assumption."

"I suppose it does. So Riley doesn't have a brother?"

"She does. Kal. They're twins." I frowned. There was no going back, no more avoiding the conversation looming before us. "Anything else you'd like to know about the Ragsdales?"

He pulled me to a halt beside him and turned so he was looking down into my eyes. "It's time for me to come clean, isn't it?"

My heart began to thud in my chest. If he said he was equally attracted to Riley, I didn't think I could stop myself from kneeing him in the groin. "Yes."

"I didn't expect to meet someone like you—to have this kind of complication."

"Whatever it is, just say it." Feeling a little sick, I dropped his hand and stepped back. "Why did you come to my shop yesterday? And don't tell me you were looking to place an order. You know the Corisis, don't you?"

He was quiet a moment, then said, "Shit," and rubbed a hand over his face. "Judy found you."

Brick by brick, walls were going up around my heart. "Yes."

"What did she tell you?"

Cold descended over me. See, this was what happened when I listened to my vagina instead of my gut. A person could wish for something as much as they wanted, but it didn't change reality. "Everything." It was a lie, but I said it with zero guilt.

He studied my expression. "And you still wanted this date, so you understand." His gaze fell to my lips.

I wish I did. I didn't want to give up my advantage by admitting how little I knew. So much for stepping outside my life for a few hours. "I do, but I'd feel better about your role in it if you gave me your side."

His forehead creased as he seemed to be weighing his options on how to proceed. I mirrored his stance, continued to look him right in the eye, and waited. Was this about my research? If so, why had they been asking about Riley? Was it a veiled threat toward the people I loved?

If they thought they could intimidate me, they had no idea who they were dealing with.

Start talking.

CHAPTER SEVEN

GIAN

I'd hoped Judy hadn't found the Ragsdales yet. I'd hoped I'd be the first to tell Teagan about our foolhardy bet. After spotting an empty bench overlooking the beach, I motioned toward it. "Let's sit."

She agreed with an incline of her head. I knew that look. She'd had that exact expression right before she'd thrown me out of her store. We sat on the same bench but with enough space between us that I didn't need to ask her how she felt about what Judy and I had done.

"So you know I went to your shop to meet Riley." I let out a slow breath, rested my hands on my knees, and looked out over the ocean as I spoke. "My original intent was to be up front with her. Then I spoke to my father and decided it might be better for everyone involved if I took the time to get to know her before saying anything."

"Because you're not sure she's who you think she is?" Her tone was ice cold. "My guess is you're probably correct to doubt your source."

I glanced her way. Was she suggesting Thomas had lied to me? "Obviously nothing will move forward without confirmation, but just by looking at her, I knew my information was correct."

"Really? What was it about her that clinched it? Because she designs logos?"

I turned to face Teagan and gave her a long look. Were we talking about the same thing? "Her jet-black hair. Her eyes as well. They're a unique shade."

It was Teagan's turn to frown. "That doesn't make sense. What does eye or hair color have to do with aptitude?"

Realization came like a kick in the pants. "Judy didn't tell you why she wanted to meet Riley, did she?"

Teagan folded her arms across her chest. "She didn't."

I nodded and let out a slow breath. "That's some poker face you have."

She held my gaze. "I don't gamble."

"Of course you don't." I ran my hands through my hair and turned my attention to the ocean. "There's no spin I could give this that would make me look good."

"I'm not interested in anything but the truth."

Nothing was going the way I'd imagined it. Not the wager. Not telling Riley. Certainly not this date. The one thing I was sure of was that no healthy relationship could be built on lies. Could I trust her with information no one outside my family knew? Teagan cared about Riley and her family. She wouldn't want to see them hurt any more than I would. "Dominic Corisi is my brother—half brother via our mother, but I don't use fractions when referring to family. We've kept that tidbit out of the news, so I'd appreciate it if you did as well."

"Judy is your niece?"

"Yes."

"And you both came to my shop looking for Riley because . . . ?"

"Because we believe she's Dominic's sister via their father."

"Dominic Corisi, Riley, and Kal are all siblings?"

"That's what we believe. What we don't know is how revealing that information to both sides would affect everyone."

"Do you think Dominic will resent discovering his father had more children?"

I chuckled, but without much humor. "The opposite. He'll swoop in and save them from their lives, even if being saved isn't what they want."

"What does that mean?"

I slumped forward, resting my elbows on my knees. How could I describe Dominic without making him sound like an ass? "He's a tsunami of helpfulness. When he finds out he has siblings his father never acknowledged, family who still struggles financially—their lives will change overnight. Shouldn't we first make sure that's what they'd want?"

I turned back toward Teagan. She seemed to be digesting what I'd said. After a moment, she said, "If what you're saying is true, it's not for you to decide how it plays out. Both sides have a right to know they're family."

"I couldn't come up with a lie this elaborate if I wanted to. There's a slim chance they're not related. A blood test would be the easiest way to confirm, but I was hoping to find out enough about the Ragsdales that it wouldn't be necessary. Either Fara slept with Antonio Corisi, or she didn't. If she did, there is no denying her children are his. They look just like him. If she didn't, she fucked his doppelgänger. Possible, but unlikely."

Teagan took out her phone and did a search for photos of Dominic. Her expression changed as her screen filled with images of him. "There is a strong resemblance." She looked up and scanned my face. "You don't look much like him, though."

I shrugged. "Different fathers. Mine was a vineyard owner. Dirt poor." I didn't know why I threw it in, but I added, "Rumor has it Dominic's father killed mine."

"Awkward."

"Very." Of all the ways to describe the fallout from that rumor, *awkward* wasn't what I would have chosen. It was fitting, though.

"Do you get along? You and Dominic?"

"Yes and no. He's a good person, just more than I can handle in large doses."

"Why?"

I sighed. "Let's just say it's been eight years since I discovered we were related, and I'm still learning how to have him in my life without him taking it over."

"He doesn't sound like a very good person."

I acknowledged a truth I often lost sight of. "He means well. He wants me to be happy. We just have different ideas about how that should look, and it's nearly impossible to get him to see that."

Teagan fell silent again. For several moments we both simply looked out over the ocean. "So you're afraid Dominic would overwhelm the Ragsdales?"

"He might." Was I superimposing my own concerns on the situation? Maybe. I gripped the bench on either side of me. "You know them; I don't. What do you think?"

She looked down at her phone again and did another internet search. I didn't know what she was looking for as she swiped through photo after photo of the Romanos as well as the Corisis. She held her phone up to me and pointed at a photo. "Who's that?"

I was glad I'd been up front with Teagan. She was not only intelligent but also extremely observant. "That's my oldest brother, Sebastian."

"He also looks—"

"He is." Twenty-eight years—that was how long it had taken me to realize Sebastian looked nothing like Mauricio and Christof. Eight of those years had been with the Corisis mixing with the Romanos. Yet somehow I hadn't seen the truth until my father had slipped up and hinted at it. Teagan had spotted the resemblance instantly. She was definitely someone who would keep me on my toes. "But we don't talk about it."

She lowered her phone. "Does Sebastian know?"

In for a penny, in for a pound. "No. That was the gist of the conversation I had with my father when he found out I was looking for more family for Dominic. Sebastian has been through hell and back. He lost his first wife when she was pregnant with their child. For a long time he was so sad none of us could reach him. He's remarried now, finally happy again, and the question we ask ourselves is if hearing something like that might send him spiraling downward again."

"I'm sorry to hear about his loss."

"It wasn't recent, but it was felt deeply by my entire family. Sebastian already has a relationship with both Dominic as well as Nicole, his sister. For now that might be enough."

I could see the wheels turning in her head. "If that's the case, why would you look for family for Dominic? And once you found them, why would you be uncertain if you should tell either side?" Before I had a chance to answer, she continued, "Because it wasn't your idea to."

"It was." I winced. The truth was worse than she'd guessed. I could have hoped it never came out, but it would, and I'd probably already told her enough to kill my chance at a second date. What needed to be done now was damage control so no one ended up hurt by the wager I'd made with Judy. "I suggested looking for more siblings for Dominic mostly as a joke. Judy took up the challenge, and we made a bet regarding which of us could find one first."

Her lips thinned. "Do you often do that? Play with people's lives as part of a bet?" Her disgust was clear.

"When you say it like that, it sounds nefarious."

"Is there another way to see it?"

My smile faded—there was no defending what we'd done. "Misguided? To answer your earlier question, we've never bet about anything like this before. Usually it's something inconsequential, like who can circumvent a high-tech security system faster."

I expected her to laugh because it sounded far fetched. She didn't, though. She looked me over, as if she were assessing someone's qualifications at a job interview. For someone who owned a printshop, she didn't seem at all fazed by the idea of hacking for fun. "Who wins?"

I took a moment before answering. This was a lot to unload on someone I'd just met, but it didn't feel as if we were strangers. "We're about even. I don't enjoy it, but I've gotten good at it because Judy can be . . . impulsive. I feel better if I'm in the mix on her adventures."

"So you join in to keep her out of trouble?" Sarcasm weighted her tone.

I let a sheepish smile be my answer. It was true. Also, part of me enjoyed the competition, but I wasn't yet ready to admit it.

Her expression tightened, and hurt filled her eyes. "Did you only ask me out so you could pump me for information about the Ragsdales?"

"No." My stomach clenched, and I reached for her hand, but she withdrew it. I took a calming breath and tried to see our conversation from her perspective. I'd just admitted to having a hidden agenda for stepping into her store. Something like that didn't exactly inspire trust. "I realize you have little reason to believe me, but I stopped caring about winning the wager as soon as I met you."

"If you say it was because you felt like you'd already won, I may vomit in my own mouth."

I held back a smile. No one could ever accuse her of not saying what was on her mind. "I wouldn't want that. Let me see if I can say how I feel in a way that won't inspire you to regurgitate your lunch. I like you. I wanted to see you again. Neither had anything to do with the wager."

Her eyes flashed. "You don't have to lie to me. It wouldn't change that I'm willing to help you find out if Riley really is Dominic's sister. I'd do anything—for *her*."

"Everything I told you is the truth."

"Says every liar." She held my gaze.

I liked that she didn't make things easy for me, but I didn't like that she didn't seem to see herself the way I did. "Do you want to know what I like about you?"

Her eyes narrowed. "Sure."

I lowered my voice. "Then come closer."

She sat up straighter, as if I'd surprised her. "No."

I made a show of shrugging. "Up to you."

We sat there for a few minutes in a battle of wills that was sexy as all hell. The advantage I hoped I had was that she might want to kiss me again as much as I wanted to kiss her. So I waited.

Another man might have swept in, but that wasn't what I wanted. There were already too many unknowns in this situation. I wasn't budging without a clear indicator of what she wanted. Her tongue flicked across her bottom lip, and I groaned. That was good, but I held out for more.

She blinked a few times, let out a shaky breath, and inched nearer.

I could have let her off the hook then, but I enjoyed the push-pull of us. "Closer."

Desire shone in her eyes as she scooted over more until the side of her leg brushed against mine. "Close enough?" she asked in challenge.

"Hardly," I answered, then cleared my throat. "But that works for now." I bent until our lips hovered a mere breath from each other's. "I like everything."

The air throbbed between us. "That's a cop-out."

"And yet true." I brushed my lips gently over hers. "You also have amazingly expressive eyes. I can tell when you're tempted to strangle me." In just above a whisper, I said, "And when you're thinking of other ways we could pass the time."

She brought a hand up to cup my cheek. "For clarification, I never fantasized about asphyxiation. I was imagining kneeing you in the groin."

I chuckled, then brought her fingers to my mouth and kissed the tips of them. "Good to know." I placed her hand high on my thigh, near but not on my hardening cock. "What else did you imagine?"

Her hand tightened on my thigh, and she shifted upward and answered my question with a kiss that quickly turned heated. Her mouth opened to mine, and I swept in, making clear where I wanted this to go. Only the knowledge that kids were romping nearby kept my hands from untucking her shirt and sliding up to cup those perfect breasts of hers. A burst of passion, deliciously contained. Never had I wanted a woman more.

She broke off the kiss and sat back, looking as shaken as I felt. My thoughts were a mess, or I would have said something to reassure her. Instead we both sat there, alternating between looking at each other and turning away to watch the waves. I was a man in my prime. I'd dated many women and slept with more than my fair share, but this was the first woman who could leave me shaken with just a kiss. I didn't know what that meant for where we were headed, but I definitely wanted to find out.

When she spoke, her voice was delightfully husky. "That doesn't mean I agree with making a bet about something as important as someone's parentage."

"Of course not. But?" I wanted her next words to be about me.

"But I do think we should find out if Fara was with Antonio before telling Riley she might have two more brothers." Damn. I felt like a teenager trying and failing to catch the eye of his crush from across the lunchroom. She continued, "Is Antonio a dangerous man?"

She wanted to talk, so that meant some of my blood needed to return to my head. "He's dead, but that's a good thing—trust me. He was a horrible person."

She sucked in a breath. "Another reason to go forward with care. Laying that on her before we've confirmed their connection would be irresponsible."

"I agree." I felt like an asshole thinking about all the ways I wanted to fuck her while she was considering the fate of her friend and my family. *Thank God women can't read men's minds.*

She sighed. "Are you certain about Sebastian?"

"Yes."

With a shake of her head, she said, "You're related to Dominic through your mother. Sebastian is related to Dominic through their father. Sebastian technically isn't your brother; he's your—"

"Cousin. It's a fucking mess. Antonio didn't have a problem with impregnating sisters."

"Wow." Her eyebrows arched.

"You don't know the half of it."

Her expression turned serious again. She looked out over the water. "I don't know that I should. Why did you tell me so much?"

I reached out and took one of her hands in mine. "I don't like secrets."

She looked down at our intertwined hands. "It's a lot of information to entrust to someone you just met."

I raised her hand to my mouth and kissed her knuckles. "I'm not looking for a one-night stand with you. I know it's early, but whatever this is between us—it feels important enough to give a real chance. Without trust, how could we move forward?"

She released my hand and stood. "I appreciate your honesty. Obviously I'm attracted to you, but I need time to think about this. It's a lot."

I surged to my feet and turned her face gently toward mine. "Take all the time you need."

"Thank you for understanding." She searched my expression. I wished I knew what she was looking for me to say.

She started walking back toward our cars, and I fell into step with her. I couldn't remember the last time I'd felt so much at a loss for what to say to a woman. We were at her car too soon.

She opened the door and paused. "I'll ask Fara about Antonio. She'll tell me."

I nodded. "I'd like to know as soon as you do."

She nodded, too, then slid into the driver's seat and closed the door between us.

A question came to me, so I knocked on her window. As soon as she lowered it, I asked, "If Judy didn't tell you about Riley, what did she say she was there for?"

"She didn't."

I couldn't imagine Judy not grilling Teagan about the Ragsdales. "That surprises me."

Teagan looked away. "She didn't have a lot of time. Her father's head of security arrived shortly after she did and wasn't happy with her being at my printshop."

"Marc Stone. No, I imagine he wouldn't be. I'll call him. Judy shouldn't take all the heat for this."

A small smile pulled at Teagan's lips. "You're a good uncle."

"I try."

We stared into each other's eyes for long enough I was wondering if she was waiting for me to kiss her again. I leaned down.

She raised the window between us, saying, "I'll text you," just before it closed.

With a goofy grin on my face, I stood in the middle of the parking lot, watching her drive off.

Smitten.

I finally understood the true meaning of the word.

CHAPTER EIGHT

TEAGAN

I kept my attention on the traffic as I pulled out of the parking lot. I didn't look back to see if Gian was still where I'd left him. I needed to put distance between us to start thinking straight again.

I cracked my window because my body was still revving hot. I would not have slept with the men I had if I'd met Gian first. I'd thought I'd known what lust was, but I hadn't. With other men intimacy had been something I'd decided I'd wanted in my head first before my body had engaged. With Gian it was the opposite. All he had to do was look at me, and my brain melted to mush. Endorphins? Pheromones? With nothing more than a softly spoken command, he'd bypassed my analytical/cautious side, and it had been a heady experience.

I'd never understood alcohol or drug addictions, but I'd read that they often started when people experienced a high so good they would risk anything to feel it again. Was that what I was doing with Gian?

The situation was far too complicated.

Riley had told me she didn't know who her father was. She'd said it wasn't a topic her mother had ever been open to discussing, so they hadn't. I hoped Fara would answer questions from me.

I knew one thing: all of us and my shop were already under more scrutiny than we'd ever been. I needed to ramp up my security at Haven Two.

Remaining invisible became exponentially more difficult once your existence had been detected. And that I had something to hide had been revealed. I'd need to do some fast programming to come up with something to keep at Haven One that might seem important enough to conceal.

Prior to Judy finding my computer lab, only Riley had known what I was working on. Everyone else thought I'd failed to find work in the technology field, even with my fancy degree, and settled for a career in custom-shirt printing.

My hands tightened on the steering wheel of my car. I'd been right to end the date with Gian early. I needed time to consider all possible scenarios.

Was everything Gian had said true? Partly true? Or all a lie? When Gian had admitted he'd come to my shop to meet Riley, I'd still assumed it was somehow related to my research. According to him it wasn't. Even if Gian had been honest about that, I couldn't tell him about NYD. He'd gushed family secrets like a burst water pipe. *I'd be a fool to expect him to keep my work confidential.*

I'd worked too hard to risk everything on a man I knew next to nothing about. Once back at my shop I tried to psych myself up to start a new program but found myself turning on Riley's laptop instead.

I spent the next few hours online reading everything available about Gian, the Romanos, and the Corisis. In all the mainstream media channels, there was suspiciously little on any of them. Even their social media accounts appeared scrubbed clean of anything of substance—a few photos, nothing more.

So I went deeper. I sought out my dark web contacts and discovered the Corisis were rarely spoken about directly. Code words were used, and conversations were encrypted. *Call me fascinated.* Just how powerful was Dominic Corisi? Even the dark web feared his wrath.

Crazy.

A collaborator from one of my open-source groups was willing to speak to me about it on a landline only. Thankfully my store had one. The hair on the back of my neck rose when he said people who crossed Dominic Corisi disappeared—in every way a person could. They were wiped from databases around the globe. Birth certificates disappeared, even in paper form. If he wanted someone gone, they ceased to exist.

Someone like that should never get their hands on a technology like NYD.

"What about the Romanos? Are they the same?" I couldn't imagine Gian wiping someone off the planet, but even an association with someone who did was damning.

"I don't have anything on them, although Romano Superstores wasn't always the 'store of the people' it currently makes itself out to be. It took over the market with a fair amount of smash-and-grab maneuvers."

"I wasn't aware of that." I wondered how that played into the story Gian had told me about his brother's sadness. "I've read several articles about the good they do in the communities they get involved with."

"That's because the news focuses on their philanthropy and the businesses they bail out rather than asking how they came into the money to be able to do either."

Not good, but not as bad as erasing people. "How reliable is your information about Dominic Corisi?"

"Very. He's generous, but when he calls in a favor, you can't refuse."

Was that what Gian had been referring to when he'd said he was still trying to figure out how not to let Dominic take over his life? I got goose bumps.

My friend continued, "If I were you, I'd stop asking about him. You don't want him to know your name."

That likely wasn't an option. "This isn't mere curiosity. It's important. There has to be someone who could answer questions about him."

"Good luck with your search for that person. Sorry I couldn't help."

"That's okay."

"And don't call this number again. Don't contact me online either. I can't be connected to you anymore."

Wow. "Understood."

Shaken, I paced my shop after ending that call. No wonder Judy thought she was untouchable. Holy shit.

It made sense, as well, that Gian might question whether introducing Dominic into someone's life was a good idea. I was questioning that myself, even if it did turn out he was related to Riley and Kal.

I rubbed my hands over my face. Well, Riley had asked for money, but like me she hadn't been specific about how it would come to her. If it ended up that she was related to Dominic, would that protect her from his darker side?

Gian had described Dominic as a good person—a tsunami of help. I'd sensed frustration in his description, but not fear. Something wasn't as it appeared.

I jumped when my phone vibrated with a message. Gian.

I can't get you out of my head.

With more than a little irony, I typed back, I've been thinking about you, too.

I want to see you again.

My face warmed, because despite everything I'd learned, I wanted to see him as well. I shouldn't, but I did. That didn't mean I was going to give in to the temptation. I need a few days. I have a tight deadline for a project I'm working on.

Anything I can help with?

I don't think so. I plan to see Fara tomorrow.

Are you okay?

Yes. I wanted to say, *No, not with any of this. I have a growing list of questions I need answered before I let you or anyone near the Ragsdales.* I didn't say that, because he didn't know I knew anything more than he'd told me. When you had an information advantage, you didn't give it up, not even to a man who knew how to kiss you until your toes curled. I'll text you as soon as I find out anything.

Or before if you miss me.

I smiled, then frowned. Where was the wand I could wave that would make everything but me and him disappear? I wanted to flirt about nothing, have lighthearted conversations, and wake up with him next to me.

I smacked my forehead lightly with my phone.

Stay in reality, Teagan. This is way too important to mess up.

I couldn't give Gian a reason to wonder if I knew something. What would I have said if I hadn't spent the last few hours researching his connection to the Corisis and shitting myself? Anything is possible.

Vague.

Could be taken as playful.

It would have to be good enough.

Good night, he wrote.

Good night.

CHAPTER NINE

GIAN

I didn't text Teagan the next morning, but I wanted to. I couldn't blame her for needing time to sort through the amount of family crap I'd vomited on her during our date. Looking back, I hated that I'd shared so much. I was two for two on delivering less than my best when it came to her.

That didn't mean I was ready to give up. There was something different about Teagan, different about how I felt when I was with her. I wanted to know her—why she'd chosen to open a printshop, how happy she was or wasn't with her life, what her dreams were.

I also wanted to fuck her, but that went without saying. I was a healthy male, and she was beautiful. Sexual attraction alone wasn't enough to have me as tangled up on the inside as I'd been since I'd met her.

It was confusing.

Awful.

And wonderful all at the same time.

My father often said he'd known well before my mother had that they were meant to be together. Now that I knew she'd been pregnant with another man's child when they'd married, it rang even more true. I couldn't imagine a better-matched couple.

And somehow he'd known.

I parked outside the front entrance of the headquarters of Romano Superstores. Sebastian exited as soon as I appeared, which meant he'd been waiting for me. I checked my watch. Five minutes late. I hoped it didn't start this off on the wrong foot. "Hope you weren't waiting long," I said as soon as he climbed into the passenger seat.

He cocked an eyebrow at me but didn't say anything. In the silence that followed I had time to be glad I'd decided to invite Mauricio and Christof to this lunch. Sebastian and I were in a good place now, but there'd been years when nothing I'd said had been right, and everything he'd said had made me want to punch him in the face. He'd seriously mellowed out since then, and I'd grown a thicker skin.

Our history mirrored my current journey with Dominic, which was interesting now that I knew they had the same father. Seriously, the only explanation for why I had missed his resemblance to Dominic was that I hadn't wanted to see it.

Now I couldn't unsee it.

He gave me an impatient look. "Are we going? You said you had something you wanted to discuss. I have an hour free, then back-to-back meetings."

I pulled away from the building. "I thought we'd have more time. I told Mauricio and Christof to meet us at the Rusty Pail. I can tell them to put in an order for us."

"When you finally get a job, you'll understand that lunch is a luxury that most times also revolves around work."

I took a deep breath and pulled into traffic. Sebastian wasn't as much of an ass as he sounded. Still, I was glad I'd chosen a restaurant that was only a few blocks away. "I'm sure I will." It wasn't the start I'd hoped for, so I began again. "Heather told me you're trying for a fourth child. I think that's great."

Normally any mention of his family was enough to bring a smile to Sebastian's face, but this time his expression remained watchful. "What's going on?"

"What do you mean?"

"You obviously have something big you want to tell me—something you thought required full-brother intervention. Did you piss Dominic off?"

"No."

"Mom?"

"No. Why do you assume I did something wrong? This could be good news."

"Is it?"

I winced. "Depends how you look at it. It's one of those things that takes a while to sort through."

"And you can't save us all the time and just say it?"

I pulled into a parking spot outside the restaurant, not seeing my other brothers' cars. "Let's start over. Ask me what I've been up to, and let's talk about nothing important until Mauricio and Christof get here."

Sebastian gave me a dark look that would have had a younger me questioning if he liked me at all. I was past that. Now I considered that expression simply a part of him. He had a resting what-the-fuck-are-you-talking-about face. Often he was thinking something much kinder.

"Just say it."

The two back doors of my car opened. Mauricio climbed in on one side, Christof on the other. Mauricio said, "So we're doing this in the car?"

Ever the easygoing one, Christof clapped a hand on my shoulder. "Wise choice. Privacy is a good idea."

"What the fuck are you all talking about?" Sebastian demanded. Okay, so maybe his expression did reflect his thoughts.

"Did you tell him anything?" Mauricio asked.

"Not yet," I admitted.

"Is someone dying?" Sebastian growled.

I forced a smile. "No, but keep that thought in mind, because compared to that possibility—this is just a wrinkle in the fabric of our family."

The car fell silent. As the youngest in our family, I half expected Christof or Mauricio to jump in and say it, but they didn't. I took a deep breath and dived in. "When I was younger, I worried about how I fit into our family because I was born your cousin, not your brother."

Sebastian's expression softened. "But now you understand how little that matters."

"I do. Family is about commitment, loyalty, and love—not the labels we're born with." We had all that. "You are my brother by choice, and that matters more than whatever circumstances brought us together."

Sebastian looked pleased for a moment, then turned in his seat so he could search the faces of his other brothers. Mauricio and Christof were nodding in support of my monologue. "This isn't about you, is it, Gian?"

I squared my shoulders and prayed I'd chosen the right time, place, and words. "No. It's about you. You and Dominic—"

"I know," Sebastian cut in with a wave of his hand. "Dominic and I discussed the probability years ago. I'm only a couple months older than he is, but the resemblance was too strong. Before you say anything else, I don't care. Basil will always be my father. I don't want to know how our mother and aunt had children from the same man, and I'm sure Mom doesn't want me to want to know. So if that was your big announcement—we're good. Let's go eat."

I wished it were that simple. "There's just one more thing."

Mauricio joked, "I don't know if I can handle more reveals. Any minute I expect to discover *my* father was an alien."

"That would explain so much about you," Christof parried.

I turned more in my seat to face the back of the car. "Not helping."

They shrugged in unison, then grinned. Brothers. I looked over at Sebastian again. "Antonio Corisi had five children."

Sebastian's eyes snapped back in my direction, and he released the door handle.

I cleared my throat. "You. Dominic. Nicole. And twins with a woman in Lockton, Massachusetts. A boy and girl. They're now in their twenties. Riley and Kal Ragsdale."

Sebastian expelled a harsh breath.

"Are you certain?" Christof asked. "Dad said you were looking into them."

I pulled up a photo of Kal from his social media and held it up for my brothers to see. "This is Kal."

Mauricio whistled. "To be safe, I guess you should get a DNA test done, but wow, just wow. Sebastian, looks like you have more family."

Christof added, "We all do. They're our cousins, right?"

"I'd need a diagram before I could answer that. Our family is getting too complicated for me to keep it straight." Mauricio threw up his hands.

Lacking the ability to provide him with a visual, I said, "Technically, they're blood relatives only of Sebastian and Dominic, not the rest of us. They had the same bio father. My bio mother had me when she was in hiding from Antonio. Antonio seems to have hooked up with their mother then. Since Sebastian is older than Dominic, that means Mom was with him before Rosella."

"Stop," Sebastian barked. "Was I not clear when I said I don't want to know?"

The car fell silent.

In what was likely an attempt to lessen the tension, Mauricio said, "You can email me that diagram later."

Sebastian looked angry, but I knew it was his go-to response when he was worried. "Mom is okay, Sebastian. Dad thinks it will be a relief to her to have the truth out." I swallowed hard. I knew this was difficult for him to hear. I'd often wished my own life story were simple. Denying something, though, didn't make it less real. "Mom didn't want you to know, because she's always been afraid it would change how you see her. It might be time to tell her it would never."

He rubbed a hand over his face, then said, "You're right."

My head snapped back. "What did you just say?"

He rolled his eyes. "You heard me."

With a grin spreading across my face, I shot a look at my other brothers. "Hear that? I'm right. This might be the start of a whole new relationship for us, Sebastian. From this day forward you'll walk around, eyes open to my genius, constantly acknowledging how often I'm correct. It'll be a burden, being the brains of the family, but I'll bear it because I must."

"Shut the fuck up," Sebastian said, but he smiled.

I laughed.

Mauricio and Christof joined in.

When the car grew quiet again, Sebastian said, "I have another brother and sister."

I nodded. "They don't know about us yet, though. Not any of us. Teagan asked for time to speak to their mother, Fara, first."

"Who's Teagan? Another sibling?" Mauricio asked.

"No." My face warmed as the memory of our kisses rocked through me. "She's Riley's friend as well as her employer."

Christof leaned forward in his seat. "Say her name again."

"Riley?" I asked, pretending not to know which he was referring to.

He wasn't letting me off that easily. "Her boss."

"Teagan," I said, realizing as I spoke how much was given away in the way I said it.

Christof laughed and sat back. "Dad said Gian met a woman he'd soon be bringing home to meet us. My guess is that's her."

"Better than the alternative," Mauricio said lightly. When I glared at him, he threw his hands up. "What? You're not related. It would have been bad, but—"

"It would have been bad—period. So bring on Teagan." Christof slugged him in the shoulder.

Sebastian shook his head, but he was still smiling. "I wouldn't trade any of you, but there are days when I ask myself why."

I couldn't help but ask, "Do you ever wonder who you'd be if you'd been raised by Antonio Corisi?"

"No," he said with finality and a look in his eye that reminded me so much of Dominic I remembered something my father had said. Sebastian and Dominic shared many of the same traits, but I treated the two relationships very differently. I didn't tease Dominic the way I did Sebastian. I didn't challenge him.

Judy's suggestion that I race her father was beginning to make sense to me. It wasn't because I needed to best him; it was because I needed to be confident enough to. Confident—not in my ability to race but in his love for me regardless of the outcome.

When I'd called Mauricio and Christof and asked them to come to lunch because I had news to tell Sebastian, I hadn't doubted they would show. In times of crisis Romanos pulled together.

To move forward with Dominic, I needed to find that level of trust. My father had said Dominic couldn't hear me because I didn't make myself clear enough with him. The older I got, the more I valued my father's opinion.

I checked my watch. "Do we still have time for lunch?"

"I didn't drive all the way out here to not eat," Mauricio said.

Christof shrugged. "I cleared the afternoon in case it was needed."

Sebastian took out his phone and sent off a text. "My afternoon is clear as well."

Mauricio and Christof climbed out of the car. I didn't when I saw that Sebastian wasn't following suit.

He cleared his throat. "If I hadn't known and Mom had dropped this on me, I might have said something I didn't mean."

"And no one could have blamed you for it. It's a lot to take in."

"Thank you for today."

"You're welcome."

The look he gave me was difficult to decipher. "I'll go see Mom tonight."

"That's a good idea."

He drummed his fingers on his knees. "As far as Riley and Kal—I trust your judgment. I'm open to meeting them, but I want to hold off on introducing them to Heather and the kids until I get a sense of who they are." That made sense. "When do you intend to tell Dominic?"

"Once I've confirmed that Fara was with Antonio."

"Do you want me there when you do?"

"No, I'm fine." Speaking to a brother shouldn't require backup.

"He might need the support."

My mouth went slack as I realized what that said about Dominic as well as Sebastian. I had a hard time imagining either of them admitting to needing people, but that didn't mean they didn't.

Something else my father had said about Dominic came back to me. Dominic wanted what I had with my other brothers. When I looked at it that way, I understood why we clashed so often. I didn't want him to buy me things, but he didn't know another way in.

Money did open doors. Helping our family in Montalcino had won him access to relationships that had been blocked for so long. The world shouldn't work that way, but sometimes it did. I hated how that experience seemed to influence how Dominic interacted with me. I wasn't our cousins in Italy. I didn't need or want to be saved.

An image came to me of where I wished we could get. I wanted to be able to pick up the phone and tell him I needed him and for him to simply be there. He didn't need to take the situation over or fix it—I just wanted him in the mix.

I wondered what he would have said had I invited him to a Romano intervention lunch without telling the whole story first.

I'd never know, because I hadn't.

I sighed. I was beginning to see how much I was shaping our relationship. I decided right then that I would do better. "Sebastian?"

"Yes?"

"I love you."

He frowned, then smiled and shook his head. "Let's go fucking eat."
I turned to let myself out. I was half out of the car when I heard him
say, "I love you too."

I smiled without turning around.

A short time later I dunked a clam cake in a bowl of New England
clam chowder, then popped it in my mouth. I nearly choked on it when
Christof asked, "So tell us about this Teagan of yours."

I finished chewing and wiped my mouth with a napkin while I
chose my words carefully. "We've only had one date. It's too early to
say much."

"If you don't know yet, she's probably not the one." Mauricio
picked up a french fry and wagged it at me. "I knew right away that
Wren was for me."

Christof shook his head. "I call bullshit. I seem to recall a rocky
patch where you thought it was over. Dad surprised you by hiring her
to inspect our sprinkler system, and you accused her of being after your
money."

"Never happened," Mauricio said with confidence.

Christof took a sip of his beer, then continued, "Tell him, Sebastian."

"I was there," Sebastian said in a neutral tone before raising his glass
of water in mock salute.

"Sure. Fine. Maybe we did start out that way." Waving both hands,
Mauricio dismissed what they were saying. "I don't hold on to the negative. I'd rather look back and remember our time in Paris." He sighed.
"I should take her back there for our anniversary. Who wants to watch
our kids?"

"We can trade off children. I'd love to steal McKenna away to Italy
again, just the two of us for once. We try to go every year, but it would
be fun to stay in the guesthouse again." Christof turned his attention
back to me. "The point is you don't have to know right away. It's okay to

get some things wrong in the beginning. If it's meant to be, everything works itself out."

"Even when you've given up hoping it ever could," Sebastian said in a quiet tone. "This Teagan doesn't have to be the woman for you, but when you meet the right one—don't give yourself anything to regret. Be the man she deserves . . . right out of the gate. No matter what else you do in life, coming home to a good family . . . one you've done right by . . . there's nothing better."

I bit into another clam cake to buy some time. My brothers were all settled with children. The same was expected of me. I didn't hate the idea, although I wasn't in a rush. "I like her. I definitely want to see her again. I don't know if I'm ready to accuse her of chasing me for my money."

Mauricio cocked an eyebrow at me.

Christof laughed.

Sebastian smiled.

And all was right in the world. I'd started the day worried about all the ways it could go wrong, but we were stronger than the twists and turns life continued to throw at us.

What would Teagan think of my family? Romanos were old fashioned in some ways; we opened doors, pulled out chairs, offered to carry anything heavy—even if our women were perfectly capable of doing it themselves. That didn't mean we didn't see women as our equals. It meant we treasured them. I'd been raised to believe that when love was done right, there was no competition, no power struggle.

My brothers felt the same and had each chosen brilliant partners. Sebastian's wife, Heather, owned an accounting business. Mauricio's wife, Wren, designed and produced high-tech prosthetics. Well, she and her father designed them. Mauricio was the pretty-boy face of the company. It worked for them. Christof's wife, McKenna, owned her own racetrack facility, where she refurbished and sold old NASCAR stock cars. They were all strong, independent, and intelligent women. Teagan would fit right in.

I looked around the table. When I was younger, I would have thought my brothers were the last people I'd turn to for advice when it came to dating, but they were all happily married and had been for years. That said something. "Teagan and I haven't actually gotten off to a great start."

I told them about the day I'd met her and how my actions had left her with the impression that I was also interested in Riley. I walked them through why I'd felt it was important to open up to her on our date, how much I'd dumped on her, and where we'd left things between us. "Essentially, she said she needed a couple of days to sort some things out."

"I'd call her," Mauricio said with conviction.

Christof shook his head. "She asked for time. Give her time."

I looked to Sebastian. "What do you think?"

He took a moment before answering. "How important is it to you that you see her again?"

I considered the possibility of never seeing her again—or, worse, seeing her with someone else—and said, "Very."

"Don't worry about anyone else's journey. When you meet the right person, there's a moment when you just know. Everything is different."

"Different how?"

"If she gets into your heart, you won't need to ask that question. For now send her something that keeps you in her thoughts without making her feel pressured."

He made it sound easy. "Like flowers?"

"Lame." Mauricio leaned forward. "You need to wow her. Go big, or go home—that's what closes the deal. I lined up a private tour of the Eiffel Tower for Wren."

Christof added, "I sent McKenna dessert, then took her to Italy."

"The important thing is she knows you're thinking about her," Sebastian said.

"Thanks. I think I know the perfect thing to send her."

CHAPTER TEN

TEAGAN

"I already ate," I told Fara as she filled a bowl with elbow noodles and store-bought meat sauce. "Plus I'm trying to cut down on carbs."

"Eat. You look fine, and you know I hate to waste food. It'll go bad if no one eats it. It's you or the dog, and the vet says Luna is overweight."

At the mention of her name the round, aged black poodle waddled into the kitchen. I accepted the bowl with a chuckle and sat at the small wooden table. She didn't need the calories any more than I did. "Sorry, all mine, Luna."

With slow, intentional movements, Fara took the seat across from me. She winced but didn't say anything. I looked around the room with loving eyes. I had so many good memories from the years I'd spent there. I'd stayed over enough that my parents had wondered if I'd moved in.

Fara lived on the first floor of a large apartment building on a busy street in a neighborhood that became dangerous after dark. Nothing about her was materialistic. I tried to imagine her with a man like Antonio Corisi and couldn't. Still, someone had fathered her children—someone who hadn't cared enough to remain a part of their lives.

I pushed the pasta around in my bowl while trying to remember the way I'd decided to word my questions. "No Riley tonight?"

"I haven't seen much of her this week. The wedding she is in is driving her crazy. I can't imagine being a bridesmaid for hire—sounds exhausting, but she says it's good money. This bride has her running errands with her like she's her personal assistant. I guess it's okay as long as she pays for the time."

"I'd give her more hours if I could—"

"You do enough for her, Teagan. She has to find her own way. And she will. I told her to stop going in late to her job for you. Loyalty should always trump money."

"She's making good money with her side job, and her schedule with me is flexible. As long as she gets her orders done, the hours aren't set in stone." Even if they were, that wasn't what I was there to discuss. "I had an interesting visitor come in my shop the other day."

"You did? Was it a man?"

I couldn't keep my questions in any longer. I looked up from my food to meet her gaze. "Does the name Corisi mean anything to you?"

All color left her cheeks, and one of her hands crumpled a napkin. "Why do you ask?"

"Was Antonio Corisi Riley and Kal's father?"

"He was never that."

I reached across and laid a hand over hers. "Biologically."

She pursed her lips and looked away, as if briefly revisiting the past. "Who came to your shop?"

"His granddaughter Judy. And a man named Gian Romano. Not together. It's a little complicated, but in short, they were looking for more family for Dominic Corisi, and their search led them to Kal and Riley."

Fara pushed back her chair. Her salt-and-pepper curls swung forward as she stood. "The Corisis are a very dangerous family. I had hoped to never have this conversation."

"Dangerous like in the mafia?"

"The mafia wishes they had the kind of power the Corisis have. There are people who are above the law, Teagan. They don't play by the same rules you and I do."

"No one is above the law."

Fara swung around, agitated in a way I hadn't ever seen her. "I don't know how to protect my family from this." She rubbed her arms and blinked several times quickly. "I should have moved away—far, far away."

I rose and went to stand with her. "What happened, Fara?"

She closed her eyes briefly and took a deep breath. "I like to think I'm a good person."

"You are."

"But I was happy the day I heard that monster had died. Only then could I begin to breathe again."

I searched her face, half-sorry I'd brought up the past, half-certain I couldn't leave without knowing what had happened. "Did he hurt you?" I asked, barely getting the words out.

"Not at first." She covered her face with her hands. "Then often enough that I thought it was my fault." She lowered her hands, and there was such pain in her eyes I thought I might be sick. "When he came into my life, I thought I'd met Prince Charming. He was good looking. Rich. He said I was beautiful, and that's how I felt when he looked at me. He said his wife had run off, and I couldn't understand how any woman would ever leave him." She shuddered. "It started with a slap I forgave because he was having a bad day. He apologized. But it quickly became darker, angrier. I think he was punishing me for whatever happened between him and his wife. I tried to hide from him, but he always found me, and when he did—it was bad. It was so, so bad. He said he would kill me one day, and I believed him. By then I had heard the rumors that he'd had his wife killed."

Tears pouring down my face, I put an arm around her. "Did you ever tell the police?"

She tensed beneath my touch. "Of course I did. They wouldn't do anything. I was no one. He was a billionaire. It wasn't until he really hurt me, broke my back, and sent me to the hospital that it stopped."

"Oh my God."

"A man came to see me at the hospital. His name was Thomas Brogos. He told me he could keep Antonio away from me, but only if I remained silent. He promised to protect me. So I told the hospital I fell down the stairs. They told me I was pregnant. I've never been so scared in my life. I never saw Antonio or Thomas again. He kept his word, and I kept my silence."

I hugged her tighter, hating that anyone had ever hurt her. If he weren't already dead, I might have hunted him down and killed him myself. "I'm so sorry, Fara."

She wiped her own tears from her cheeks and squared her shoulders. "It was a long time ago. Sometimes I pretend it didn't happen. So yes, the Corisi name means something to me."

I sniffed and stepped back. "I don't even know what to say."

She gave my cheek a pat. "There's nothing to say. Eat your pasta."

I didn't move. "No one deserves what happened to you, Fara. No one. I hope that bastard is burning in hell."

"I'm sure he is. Money doesn't protect you on the other side."

After a long pause, I asked, "What do you know about his son Dominic?"

"Only what I read in the news." Her eyes rounded with fear. "Does he know about me? About Kal and Riley?"

"Not yet."

She gripped my hands. "How much does Riley know?"

"Nothing about the Corisis."

"Promise me it'll stay that way."

My stomach twisted and churned. "I don't think that's possible, Fara. People already know."

"Promise you'll try. I couldn't bear it if my children were hurt because of a mistake I made."

Her grip on me turned painful, but I didn't flinch. "No one is going to hurt them." Even as I said the words, though, I thought about what my open-source friend had told me. Dominic sounded as dangerous as his father had been, but was he as vile?

"You don't know what they're capable of. The only protection we have is our silence."

"Nothing is going to happen to you, Riley, or Kal. I won't let it."

She wiped the corners of her eyes. "You're a good person, Teagan, but good doesn't always win against evil. You shouldn't get involved in this. I don't want to see you hurt either."

"The Corisis will never hurt anyone in this family again, Fara. That's the promise I'll make you."

Still looking lost in her memories, Fara said, "If they come for us, there's no way to stop them."

Between gritted teeth, I said, "There's always a way. Put this conversation out of your head, Fara. I'll handle the situation."

She shook her head. "No. I'll—I'll—I don't know what I could do."

After giving her hands one last comforting squeeze, I stepped back. "Do you trust me?"

"Of course I do."

"Then believe me when I say you're safe."

She nodded.

We spent a moment in silence; then she said, "Your pasta must be cold."

I shot her a sad smile. "Don't give it to Luna. Just this once, let it hit the trash."

Fara agreed to, but when I left a few minutes later, it was still in the bowl, and Luna was on the floor beside the table—begging. I could worry about only so much at a time, though.

Rather than immediately getting into my car, I went for a long walk first. Domestic violence was something I knew existed in the world, but I'd never seen it firsthand.

Some people asked why the abused didn't leave, as though it were their fault. As if anything so horrific could be deserved. I let what I knew about the whole situation steep. So much of what Gian had said about his family had seemed over the top until Fara had described her own experiences with Antonio.

Gian had said there was a rumor that Dominic's father had killed his. Suddenly that was very believable.

What would the Corisis want with the Ragsdales? I couldn't imagine a happy family reunion was possible.

How much of what Gian had said could I believe?

After a sleepless night, I drove back to my shop. A wrapped box had been delivered. I carried it inside, placed it on a counter, and read the card.

I hope to spend time with you soon. —Gian.

I ripped away the wrapping paper and packaging to find a delicate wooden clock.

A clock. Just how naive did Gian think I was?

I picked it up, turned it in all directions, but saw nothing unusual.

I retrieved a screwdriver from a nearby drawer and began to unscrew the back portion of the clock. Gifts were the perfect way to disguise a listening device or camera. The more advanced technology became, the smaller a covert device could be.

I had the entire clock dismantled and spread out over the counter when Riley burst in. "Sorry I'm late. You would not believe my day."

I could say something. But I won't. "Don't tell me—the same bride?"

"You guessed it. Do you remember when we thought being a bridesmaid for hire would be easy?"

"I never thought that."

"Well, it can be. Sometimes all I have to do is walk with the odd-numbered groomsman. Once all I did was mail out the invitations. Seriously, this woman needs better friends. She has people in her wedding party. Why does she want to spend so much time with me?"

"Because she's lonely," I said. Lately I knew the feeling. I missed being a larger part of Riley's life. There was so much I wanted to tell her, but she was smiling, and I hadn't decided what to do yet with what I'd learned.

"If she is, I understand why. All she does is brag about what she owns, how rich her fiancé is, how wonderful her life will be. I don't think it will be. She's not easy to be around now. I doubt that will change when he puts a ring on her finger."

A tight smile twisted my lips. "See, money doesn't make people happy."

"So true. I tell that to my credit card company every month, but so far they don't get my humor." As she stepped closer, her attention was drawn to the clock pieces that were laid out carefully on the counter. "What are you working on?"

"A clock."

She picked up a torn piece of wrapping paper. "Someone gave you a broken clock as a gift?" She read the card. "Oh, Gian—as in Romano. I meant to ask you how your date went, but we keep missing each other." She sat on a stool beside the counter. "So tell me why your new boyfriend is sending you broken clocks."

I opened my mouth to say Gian wasn't my boyfriend, but she started speaking again before I had a chance to.

"Let me guess; it's not broken—it's a kit. He knows you're brilliant and how you love figuring out things and gave you a challenge." She propped her chin on her hand. "That's so romantic."

"Romantic. Sure." I wished I lived in Riley's reality. Unfortunately, my head was still spinning from everything I'd learned from Fara. If only the clock were a time machine and I could go back to when my biggest worry was if Gian liked Riley the same way he said he liked me.

Riley rolled her eyes. "Don't even try that with me. I know you too well. I saw the way you were looking at Gian and the way he was looking at you."

"We definitely had a connection, but—"

"But nothing. You like him."

I couldn't lie to her. "I did, but I ended the date early."

"That's awful." Her smile faded. "I'm sorry. What happened?"

Nothing that made sense.

Snippets of our date flooded my head. His kiss. His hands in my hair. God, I loved the way he'd looked at me—like we were alone even when we weren't. "He wasn't my type."

"Your face is not saying that at all." She gave me the look only a best friend who'd known you forever could. "Your problem is you want a man to be romantic, but you don't believe him when he tries to be."

"Oh, so that's my problem. Thanks for clearing that up for me."

Riley picked up an internal piece of the clock and looked down at it as she spoke. "Did I ever tell you my lake theory?"

I pulled up a stool. Even with all the things racing through my head, it was incredibly calming to be sitting and chatting with Riley, as if both of our lives weren't about to be turned upside down. "No, but I'd love to hear it."

"Have you ever stood on a hill overlooking a beautiful lake, with the wind in your hair, and thought there was nothing more perfect than that view?"

"Probably?" I had too much on my mind to call up such a banal memory.

She put two pieces of the clock together. "If you wanted to find something ugly about the lake, it would be easy enough to. There are always dead fish, invasive species of weeds, pollution from either factories or runoff sewage from homes built nearly on top of each other along the shore. In fact, if you did a water-safety test, you'd probably never swim in a lake again."

"Thank you for ruining my desire to?"

She connected another piece. "You're too smart to not get my point."

I started to put the clock together with her. "So romance is about overlooking the dead fish and sewage? I can't do that."

"There's always some sewage. You can ask the universe to send you a thousand different men, and you won't find one without something wrong with them."

I grimaced. "I thought your last boyfriend was nice."

"He was, but he was only human. I was sad when we broke up, but I don't regret that we dated. We had some good times. That's what you don't let yourself have with men. You never let go and enjoy being with them in the moment. You think if you can't let them know everything about you, then they aren't worth being with. I don't agree. Not every relationship is meant to be forever. You don't have to go looking for dead fish on the first date."

We reconstructed the clock, exchanging parts naturally as we did. I'd taken it apart, so it was easy enough for me to remember how it went together. As far as I knew, Riley had no experience with the internal workings of one, but she was as good at it as I was. She was so much more intelligent than she gave herself credit for. Even if I hadn't been there to help her, she would have found a way to pay off her mother's bills. I hoped she saw that and knew I needed her every bit as much as she needed me. "He was an amazing kisser."

"I knew it," Riley crowed. "I like him. You should definitely sleep with him."

I coughed back a laugh. "Not going to happen."

"Because he's not your type?"

"Exactly."

"So give me his number."

My mouth dropped open. "Why?"

"My taste is well-dressed, good-looking men. If you don't want him—"

"I'm not giving you his number."

Her eyes were wide with feigned innocence. "Because he *is* your type?"

"I thought you said there was no connection between the two of you."

She sighed. "There wasn't, but I have other single friends. One of them might hit it off with him. When you reel in a fish like that, you don't just toss him back."

I shook my head. "What's with all the fish analogies? Forget it. I'm not giving you his number, because I haven't decided what to do about him yet." There, that was true.

"Okay."

"Okay."

She smiled. "Fucking him might help you make up your mind." She tightened the last screw on the clock, and looking pleased with herself, she pushed it back to the middle of the counter.

I found myself smiling along and blushed as I too easily imagined being intimately entangled with Gian. "It's not that simple."

"It is." Her grin was the same she'd used while talking me into skipping school with her when we were children. I didn't regret any of the times I'd sneaked away with her. She and I were a good balance. She pushed me beyond my comfort zone, and I made sure we were never caught. Not that my parents would have cared. Hell, they probably would have been relieved that I'd done something they considered normal. All we ever did, though, was sit in coffee shops and plot the rest of our lives.

"Did you thank him for the gift?" Riley asked.

"Not yet."

"No one ever gave me a clock. The note with it was so sweet. You have to see him again."

"I intend to. At least one more time." I needed to convince him to not move forward with his plan to tell Dominic Corisi about the Ragsdales.

"I bet he's checking his phone every few minutes. Put the poor guy out of his misery."

I took out my phone, then looked around. "Do you have an order to work on?"

"No."

"Could you pretend you do?"

She laughed. "Okay. Okay. But remember what I said, and give him a fair chance. You just might discover you enjoy swimming in that lake."

I shooed her away. My head was tangled up enough without imagining polluted water every time I pictured having sex with Gian. After Riley disappeared into the back room, I opened my messages and began to type.

CHAPTER ELEVEN

GIAN

I breezed past the security at the rooftop helipad entrance of the Corisi building in New York. Although I'd flown down to see Dominic, he wasn't what filled my thoughts.

Waiting to hear from Teagan was harder than I'd expected, and that was its own delight. It felt good to have found someone I cared that much about seeing again. So often my feelings for a woman were more ambiguous. There had been women I'd wanted, but I had known right out of the gate that they weren't long-term potential. Others had been a slower burn, followed by a level of attachment, but over time those had waned as well.

This felt different.

I found it difficult to think of anything beyond her and what her reaction would be when she received my gift. Would it be enough to convince her I was worth a third try? I hoped she'd already spoken to Fara, because that meant she'd be calling soon to tell me what she'd learned. Yeah, I had it bad.

Marc Stone met me in the hallway. We shook hands. "Good to see you, Gian," he said with a warm smile.

"You too, Marc. Is Dominic in a meeting?"

"He cleared his morning when he heard you were flying down." His expression turned serious. "Is there anything I should know about?"

"No, just visiting." Marc was a retired Marine. I'd heard Dominic had recruited him despite his lack of experience in the field because he'd shown loyalty in battle. If the quality of a person's friends was a reflection on their character, then Dominic's said nothing but good about him.

The smile returned to his face. "Seeing you always puts Dom in a good mood."

I nodded. It was time to stop second-guessing myself when it came to Dominic. I needed to see him the way I did my other brothers. Only then could we get to the same comfort level.

Marc left me at the open door of Dominic's office. If I had a safety issue, Marc would have handled it immediately and discreetly. He was everywhere, but not in a way that had ever made me feel uncomfortable. More like a guardian angel?

As soon as I stepped inside, Dominic ended the call he was on and stood. "Gian. Come on in." He stood and walked out from behind his desk.

Although he was graying around his temples, he still had the physique of a man in his prime. I hoped I aged that well. We stood there for a moment as I shifted gears in my head. In the past when we'd met, we'd shaken hands—sometimes not even that. I wasn't as restrained with my other brothers. *Okay, here goes.* I stepped in and gave him a warm, back-thumping hug.

Dominic straightened in my embrace, as if taken off guard, then briefly returned the hug before we both stepped back. "Everything okay?" he asked with a frown.

"Does anything have to be wrong for me to visit?" I said as I took a seat in one of his office chairs.

He stood above me, as if weighing my question. "I guess not." With that, he took a seat across from me. "Judy told me you're not thrilled with the idea of running a research facility."

Oh, Judy. "That's not why I'm here, but she has it partially correct." This definitely wasn't how I wanted to start my visit. I remembered how open I'd been with Sebastian, Mauricio, and Christof when they'd asked me what my plans were. My father was right; I was like that with them because I knew things could get heated between us, and yet it didn't change how much we loved each other. Dominic and I were brothers. Time to stop tiptoeing around him. "I appreciate that you want to help me start my career, but if you build it for me . . . I won't ever feel that it's mine. I don't want to join Romano Superstores for the same reason. I need to find my own path and build something on my own."

His annoyance was clear. "You should have said something."

"I did. A hundred different ways." As I said the words, I remembered something Sebastian had said about Dominic needing support as well. This didn't have to be an argument. I added, "But I didn't say it as clearly as I am now."

"The building is complete. I've already started interviewing."

His tone was harsh, and it was easy to see why people caved in the face of his displeasure. He had an intimidating presence and an expectation of things going his way, but this time I wasn't going to back down. I wouldn't have with Sebastian. So I looked him in the eye and said, "Then it looks like you are now the head of a research facility, because although I love you, I don't want it."

Dominic folded his arms across his chest.

It was tense, but I had the advantage in the situation. I'd been raised by phenomenal parents who had made sure my brothers and I always made up. No matter how dicey things got between us, we started with the love we had for each other, and that was the path back. I knew how to handle this situation, even if he didn't. "Quit looking at me like I'm an employee you want to fire, because I know you love me."

His expression relaxed. "I do. What the hell am I going to do with another research facility?"

"Donate it to a hospital, fund it, and use it as a tax write-off?"

"I like that idea." He smiled. And just like that, tension left the room. "Glad we worked that out. Now there's something you can help me with."

He'd heard me. A grin spread across my face. *Holy shit. Miracles do happen.*

Even though I'd probably never tell him what kind of research interested me, I could at least imagine us racing at Decker Park without it mattering which of us won. "Sure. What do you need?"

"Parenting is not easy. Thank God Leonardo is doing well in school. He's bright, but in a different way than Judy. He doesn't test the rules. Must take after Abby."

"This is about Judy?" If so, I was on the same page.

"Oh yes. Abby says I've spoiled her. Maybe I have, but I raised her to be strong and confident. She's intelligent and has always had access to people with knowledge beyond what could be taught in school, so it isn't that she lacks in education. My concern is that she's beginning to think she is smarter than everyone else. People get hurt when they get cocky."

"I agree."

"She was always curious and strong willed, but not in a bad way. She used to be respectful." His mouth twisted in an ironic smile. "Lately, she's been going head to head with Marc and testing his patience. How she is acting toward him is . . . disappointing."

Having never had a child, I was far from an expert on parenting, but I did know Judy well enough to agree that she needed to be reined in before she did something that got her hurt. "Have you spoken to her about it?"

Dominic groaned and motioned toward his desk. "There's not a world leader who wouldn't pick up if I called, but do you think I can get Judy to answer my texts today? No. She came to me last night with this crazy idea of wanting to start her own business with someone she wouldn't tell me the name of. I said I'd need a full background check on this person before I even entertained the idea of her working with them, and she said I'm overbearing and controlling. She's never spoken to me like that before."

"I haven't seen her in a couple of days, but I'll hunt her down."

Dominic nodded. "I'd appreciate that. Judy needs to go to college, to be surrounded with people who challenge her, and learn that she doesn't know everything. I can't get her to see that. Abby thinks we've made things too easy for Judy, but don't we all want better for our children than we had for ourselves?"

This was a whole new side of Dominic. I couldn't remember him ever coming to me with a concern. Had this type of realness always been possible, and I just hadn't understood how to bring it out? "My parents were strict, but we always knew they loved us. They supported us, but they didn't do for us. When we struggle, we grow. It's okay to say no to Judy. She'll survive it, and she'll come out the other side better for it."

"You sound like Abby."

"You chose her for a reason. She grounds you."

A smile returned to his face. "That's what first drew me to her. No matter how insane my life felt, when she was at my side, I felt calmer."

"Your harbor in the storm."

"Exactly." His expression warmed. "We just celebrated our twenty-year anniversary—only us and the kids. That's all she wanted, and it was the perfect day. Twenty years. Hard to believe time can fly by that fast." His gaze met mine. "I'm far from perfect, but Abby brings out the best in me. When you find that quality in a woman—marry her."

"I'll keep that in mind." I was enjoying my glimpse into this softer side of my brother. Dominic did have his flaws, but so did I. Yes, he was larger than life. Sure, it was difficult to include him in anything without him taking it over, but then there was this Dominic. Maybe, just maybe, if I did this right, this would be our new normal.

I thought about Riley and Kal. Dominic would be good to them. I was tempted to tell him about them right then, but I had enough of my father in me to understand that things went better when they were allowed to play out on their own. Some might have looked at the years Dominic and I hadn't known about each other and seen them as time we'd missed out on. I didn't. I wouldn't have been the brother Dominic needed if I hadn't been raised with the ones I had.

Teagan had asked for time to speak to Fara, and although I was impatient to hear what she'd discovered, I would respect her request. I inhaled and remembered the light scent of her, followed by the look on her face just before we kissed. Warmth spread through me as I remembered how good it had felt to have her in my arms. Waiting for her to contact me was slow, sweet torture.

"What's her name?" Dominic asked.

His question brought me back to reality. I blinked a few times, then said, "Teagan."

"Why is this the first I've heard of her?"

"We've only been on one date so far."

"How did it go?"

I shrugged. "She asked for a couple of days to sort out a few things before seeing me again. So I sent her a clock."

He frowned. "A clock?"

"As a way to stay in her thoughts without pressuring her."

He took a moment to digest what I'd said. "One to ten, how important is she to you?"

Without missing a beat, I answered, "Seventeen. Possibly eighteen."

"You can do better than a clock."

Here we go. "I was shooting for sensitive and supportive." I also liked the idea that the clock measured what I wanted to have with Teagan. We needed time to figure out what we could be to each other.

He shook his head. "Women don't want sensitive."

"They don't?"

Dominic stood. "No. Supportive—sure, later. No relationship lasts without a good basis of friendship and mutual respect. But you don't win a woman's heart with a clock."

I rose to my feet as well. I'd heard the PG version of how Dominic had wooed his wife, and it still hadn't been tame. Before that day I never would have dared to say, "Are you suggesting I kidnap her and steal her off to a private island? Because I, one, don't want to go to jail and, two, don't have my own island."

"You can't kidnap the willing," he said with a grin. "Abby wanted to go with me." Then, as if he realized how much he'd shared, his expression sobered. "Either way, that wasn't how we started. I had Marie set up a spa day for her."

"She wasn't offended that you thought she required a makeover?"

"No. It wasn't like that. I was bringing her to the reading of my father's will, and Marie suggested Abby would want to look like she fit in."

It was my turn to look skeptical. "Yeah, still insulting. So far I'm not seeing how that's better than our walk on the beach and a clock. In fact, I'll go out on a limb and say I'm ahead of where you were."

A glitter of challenge lit in Dominic's eyes. "I highly doubt that."

"You'll see," I said with an answering smile. This was exactly the kind of ribbing my brothers and I often gave each other. "When she contacts me, and she will, you'll witness the power of consideration and thoughtfulness."

Dominic smiled. "I look forward to standing corrected."

My phone vibrated with a message. Do you have time to see me today? Teagan. I nearly dropped my phone. "It's her. She wants to see me."

"That's good."

"It is," I said, a huge smile spreading across my face. "Do you mind if I cut out and head back?"

"Not at all. Call me later, and tell me if it was the clock that closed the deal."

I'd never thought to call Dominic with something like that, and it lifted my spirits to think that he wanted me to. "I will." I walked to his office door, then turned back. "I told you the clock would work."

He laughed. "You might want to consider answering her text, then."

"Oh, shit." Only then did I realize I hadn't. "I really like her, Dom."

"I look forward to meeting her."

"Soon." I nodded. There were a few things to work through before that happened, but I could see us heading in that direction. I walked back to Dominic, gave him a quick hug, then raced out of his office toward the helicopter waiting for me on the roof.

After speaking to the pilot about a flight path change, I texted Teagan. I'm out of town, but heading back. How about an early dinner? Five o'clock? Do you have a favorite restaurant?

I was hoping we could meet somewhere more private. My place?

Absolutely.

Abso-fucking-lutely.

CHAPTER TWELVE

TEAGAN

Later that day, I walked from room to room of my already immaculate apartment, adjusting the placement of things. I'd only asked myself about a hundred times if it was a wise choice to let him into my home.

We needed to talk, though, about things that couldn't be discussed in public. Things Riley couldn't overhear. I could have met him at the beach again, but I didn't want this to feel like a date.

So why had I worried about what to wear? Why was my hair down and my makeup touched up?

Because I'm an idiot.

I'd promised Fara that the Corisis would never hurt her family again. That was all that mattered. I hadn't decided how I'd convince Gian to not tell Dominic about Riley and Kal, but I was confident I'd be able to. I'd always been able to think on my feet.

I wouldn't lie. In my opinion, that never led anywhere good.

That didn't mean I had to gush details.

I checked my appearance in a mirror in my living room. My cheeks were flushed. My eyes were bright and dilated. I groaned. There was no denying I was also excited to see Gian again. I just hoped it wasn't as obvious to him as it was to me.

I jumped at a knock on my door and checked the time on my phone. Exactly five o'clock. I tried to flatten my springy curls, then gave up. They'd looked worse, and I'd survived.

Not that it mattered. I'd invited him over to *talk*.

Sure, I'd shaved my legs, but only because I'd had time to waste, and they had been getting stubbly.

The condoms I'd purchased on the way home? Every modern woman should own some.

And wine had a long shelf life. Picking some up didn't mean I intended to share the bottle with him.

This was not a date.

I opened the door, and heat flooded me as soon as our eyes met. Was it possible for him to have gotten even better looking? If I didn't tell him about NYD—if I was able to convince him to keep the Corisis away from the Ragsdales—could we . . . should we . . .

He stepped forward, pulled me into his arms, and gave me the kind of kiss every woman dreamed of her man greeting her with—passionate without being greedy, wild without being out of control. I wound my arms around his neck and gave myself over to the kiss.

Nothing so uncertain should have felt so right, but it did.

When he raised his head, I felt . . . shattered, but in the most amazing way.

With his hands still on my hips, he smiled down at me. "Hey, you."

"Hey," I said because I couldn't think of anything wittier to say.

"So your hallway is nice."

I laughed and stepped back. "I suppose I could let you in."

He raised a hand between us. "If you didn't already make dinner, I brought food." With that he bent down and retrieved a bag of groceries. "Did I mention I can cook?"

"I—I didn't make anything." Mouth hanging open, I shook my head and closed the door behind him.

"Good." He continued, "I didn't know what you like to eat, so I have a few options."

I followed him to my kitchen. "That's really considerate of you."

He put the food on the counter, then turned toward me. "Sweet can be sexy."

"It sure can," I said just above a whisper. "I'm a decent cook as well."

Walking toward me, he asked, "Is that a challenge?" He stopped just a few inches from me, his face just above mine, so close that if I shifted, we would have been kissing again.

I was smiling up at him, wondering what I would have thought of everyone before him had I known my body could ignite like this for a man. He didn't have to do more than stand near me.

"Did you like my gift?" he asked.

"Your gift?" I struggled to think of anything beyond him and how delicious it felt to have all his attention on me. "Oh, the clock. Sorry, yes, I should have thanked you for it."

His smile was all sex. "You can thank me now."

I swayed forward and ran a hand up the back of his neck, then pulled his head lower and brushed my lips over his. He wrapped his arms around me. I writhed against him. The hunger in both of us overshadowed everything else.

His shirt hit the floor.

Mine followed, along with my bra.

I couldn't get enough of him. I dug my fingers into the strong muscles of his back, teased his chest with a brush of my nipples. His touch was confident but gentle. Even when he dug his hand into my hair and pulled my head back to arch me over his arm, the move was smooth without feeling practiced. He kissed his way down my neck, then made his way to one breast and then the other.

He rewarded each of my moans with more pleasure.

I rewarded his efforts by shedding the rest of my clothing and helping him out of his.

When his mouth closed over mine again, one of his hands slid down my stomach to my sex. The finger he dipped between my folds was met with wet eagerness. I parted my legs more and closed my hand around his fully excited cock.

As he circled my clit, I pumped my hand up and down his shaft.

When he thrust a finger inside me and pleasure shot through me, my hold on him tightened, and he chuckled, "Easy there."

I released him. Possibly for the safety of his manhood, he lifted me off my feet and sat me on the counter, then stepped between my legs. Those fingers of his were magical. His mouth was hot and everywhere, bringing my body alive.

Our tongues circled each other's, our breath mingled, and I felt myself nearing an orgasm. He took me right to the edge of one, then broke the kiss off long enough to wrap himself in protection.

We were kissing deeply again when his cock dipped between my folds and entered me ever so slightly. I shifted my hips forward on the counter. His first thrust filled me; his second had me throwing my head back and gripping his shoulders.

With his hands on my ass, he lifted me off the counter and thrust even higher up into me. My breasts danced against his chest. I yanked his head down so I could taste his mouth again.

He shifted again so my back touched a wall, and he murmured things I was too lost in the moment to hear as his moves became stronger and faster. I clung to him and met his thrusts with my own.

Then I started swearing—something I'd never done before. It just felt that fucking good. I didn't want it to stop, and I wanted him to know just how fucking important it was that he didn't.

His midsex chuckle was hot as hell. It was on after that. When I approached an orgasm again, I was mindlessly begging him to go harder and faster.

And when I came, it was a head-to-toe, whole-body-racking glorious release. He came soon after me, then buried his face in my neck, and we stood there, still connected, as we both came back to earth.

"I like the way you say *thank you*," he said into my ear.

I raised my head. I would have responded with something snarky, but there was still hot desire in his eyes, and I still felt like I was floating. I tightened and released my inner muscles around his cock in a rhythm as old as time. His nostrils flared with pleasure. "You should see the way I say *fuck you*."

"I'm in for whatever you want to say."

Whatever I want to say.

There are things I need to say.

Shit.

I pushed my hands on his shoulders. "Put me down, please."

"Sure." He looked concerned as he slid me back to my feet. "You okay?"

"Yes." *And no.* I hunted for my shirt on the floor and slipped it back on. I didn't regret what we'd done, but I'd disappointed myself. I didn't act with impulsive abandon. Totally uncharted territory. I'd never accidentally had sex with someone I'd invited over to warn away from my friend. Who was I kidding? It hadn't been an accident. "I wanted to have sex with you."

"I kind of got that when you ripped off my pants."

"I did not—" I stopped and blushed, because I had. "Whatever. Could you put them back on now?" I picked them up and threw them at him.

He did, then rubbed the back of his neck while dipping his head to one side. "Do you want me to go?"

God, he had a beautiful chest. I swallowed hard. "No." I stepped into my underwear, then pants. I would have put my bra back on had I thought about it before I'd put on my shirt, but since I hadn't, I kicked it aside. "Sorry. This is awkward."

He stepped closer. "It doesn't have to be."

I kept my eyes averted. I didn't see how it could be anything but. "I invited you over because we need to talk."

His bare feet appeared in my view. "Teagan, look at me."

I raised my eyes slowly to his, lingering briefly on his yummy bare chest. I gave myself a mental shake. Seriously? I needed to get control of myself. When my gaze locked with his, I felt a delicious warmth spread through me. I wasn't used to being wanted so openly. It made me feel both sexy and a little giddy.

He caressed one side of my face gently. "I like you."

God help me. "I like you too."

"I'm open to hearing whatever it is you want to tell me, but—"

"But?" I tensed.

"I'm also hungry. I skipped lunch today. Let's talk while we cook."

A smile pulled at my lips. He had such an easy way about him. I nodded. "What did you bring?"

"All the ingredients for a shrimp scampi that could blow your socks off, chicken in case you aren't into seafood, and salad. Do you like garlic bread?"

I tried to warn myself I didn't really know him, tried to be upset with myself for already having had sex with him, but it felt too good to be with him for me to regret a single moment of it. "Everything you listed sounds delicious."

He kissed me gently, then said, "Good, then lead me to your kitchen, woman."

I stood there, looking up at him, wondering why the hell I'd put my clothes back on. I thought about what Riley had said about how I wanted romance but had a hard time believing in a man trying to be romantic. My problem was not being able to let go and enjoy.

He likes me. I like him.

We have some serious shit to talk about, things that may make him not want to see me again. But does that have to stop me from enjoying the time we do have together?

For one day, would it be so bad to be like Riley?

"Sure, follow me." I turned and did a little sashay as I started walking, then looked over my shoulder to see if it had caught his attention.

His gaze flew from my ass to meet my eyes. "Sorry, where are we going?"

My pleasure bubbled out as a laugh.

When I turned forward again, I frowned. It was so easy to forget what had brought us together. He was nothing like the deceased, abusive Antonio Corisi or the very much alive and equally dangerous Dominic Corisi. At least, he didn't seem to be. Yet Fara had found Antonio charming at first. Was I playing with fire?

CHAPTER THIRTEEN

GIAN

Having sex with her as soon as I walked in the door wasn't how I'd imagined this date going, but I wasn't complaining either. I wasn't sure what to make of her desire to instantly get dressed again afterward, but women were complicated creatures. My father joked that the secret to understanding them was holding your own tongue. If you gave a woman your attention, she was usually more than willing to tell you what she was thinking.

She'd said she didn't want me to leave.

She'd invited me over to talk.

Okay, so we'd talk.

I followed her with my pants back on but my shirt off, because—well, a man could hope. Once inside her small kitchen, she stood over the bag of groceries, looking lost in thought. I wanted to wrap my arms around her, kiss her neck tenderly, and tell her everything would be okay, but if I did that, all the blood that I required to be an attentive listener would head south. Instead I leaned against the counter near her. "All you really have to decide is chicken or shrimp."

She raised her eyes to me. Did I mention how easy it was to forget everything else when she looked at me? "That's all? I wish it were that simple."

There was obviously something weighing on her mind. I wondered what Fara had told her about Antonio. Nothing good, I was sure. "I have no idea what you're about to tell me, but I'm not worried."

She held my gaze for a long moment. "No?"

I ran my fingers lightly through her curls, then let my hand drop. "No. Life is a tangled, complicated, unexplainable mess. Very rarely does it go according to plan. I don't let that stop me. My father says every single morning a person decides how happy they will or won't be, and that determines how their day unfolds. Almost every problem is surmountable."

"I went to see Fara." Her voice sounded low and tight.

I nodded. "I figured that's what you wanted to discuss."

She braced herself with both hands on the counter on either side of the grocery bag. "I thought you were exaggerating about Antonio Corisi, but he was a horrible, horrible man."

"Yes, he was."

Her eyes darkened. "He hurt Fara."

My gut twisted. I wasn't surprised about Fara, considering Antonio's violent history, but it was hard to hear regardless. "I'm sorry."

"She met him when his wife left him."

"My bio mother didn't just leave him; she faked her own death to keep him from finding her. He was physically and emotionally abusive to her. She believed he'd kill her if he ever found her." I'd had eight years to assimilate that part of my family's history into my own life story, but it still felt alien to me. There'd been no violence in my childhood. Arguments had gotten heated, but never cruel or physical.

"That bastard is the reason Fara has back issues. He beat her so badly it landed her in the hospital."

"There has to be a special level of hell for someone like him."

"I hope so. When she was in the hospital, a man came to see her. His name was Thomas Brogos. He's married to Rosella Corisi."

She'd obviously done her homework on my family since we'd last spoken. "My stepfather. He helped Rosella hide from Antonio."

Teagan's hands fisted, and she straightened. Fury flared in her eyes as she said, "He told Fara he could protect her, but only if she kept her silence. If he knew what Antonio was doing to people, why didn't he stop him?"

I'd asked myself that same question so many times. Once, years ago, I'd worked up the courage to get the answer directly from him. "I asked him that once. He compared working for Antonio Corisi to watching an apartment building full of families burn. He couldn't stop it, but he saved those he could."

"Not good enough."

I took a deep breath. "It's difficult not to think he could have done more. He let Dominic believe his mother was dead. He didn't stop Antonio from ruining the lives of anyone who helped hide Rosella. I'll tell you the rest of this story another time, but there's a town in Italy that still calls Antonio the devil because of how much they suffered at his hands. Thomas said he promised Rosella he would keep her safe and that his vow shaped all his decisions. He loved her so much he wouldn't do anything that put her at risk."

Teagan made a face. "That's an ugly version of love. I wouldn't want anyone to love me so much they sat back and let others suffer."

I closed my eyes briefly, understanding her point but also having had years to see how the hurt was on all sides. "I'm sure he had some dirt on Antonio—enough that he could use it as leverage, but not enough to take him down. What should he have done? Killed him? I don't know. He believed that if he tried to take on Antonio, Rosella would have been killed. As the son of a man who might have been murdered by Antonio, I have a certain amount of sympathy for the tough choices Thomas had to make. Was he a coward or a hero? I don't know."

Her hands shook. "Fara doesn't believe Antonio knew about Riley or Kal. Would he have hurt her more if he had? Hurt them?"

"We'll never know."

"Fara went to the police. She said they did nothing."

"He was a powerful man."

"Doesn't Dominic Corisi have even more money and influence than his father did?" Her terse question hung in the air between us.

"Dominic isn't his father."

"Isn't he?" Her eyes flashed with sparks again. "Even you said he would take over the Ragsdales' lives."

I grimaced. In this context my words sounded more damning than I'd meant them. "Yes, I said that about Dominic, but I periodically bitch about all of my brothers. Sebastian is a grump. Mauricio thinks his shit doesn't stink. Christof never lets a joke die. That doesn't mean they aren't amazing people or that I'm not grateful to have them in my life. Dominic is nothing like his father."

She was quiet a moment. "You can't tell him about Riley and Kal."

I might have agreed with her a few days earlier. I didn't any longer. "Yesterday you said they deserved to know about each other."

"I was wrong."

"Because Antonio hurt Fara." It was a statement rather than a question.

She pushed away from the counter and stood toe to bare toe with me. Hands on hips, she said, "I promised Fara that the Corisis would never hurt her family again. I don't know how I'll stop them, but I will if I have to. Their best protection for now, though, is to remain off the Corisi radar."

Unfortunately, with Judy already having found them, that wasn't a possibility, but she wasn't ready to hear that yet. "Dominic would never hurt the Ragsdales—any of them. It would cut him deeply to hear that his father had."

"But he won't hear it, because you're about to promise me that you won't tell him."

A thought came to me that had me tensing. "You didn't fuck me to keep me quiet, did you?"

Her eyes narrowed, and the sound she emitted was not a pretty one. "Is that what you think?"

I remembered the desire in her eyes when she'd met me at the door. There had to be a way back to that. "No." I released an audible breath. "Sorry, I shouldn't have said it."

She seemed to relax a little as well. "It was a valid question. I would have asked you if our roles were reversed."

I'd never found a woman sexier. Her legs were planted slightly apart in an aggressive stance, and I imagined her in one of those little leather outfits the movies always dressed ancient female warriors in. "Did you know that Amazon warriors are now believed to have been Scythian nomads? Homer wrote about them, and for a long time people believed they were a myth, but archeologists are uncovering grave sites that support their existence."

"What?" Her expression turned puzzled.

"The Greek poet Homer."

"I know who Homer is." She shook her head. "I don't get how he's relevant to what we're talking about."

Sometimes a man's best defense is an ambiguous smile. She didn't look as if she'd be amused by where my thoughts had taken me.

She studied my face for what felt like an eternity before she said, "I don't regret having sex with you."

Whew. I joked, "We're completely on the same page about that."

"Sex is a biological urge. We're both single. We did nothing wrong."

"Exactly." Was she trying to convince herself? I was already sold on the idea that what we'd done was great and doing more of it would be even better.

"You can't tell Dominic about Riley and Kal."

"Is this where you tie me up and ply me with oral sex until I agree? If so, I should warn you it may require several sessions."

She held my gaze for a long moment; then a corner of her mouth lifted in a smile. "I'm serious."

I took one of her hands in mine. "So am I. Listen, I don't know what the right thing to do is in this case, but I do know we don't have to make the decision now. Let's cook up some shrimp scampi and open a bottle of wine. Do you have any?"

"I do, actually." She appeared embarrassed about the admission, although I wasn't quite sure why.

"A lot of answers can be found at the bottom of a bottle. We'll figure this out."

She looked down at our linked hands. "I don't get drunk."

"I don't want you drunk."

When our eyes met again, there was a sizzle in the air. If she hinted for me to leave, I'd go, but if she wanted me to stay, I was all in for the night.

I kissed her hand, then let it go and began to unpack the bag of food. First I handed her the wrapped, raw chicken. "You'll want to refrigerate that."

She walked away with it, then returned to my side.

Unable to resist, I gave her a brief kiss that brought a surprised smile to her face, then said, "Fun fact, shrimp scampi is an American Italian dish with a name that amuses actual Italians. The word *scampi* in Italian refers to a crustacean very similar to a shrimp. So the name of this dish is *shrimp shrimp*."

"You are just a well of trivia," she said, looking over the ingredients I was organizing on the counter. "That's interesting, though."

I didn't spew trivia at most people, but it was often circling in my head. For some reason it was important for me to let Teagan see the real me. "We'll need a pot to cook the pasta and a pan to fry everything up."

She gathered what I'd asked for and filled the pot with water, and we began prepping. I didn't have to tell her to mince the garlic or chop the parsley. Meanwhile I peeled the shrimp and washed it off. The comfortable rhythm eased me into relaxing as well. "So how did you get into the printshop business?" I asked.

She paused and gave me an odd look. "I like T-shirts, and it seemed like a fun way to make money."

"That's great. It's important to love what you do. And you've got your own business—I admire that."

She dropped pasta into the boiling water. "Don't patronize me."

I turned on the heat beneath the pan. "I'm not. I don't say anything I don't mean. If you're not proud of owning your own business, you should be. It takes real grit. Far more fail than succeed every day."

"You mean that."

"Why do you sound so surprised?"

"I didn't think you'd be so down to earth." As she spoke, she opened a bottle of white wine, poured two glasses, then handed me one.

"Because I'm a Romano."

"Yeah, I thought you'd be pretty full of yourself."

I shrugged. "My family might have money, but mostly because Sebastian threw himself into work after his first wife died. For a while he was a one-man demolition company when it came to taking out his competition, but he's mellowed over time. Christof stayed with the family company, but I'll probably go the way of Mauricio and branch out on my own."

"What did you go to school for?"

"Biomechanical engineering and business. You?"

"Interesting combination. Computer science and system design."

"Really? Where did you go to school?"

She hesitated, then said, "MIT."

"I bet your design software is top notch, then."

"You could say that."

"That's awesome."

She sipped at her wine, then asked, "You don't think it's odd that all I've done with my MIT degree was open a printshop?"

"Do you think it's odd that I have multiple degrees and zero jobs?"

"I do." She frowned. "With all the resources you have, it's hard to believe you haven't found anything that interests you."

"Let's just say that what has intrigued me so far hasn't aligned with what my family would approve of."

Her eyes widened. "So it's not that you haven't found something you want to do; you just feel like you can't do it." She laughed. "You want to be a stripper?"

"Could I pull it off?" I flexed my chest muscles.

She rolled her eyes, but her cheeks were flushed. "I'd have to see your moves."

I didn't dance—and certainly not for money—but a man was willing to do some pretty silly things when more sex was a possible reward for getting it right.

She burst out laughing at my brief efforts. "Don't quit your day job."

I pulled her to me and swung her around. Between kisses I growled, "Do you think you could do better?"

"Definitely," she purred, then moved her body rhythmically up and down across mine.

Everywhere our bodies touched ignited. My brain completely turned off, and the crotch of my jeans became painfully tight.

She turned in my arms, arched her back so her ass brushed across my bulging cock. I spun her back to kiss her deeply before sliding her shirt up over her head and spinning her in my arms again. Her breasts bounced against my chest as I drew her to me again.

Without music we danced our way slowly out of our clothing. Whatever embarrassment I might have felt during my first attempt completely fell away as I kissed my way slowly from one beautiful breast to the other, then turned her toward the stove and pulled her roughly back against me. "Have you ever fucked while cooking?"

She shuddered. "Sounds dangerous."

I pulled back, sheathed myself in protection, then slid my cock back and forth over her sex from behind. "It takes concentration and care, but I'm confident we could pull it off."

The wiggle of her ass against me was all the *yes* I needed. She bent slightly forward; I held her hips in place in front of me, and I thrust myself deeply into her sex. Once inside I kept my movements slow and sure—deep and strong. Then I began issuing commands.

"Turn on the heat beneath the saucepan. Add butter; then add the garlic. Shrimp and parsley are next."

As she worked, I fucked her slowly, in and out. I brought my hand around to the front of her sex so I could bring her even more pleasure. She added the shrimp while I was kissing her back. She added the parsley as I teased her hardened nipples with my thumbs.

All the while I kept my movements slow and sure.

"It looks ready," she said in a strangled, excited voice.

"Are you?" I asked in a similar tone.

"Yes." Oh, a man could come from the breathy sound of her voice alone.

"Then turn the stove off."

She did, and we edged over so her face was over the counter rather than the stove. I pulled back and pounded into her, loving the sound of pleasure she emitted. It was on after that. She met me thrust for thrust, her hair flying wildly around her head as I fucked her from behind.

When an orgasm rocked through her, she braced herself against the counter and called out, "I'm coming."

I slammed into her harder and faster until I joined her. If possible, this orgasm was even better than the first, because we'd taken our time getting there. As I came back down to earth, I eased out of her, cleaned off, then returned to pull her into my arms. We stood there for several minutes, our breath slowing and our hot bodies wrapped around each other. I kissed her forehead and said, "I like cooking with you."

She tipped her head back to meet my gaze. "I'll never look at this counter the same way."

I chuckled. "Is that a bad thing?"

She framed my face with her hands. "Not at all."

Our kiss was the warm, easy one of sated lovers. "Good, because I know a lot of recipes."

She smiled up at me. "I don't know you well enough for it to be this good."

"When it's this good, it might be worth spending time getting to know each other." I kept my tone light because I didn't want to spook her.

She nodded.

My stomach growled.

She smiled. "Seriously? That's what you're thinking about right now?"

I kissed her neck and murmured, "A man has needs. I do know of this great restaurant, though, where clothing is optional. It's called One Room Over."

"I can't eat naked."

Who had she been with who had left her feeling inhibited about that gorgeous body of hers? "Even if dessert is me pushing your chair back, dropping to my knees, and eating *you*?"

Her face went bright red, and her gaze fell to my chest before rising to mine again. "Sounds like a place I should try at least once."

We separated to set the table and transfer the food to the plates. I was comfortable with my body, but I'd never shared a meal naked—at least not out of the bedroom. I would have suggested anything naked, though, to distract Teagan from retreating back into her clothing.

We sat across from each other, vulnerable—real.

Those gorgeous breasts of hers bounced delightfully each time she moved. She was looking down at her food on her plate, as if it were the reason either of us were there. For someone who had just had two incredibly intimate experiences with me, she seemed self-conscious. "You're beautiful," I said.

When she didn't say anything, I wondered if I'd pushed her too far out of her comfort zone. I leaned, stabbed a shrimp with my fork, and held it up an inch from her mouth.

"Don't," she said. "I don't do the whole feed-me thing."

"I do," I said in challenge.

When her eyes met mine, they were flashing, and I preferred that to guarded and uncertain. "And what you like matters more than what I do?"

"Never," I said as I ran the shrimp lightly along her bottom lip. "But have you ever let anyone feed you?"

She swallowed visibly. "No, but I've also never seen the appeal."

"Open your mouth," I said.

She met my gaze and didn't do as I'd asked at first. For me, the exchange had very little to do with feeding her and everything to do with trust. We'd had sex—twice—but she still had her guard up with me. I was about to lower the fork when her mouth opened.

I fed her that one shrimp, then sat back in my seat. "Don't ever do anything you're not comfortable with, but it is also good to try new things."

Her forehead furrowed, which didn't seem like a good sign. "You and I are very different people."

"Does that have to be a bad thing?" I didn't think so. I found our differences exciting—okay, I found everything about her exciting.

Even that it was taking her a little longer to get where I was.

"I haven't decided yet."

I smiled because I was perfectly okay with helping her get there.

CHAPTER FOURTEEN

TEAGAN

I took a sip of my wine and lowered my gaze. I tended to look at men through the same lens I did code. At first glance they might look executable, but if I looked closer, I almost always found a fatal error. I was still glowing, still in awe of how intense our attraction to each other was—but that didn't stop me from digging for a reason it couldn't work.

Every lake had dead fish, and every relationship had sewage? Gian was the first man I'd met who made me want to turn off the little paranoid voice in my head. Each time I thought I had him figured out, he surprised me. Every time I thought I could control myself around him, I surprised myself.

Seriously, I was sitting across from him, buck naked, eating a meal we'd cooked while fucking. A mind-blowing first for me.

I would have said it was an amazing date, if I weren't as freaked out by it as I was excited. This wasn't me . . . or was it? Could it be?

I kept trying to pull us out of our sexual haze and back to reality, but did it have to be all or nothing? Not according to Riley.

Part of me was panicking because I couldn't see myself ever telling him about NYD. There was too much at stake. He'd already proved he was free with sharing secrets—at least his family's. I hadn't yet convinced him to keep Fara's. There was no way I could share more with Gian.

Was it possible to let him only halfway into my life?

"What are you thinking?" he asked.

I decided to be honest. "I'm not good with relationships."

He reached across the table and laced his hand with mine. "Before you I would have said the same, but I'm wondering now if I'd just never met the right person."

The way he looked at me made me want to believe he meant every word. "How many women have you used that line on?" I cringed inwardly at my own defensive joke. Half of me wanted to relax, ride this—him—out, possibly wake in his arms. Half of me wanted to throw his clothes at him, tell him it was time to leave because I didn't like feeling out of control.

"One, and it didn't impress her at all." His smile was all charm.

I melted, then panicked and took a healthy gulp of wine. The intensity of my responses to him scared me, but I was not and never had been the type to let fear stop me. I wouldn't have respected myself if I'd turned tail and run then. As far as I could tell, he'd been nothing but honest with me, more honest than I'd been with him, so I said, "She might have been a little impressed."

He plopped a shrimp into his mouth and grinned. "Tell me about your family."

I sat up straighter in surprise. "We can't talk about them right now."

"Why? Can they hear us?" He made a show of looking around.

I waved a hand over my bare chest.

His gaze dropped to my breasts, lingered, then returned to my face. "Nudity isn't always sexual; sometimes it's about being comfortable enough with someone to let your guard down. I'd like to hear about your family. If you have to put a shirt on to discuss them, I'm okay with that, but I want to know you."

My sex was still swollen and sensitive from our earlier romps. My nipples puckered because every time he looked at me, my whole body hummed for his. It didn't feel like a time when we should be talking about anything but how that felt, but I wanted to know him as well.

And I didn't want to put my shirt back on.

He poured us each another glass of wine, and I started talking. I told him about how I'd practically grown up with Riley and Kal, about how much time I'd spent at their house and how my parents had felt about it. The more wine we drank, the more easily the stories flowed out of me.

Not a single one about NYD or NYSM, but enough about my relationship with the Ragsdales and my own parents that he had a pretty good idea of who I was by the time I realized I was the only one speaking.

I asked him to tell me more about his family. It might have been the wine, but the picture he painted warmed me from head to toe. Once beyond the craziness of how he'd become a Romano, there wasn't anything not to love about the life he'd had with them. Big family meals. Parents who raised their children to support each other. By the time he was done describing how an average day at their home now was full of love, laughter, and a herd of nephews and nieces, I felt a little envious.

I wanted that in my life. My parents were good people. I'd always had nice clothes, my own bedroom, and their support when I shared my goals with them. They'd always had their own lives, though. When Gian said he spoke to his parents and at least one of his brothers every day, I couldn't imagine my own family being that connected.

"So your whole family knows about me?" I asked, mostly joking.

"They do," he said, and my eyes flew to his.

"What did you tell them?"

Gian sat back and rubbed a hand over his chin in a comical manner. "I'm not sure I should say. Doesn't every relationship do better with a little mystery?"

Ours already had its share of that. "I'm curious."

Holding my gaze, he said, "I told them I found someone who makes me smile every time I think about her."

I swayed a little in my chair. Never had anyone been as direct with me as he was. Never had I wanted to believe in anyone as much as I wanted to believe in him.

"Do your parents know about me?" he asked.

I didn't want to lie to him, so I didn't. "I haven't spoken to them recently."

He reached out to take my hand in his. I tensed. "Hey, it's okay. This is all new. No pressure."

I still felt a little cornered. "They don't normally hear the names of anyone I date."

A smile returned to his face. "They'll hear mine."

His blend of sweet and cocky, sensitive and bold kept me breathlessly unsure. "Maybe."

I didn't hear the sexy challenge in my words until I'd uttered them. He rose, literally, to meet it by standing and walking around to my side of the table.

With one strong move he turned my chair away from the table and bent until his mouth hovered just above mine. As he spoke, his lips moved gently over mine. "I'm ready for dessert. How about you?"

I darted my tongue out and over his lips. "Guess it depends what it is."

He sank to his knees before me, yanked my legs forward and over his shoulders. "Chef's specialty."

"Oh yes." My head rolled back. I held on to the sides of my chair and closed my eyes.

He started slowly, kissing the insides of my thighs while running his hands up and down along the outsides of them. His hot breath was its own delightful caress. I was more than ready when he parted my sex with his fingers and began to love me with his tongue.

Everything beyond him and how good he was making me feel fell away. The voice in my head didn't dare make a peep.

Were people really as happy as they made their minds up to be? Call me converted to that philosophy if it meant I could experience this again. It was more than the act of his tongue flicking over my clit. Men had done that before, but somehow this was entirely different.

His every caress echoed through me. So often with sex I held a part of myself back, but I couldn't with him. The line between where I ended and he began blurred.

When I came, it was as close to a religious experience as I'd ever had, and I burst into tears. He didn't ask me to explain why—and I was grateful for that because I couldn't have.

He picked me up, as if I were light as a feather, and carried me to the couch. I wasn't a small woman, but I felt as if I were when he sat and cradled me in his lap. I couldn't say how long he simply held me in his arms, but my tears dried, and all my fears were replaced by a sense that I was where I belonged.

He kissed the top of my head and said, "I read a study where forty-five percent of women reported they'd experienced postcoital tristesse at least once in their lives. It's usually a release after anxiety."

I smiled against his chest. My worries still felt far away. It was kind of sexy, though, that he tossed around medical terms, when another man might simply have asked me if I was okay. "I'm fine," I murmured.

He nuzzled my neck. "That's the oxytocin your body is still releasing talking. Studies show women are more likely to continue producing it after orgasm than men—which is why they are more likely to want to cuddle."

I raised my head to look him in the eye. "If you're about to tell me you're not a cuddler, I'm prepared to call bullshit."

His smile sent a flush of warmth over me. "Did I mention that I like you?"

I laid my head back on his chest. The sound of his heart beating steadily soothed me. "I don't want to think about anything right now."

He settled himself back into more of a reclining position on the couch, taking me along with him. "That's perfectly normal as well. The orgasm signaled your parasympathetic nervous system to start down-regulating your body. We can just lay here for a while and enjoy the effects of the serotonin rushing through us."

I didn't have the energy to raise my head again, but against his chest I asked, "Is this what you consider after-sex pillow talk?"

He didn't laugh the way I'd expected him to. Instead he said, "Actually, no. I've never been able to be the real me with anyone."

I hugged my arms around him. Those women had been fools. Something he'd said earlier came back to me about nudity not always being sexual. His cock rested against the side of my thigh, as relaxed and sated as I felt. The intimacy we were sharing wasn't about having more sex, nor was it entirely about what we'd just done. This level of connecting was new to me as well. I loved the idea that he might not have shared this side of himself with others. "I can't say I've thought that much about the mechanics of an orgasm, but I do enjoy understanding how things work."

"I took a class on human sexuality and the biomechanics of it—fascinating stuff." This time he did chuckle. "I may have enjoyed the subject too much."

"You know you need to expound on that."

His chest rose and fell as he took a deep breath, and my curiosity was piqued even more. "When I started college, I imagined myself becoming a family practice physician. The more I learned about human sexuality and all the issues people have with it, the more interested I became in the topic." He ran a hand through my hair. "My study partners had lofty goals of curing cancer and eradicating disease in third world countries. I proposed writing my thesis on mindful orgasms, their ability to rewire pleasure pathways, and how biometric devices could revolutionize sex."

"And?"

"And then my department head asked me if I'd lost my mind or if my topic choice was a form of rebellion. I lost my medically inclined peers when I wove pleasure into the equation. I lost my psychology peers when I suggested pleasure can and should be measurable."

"Are you referring to smart vibrators?" *Call me interested.*

"Yes and no. That's a part of it. Either way, I chose a mundane topic instead and decided medicine wasn't a career path I wanted to pursue. Since I couldn't do what I wanted to, I switched over to business and got an MBA. I circled back to medicine, but my heart was no longer in it."

"Your family wouldn't approve if you became a sex therapist?"

He took a moment to answer. "It's not about becoming a therapist— it's about creating the tools that bring science to what is still a field full of unknowns. I don't like that our puritanical society shames those who admit they struggle to enjoy sex. I've dated women who thought they were unable to orgasm, and they'd accepted that they were somehow different. Their only problem was a lack of understanding of their own bodies. I'm a considerate lover, but when people doubt themselves long enough, their perception of themselves blocks them from reaching for better. I was studying medicine when I met a woman who couldn't let go. Ever. I couldn't please her. It was humbling, but I thought about her welfare rather than my pride, and I knew I had to do something. I bought her a smart vibrator and taught her how to use it. When she saw her own biometrics graphed on her phone and how she could control them herself, it was a game changer. She sent me a screenshot of her first orgasm. I wasn't there for it, but that was okay. That was it—after that I was sold on data-driven pleasure."

I could honestly say I'd never met a man like him before. "She must have been devastated when you broke up."

"I don't believe she was. We'd had sex, but we were never actually a couple. She wanted to be with someone she could have a fresh start with sexually, and I understood that. She's happily married now to a great guy. I went to their wedding. She told me I helped make a family possible for her, and it might sound corny, but I feel pretty damn good about that."

"You should. What you did for her was beautiful. Does he know your contribution to their happiness?"

"I doubt it, and that's okay too. Sometimes a little mystery is good for a relationship."

I tensed in his arms as I made the correlation between what he'd shared and our own situation. "Some people would call it a lie of omission."

He looked down at me. "Do you have something you're not ready to tell me?"

"If I do?"

He caressed my cheek. "Are you married?"

"No."

"Does this secret of yours have anything to do with hurting anyone I love?"

Not unless they come for me. I shook my head.

"Then tell me when you're ready to."

I nearly burst into tears again. "Gian, you're a better person than I am."

He frowned. "I don't believe that. All I'm saying is that I understand that there is a time and place when things are best shared. My family doesn't know about my first thesis topic. They may never know. If you have something you're not ready to share, why would I pressure you to?"

Why indeed?

I lifted my head and ran my lips over his, losing myself in the wonder of how each kiss felt incredible in a different way. This one was comfortable and open. "Would you like to stay over?"

"To hold you all night? Find out if you snore? Wake with you in my arms and start the day with a shower where you discover the joy of having my cock in your mouth?"

Heat seared through me. "Yes, all of that."

Against my lips he growled, "I'm in."

CHAPTER FIFTEEN

GIAN

I was still smiling the next day when I visited my parents. I'd hated to leave Teagan, but she'd said she had work waiting for her, and I knew I could use the time productively.

My parents were seated together on a porch swing. I was leaning against the porch railing, enjoying the warmth of the sun on my back. "What a beautiful day. Did you do something different with the backyard? It looks amazing."

"We had all the shrubbery rearranged," my father joked. "Glad you like it."

My mother shushed him. "He's in love, Basil. Let him bask in it."

I hadn't taken offense. My father was the original ballbuster in our family, and it had given all of us a thicker skin. "Can love happen this fast?"

My father put his arm around my mother's shoulders. "I knew right away."

Ever a little cheeky, she said, "It was slower for me, but your father believed we were meant to be."

He kissed her cheek. "And I was correct."

She cuddled closer to him, love shining in her eyes as she looked up at him. "Yes, you were."

Right there—that was what I wouldn't settle for less than. After more than forty years of marriage, they were still very much in love. Could I have that with Teagan? My head said it was too early to know, but I couldn't deny how right it felt to be with her.

Turning her attention back to me, my mother asked, "So what's her name?"

I folded my arms across my chest. "Do you think I believe Dad didn't already tell you?"

Her smile was shameless. "Tell me anyway."

"Teagan Becket." I loved the feel of her name on my lips.

"When do we get to meet her?" my mother asked.

I ducked my head a bit. "It's still early. I don't want to rush her."

"Good boy," my father said. "When it's forever, there's no need to."

"Forever," my mother repeated in a sigh. "I'd love to see you with someone who makes you as happy as your brothers are. What do we know about her family?"

"Her parents retired to Florida. They sound like nice enough people. From the way she described it, she had a very normal childhood." I winked at them. "Which means it was nothing like what you two served up."

They laughed. My father asked, "Is she close to them?"

I shrugged. "Not everyone is like us, Dad. A lot of people talk to their parents once a week and visit only for the holidays."

My mother pursed her lips. "I hope we won't be too much for her."

"We have time before we need to worry about that." When I'd left Teagan's, I'd promised to give her a call. I already knew I didn't want to be anywhere but with her tonight.

My father nodded toward me. "I heard you flew down to see Dominic. How did it go?"

That he knew was not a surprise. "Better than normal, thanks to you. I took your advice and spoke to him the way I would have

Sebastian. I told him I loved him but I didn't want the research facility."

"How did he handle that?" my mother asked.

"Better than expected. Then—and this is still hard to wrap my head around—he asked for advice on how to handle Judy. She's pushing boundaries lately, not being as respectful as she could be, and is still not at all interested in going to college. He worries he spoiled her."

"Twenty is a tough age," my father said. "Too old to punish, too young for the brain to be fully developed. You gave us some grief at the same age."

"Me? I don't remember us ever having a problem." I did, but I liked to play with them as well.

My mother shook her head with a slight smile. "Ah, the memory of the young. Gian, when you left to live in New York, to get to know Dominic, you said a few harsh things. We understood that you were afraid and saying what you had to so you could feel better about leaving, but parenting isn't always easy."

I shrugged, even though the memory still made me sad. The past was something I could do nothing about. "I know how lucky I am to have you for parents."

My father smiled in approval. "We feel the same about having you as a son. Judy will come around."

I nodded. "Dominic tends to support whatever she does. I told him it might be time to say no to her. You said no to us all the time, and we turned out okay."

With one hand waving in the air in classic Italian style, my father said, "The older I get, the less I believe there is one best way to parent. Dominic and Abby love their children. Their children know that. In the end that's what matters most." Then he smiled. "Although if Judy is new to the word *no*, it might be time she heard it."

"I agree." My mother made a face. "Although it won't be pretty."

Despite how strong willed Judy was, I adored that kid. "Abby will rein her in if she goes too far."

"I can see that," my mother said.

After a pause, my father asked, "You haven't mentioned the Ragsdales. How did that turn out? Did you tell Dominic about them?"

I clenched the railing on either side of me. "I didn't. That's actually part of what I wanted to talk to you about today." I gave my parents a G-rated version of how my time with Teagan had gone the night before. It wasn't easy to tell them Antonio had hurt another person, especially since my mother had also been with him, but it was essential to their understanding of the situation. "So Teagan doesn't want me to tell Dominic about the Ragsdales, and I see her point, but I also think Dominic has the right to know he has more family."

Neither of my parents said anything at first. When my mother spoke, her voice trembled. "The conversation I had with Sebastian the other day wasn't an easy one to have, but I'm glad we had it. He told me you'd encouraged him to talk to me, and I want to say thank you for that, Gian. I've carried that secret for too long, given it too much power. I didn't want him to be Antonio's son, and I thought if he knew, it would change how he saw Basil—as well as me. It didn't."

I understood that. "I have two mothers, but only one *mom.*"

Tears filled her eyes, but she blinked them back. "You were a gift I never expected but have always been grateful for."

I let her words soak in. "I can imagine Dominic looking at the Ragsdales the same way. And if they get to know him, they'd feel that way as well."

"So you intend to tell him," my father said.

"Teagan wanted me to promise I wouldn't, but I don't think I could keep that kind of secret from him."

"What will you do?" my mother asked.

"Change Teagan's mind." It was the only choice that made sense.

"One more thing," my father said. "Have you spoken to Judy about the change in direction of your little bet?"

"Not yet." In the chaos I'd almost forgotten about her involvement. *Shit.*

CHAPTER SIXTEEN

TEAGAN

I unlocked the door of my printshop the next morning but left the CLOSED sign up. Now that NYD was at a new location, I had no reason to be at my shop other than to see Riley. How much longer would it make sense to keep it open? Things were changing so fast I didn't know what to expect next.

I was so confused. I needed to talk to someone who knew me well enough to know this wasn't me. I had work waiting for me, but instead of diving into it, I was waiting for Riley like junior high kids about to gossip in the bathroom.

And what was with the smile I couldn't get off my face? Sure, the sex had been good, more than good, but it hadn't been life changing . . . unless it had been.

One amazing day couldn't change a person, could it?

Was this a temporary glitch that time away from him would reset and resolve?

I normally had firm boundaries. Men didn't stay over at my place. I was breaking all my own rules for Gian, and what scared me was how much I was enjoying it.

Somewhere between breakfast in bed and shower sex, I'd lost all desire to spend the day working with NYD. That wasn't good.

I'd wanted to curl up next to him in bed and nap all day. Or worse, follow him like a puppy wherever he went. What was that about? I'd taken some of Gian's advice and decided to learn more about my own body. On my way to my shop I'd listened to an audio research paper on the chemical breakdown of orgasms and how they affected the brain.

A large dose of oxytocin was linked to a sensation of trust. Was that why after several orgasms I believed Gian would respect my request that he not tell Dominic about Riley and Kal? And what about my feeling of loss? Also easily attributable to hormones. At the end of the day, we were mammals. I could also be close to ovulating, which was a real mind-bender for women that many weren't even aware of. We were designed to want to procreate.

Was that what all this was? Had I somehow hit the trifecta for temporary postorgasmic attachment? The right man with the right moves bringing me pleasure at the peak of my monthly cycle?

I needed Riley.

The clock Gian had sent me was still on the counter where Riley and I had worked on it. I sat beside it and sighed. "I don't like this," I said to the clock. "No one is as perfect as he appears to be."

It didn't answer me. *Thank God.* I would have shit myself if it had. I already felt like I was losing my mind, but that would have taken my concerns about my mental state to a whole new level.

The door of my shop opened. Every muscle in my body tensed as I watched Riley walk toward me with a young woman—a woman I recognized. Judy Corisi.

Whoosh. Just like that my good mood was gone. I stood.

Riley, all smiles, hadn't noticed my mood change. She looked over at me. "Teagan, I didn't know you'd be here this morning."

"Well, here I am."

"I have news that is going to make your day," Riley said.

"I doubt it," I muttered under my breath.

"This is Judy Corisi. *Corisi.* We just met at the coffee shop. Life is so random, isn't it? And she's in the process of designing a new logo for one of her father's businesses. I brought her in to show her my software."

Wide eyed and doing her best innocent act, Judy said, "I'm sure we can come up with something I could use."

"Absolutely." I wasn't quick to anger, but it was bubbling within me. This youngster had a lot of nerve, but no street smarts, if she thought she could corner me. I forced a smile to my lips. "I have some time before I head out. Riley, why don't I show her around and crunch some numbers with her?"

Riley looked confused. She walked over to me, and in a low tone she said, "One order from her could make this shop turn a huge profit. I could finally feel like I'm repaying you for all you've done for me."

"You already have a thousand times over with your friendship." I needed her to step away, though, so I could have a real conversation with Judy. "Could you do me a favor and pick up our ink order from Staffers?"

The smile returned to her face. "Sure. You want to close the deal yourself. I get it." She smiled at Judy. "You couldn't be in better hands. She's the brains behind this shop."

"Then I found what I was looking for," Judy said.

I smiled until Riley left the building. As soon as the door closed behind her, I looked Judy in the eye and said, "In consideration of your age, I will say this as nicely as I can—stay away from the Ragsdales. I know about the bet you made with Gian. That whole situation is already being handled."

Judy's eyebrows came together briefly. "Who found you first, Gian or me?"

Her question only inflamed my anger. "Irrelevant. Your little game is over." My hands clenched at my sides.

Sadly, the girl before me was so full of herself she either didn't pick up on my warning cues or dismissed them. "If you know who I am and the backstory to why I'm here, then you know Riley and I are family . . . you don't have the right to tell me what I can or can't do when it comes to her."

I tried self-calming, telling myself she was too young to go to battle with, when she continued, "Good news, bad news? Good news, I'm still very interested in whatever you're working on. My gut tells me it's something amazing, and my gut is never wrong. Bad news, my father won't fund anything he hasn't fully researched. If I can bring him real data, though, and designs, he said he was open to discussing it again. We could be business partners even if he says no. I know some pretty influential people."

Between gritted teeth, I said, "I'm not interested."

"Too late. I am."

That was when I lost my shit. I advanced on her, finger waving in her face. "Who the *fuck* do you think you are?"

She took a step back, hands splayed, eyes widening. "Hey, why the anger? I'm offering you an opportunity."

"The only opportunity you're offering me is prison time if I follow through on the ideas running through my head."

She took another step back. "Are you upset because I broke in the first time? You should be thanking me. People pay my aunt big money to test their security systems, and yours was flawed."

Maybe it was the thought of how powerless Fara must have felt when facing off with the Corisis, or maybe I just had no stomach for Judy's level of arrogance, but I advanced on her again and said, "You ignorant, entitled, spoiled little girl. Why would I want to partner with you on anything?"

Another advance. Another retreat.

I continued, "Outside of your father's cash, what could *you* offer me? After your visit I looked into you. You haven't done shit with the advantages you were born with. College? No. You're too good for it, aren't you? I can't imagine what skill you think you have that I'd need. As far as I can tell, you're nothing without your father's money."

"That's not true." Her eyes darkened, and I knew my words had struck home.

I went in for the kill. "I feel bad for you because you actually believe you're special. Honey, people are paid to make you feel that way. Welcome to the real world, where what matters is what you bring to the table. As far as I can see, that's nothing."

Her mouth rounded, then quivered. Tears filled her eyes, which might have worked with some but only made me angrier. "Don't cry. Don't you dare fucking cry. If you're old enough to think you could run a business, don't be one of those women. You think men fucking cry when they negotiate deals? All you're doing right now is living down to my already low opinion of you."

"You can't talk to me that way." She glared at me, shaking. *Good, I hope these truths help her.*

"What was it you said? 'You don't have the right to tell me what I can or can't do,'" I growled. "Don't come near my family again. Yes, you heard me—*my* family. The Ragsdales might be blood related to you, but if you think that gives you a right to play with their lives . . . I'm prepared to teach a harsh lesson in how the world works. I'm not afraid of being erased, because I want to be invisible. Can you say the same? Come for me or those I care about, and I'll take you and your father down. That's not a threat; that's a promise."

I almost laughed when Judy backed right out of my shop. The shock on her face was pretty comical. It didn't look as if anyone had ever spoken to her that way before.

As my adrenaline slowly ebbed, I did ask myself if I could have handled the situation with more finesse. I locked the shop front door and hugged my arms around myself. If Judy took what I'd said back to her father and he came after me, I had no way of backing up the threats I'd made.

Take down Dominic Corisi? Not alone.

Gian's face flitted through my head. Threatening the Corisis probably had killed our chance of being a couple.

How would Riley respond when all of this came to light? Would she understand that I was trying to protect her? Would she hate me for not telling her?

My phone beeped with a text from her. The bride she was working with wanted to see her—could she bring the supplies by the next day?

Sure, I texted back, even though I was disappointed we wouldn't have a chance to talk. Nothing I wanted to share with her belonged in a text.

Is Judy Corisi still there?

I replied: **No, she's gone.**

How did it go?

I took a moment to choose my words carefully. **Hard to say.**

It'll work out.

I sighed, then typed: **I sure hope so.**

I closed up the shop and headed back to my apartment. I'd been given a temporary reprieve from deciding what to do with Riley. Had she returned, I didn't know that I would have been able to *not* tell her what was going on. I went back and forth between what I thought was best for her and what I would have wanted if our roles had been reversed.

I considered going to my new lab to work, but I wasn't sure if I was being followed. The one thing Judy had said that I agreed with was that my security system was flawed. I'd prepared for many situations, but never for something like a billionaire coming for me with a vengeance because I'd insulted his little princess.

Protecting what I had wasn't impossible; it just meant I had to rethink my strategy. Hiding wouldn't be enough.

138

Back at my place, a text from Gian came through. You're all I can think about. I want to see you tonight.

My breath caught in my throat. Earlier that would have been enough to make me rush to wherever he wanted to meet me. I was even more confused now, though, than I'd been earlier.

My apartment was wall-to-wall memories of how that had gone. Even as my head filled with reasons why a repeat performance was a bad idea, my body hummed for him.

I wanted to curl up on his lap again and tell him all about Judy. In general I handled things on my own, always had, imagined I always would. I didn't need a man to fix this for me.

Damn you, oxytocin!

I found the half bottle of wine Gian had said we might find the answers at the bottom of and poured myself a glass. I took it as well as the bottle to the couch. In the emptiness of my apartment, I downed the glass and asked myself some tough questions. Had Judy deserved what I'd said to her? Why had I gotten as angry as I had?

I wasn't that person. I didn't tear people down. I'd not only hurt her, but when I'd sensed she was backing down, I'd ramped up. Why?

I went over our conversation again and again until I found what had triggered me. When I'd said, "I'm not interested," she'd said, "Too late. I am."

Looking back, I recognized how in that moment she'd stopped being a cocky twenty-year-old daughter of a billionaire to me and had become Antonio Corisi telling Fara there was nothing she could do to stop him.

Classic transference.

Funny, when I'd read about it in school, I'd never thought I'd succumb to it. I was too much of an analyzer to let myself get away with shit like that. At least I was an equal opportunity dissector. I could spot the sewage in myself as well as others.

And my rant about her not crying? I'd cried with Gian, and I'd felt vulnerable because of it. Vulnerable. Yes, that was how everything about the last couple of days had left me feeling.

Even with my friendship with Riley. Before Gian had walked into my shop, our friendship had been simple. Now for the first time I had a secret I was afraid would change Riley's life—our lives—forever.

It took until the bottom of the second glass of wine for me to see how selfish that was. Fara had made me promise to keep the truth from Riley, but hadn't that also been a selfish request?

Riley and Kal had the right to know the truth. What they did with it—whether they reached out to the Corisis or wanted nothing to do with them—should be their decision.

Sadly, I ran out of wine before I figured out how to respond to Gian's request to see me.

CHAPTER SEVENTEEN

GIAN

I wasn't a vain man, but I couldn't get over the fact that Teagan hadn't answered my text. I thought about it on the ride from my parents' home to the gym. I thought about it straight through my workout. While showering and changing, I tried to figure out how a night I'd considered perfect hadn't been so for her.

We'd kissed passionately as we'd parted that morning. I wanted to call her and ask her what the hell had changed since then, but I didn't want to be that guy. The chance that she was merely spooked because I'd been too good in bed for her to handle was slim.

I must have said something stupid that had hurt her feelings or pissed her off. I had no idea what it was, though.

Judy opened the door of my apartment and walked in, as if I'd left the door unlocked. *Looks like I'll be changing my code again.* She plopped onto the couch, crossed her arms over her chest, and sighed.

I probably should have lectured her on boundaries, but we'd had that talk multiple times before, and yet there she was. Plus, she genuinely looked upset. "What's wrong?"

She sighed again. "You have multiple degrees from some of the best universities in the country, and I've won against you."

I sat down on a chair near the couch. "Once or twice."

"Every tutor I've ever had said I was above average in intelligence."

I wasn't sure what to say to that. "Did something happen?"

Her eyes were shooting daggers when she looked at me. "Yes, I spoke to the most horrible woman today. Just nasty. I hope whatever she is working on is a huge flop. You know what? It probably will be. Her opinion of me doesn't matter, because she doesn't."

"I'm lost. Who are we talking about?"

"Teagan Becket." Judy said her name as if it were an insult.

"Whoa. Stop right there. You went back to the printshop?"

Her eyes narrowed. "How do you know it wasn't my first time there? Oh, right, because you found Riley before me, didn't you? Why didn't you tell me? It also would have been nice if you'd given me a heads-up that she was friends with Cruella."

This is likely why Teagan didn't answer my text.

"What did you do, Judy?"

"Me? Nothing. Nothing bad anyway. I offered Teagan a chance to work with me on a project, and she started spewing insults at me until I had enough and left." Judy sniffed. "You should have heard what she said to me. I can't even repeat it. It was so nasty."

I couldn't imagine Teagan doing that. "I'm going to need to hear this story from the beginning."

She pursed her lips. "I can't. It was too hateful. All I need from you is a suggestion on how to get her voice out of my head. She called me . . . *entitled.*"

I grimaced. "You do have an issue with respecting boundaries."

If looks could kill, the one Judy shot me would have dropped me dead. "She said I'm nothing . . . that I only think I'm special because people are paid to make me feel that way."

"Okay, that was harsh, and it's not true. However, something must have led up to her saying that. I doubt you walked in the front door of the store and she started yelling at you for no reason."

"I didn't break in." I heard her add "This time" under her breath.

"But you broke in the first time? And she caught you? *Judy.*" I turned her name into a reprimand.

"I did her a favor. Now she knows her system was subpar."

Judy's biggest problem was that there were no consequences when she broke the rules. Since she was even buffered from people's opinions of her actions, she didn't see them in the light others did. "I don't agree. You broke the law. If you were anyone else, you'd be in jail."

She shook her head. "No."

I nodded. "Yes. It's called breaking and entering, and it's illegal."

She sulked deeper into the couch. "Overlook the fact that Alethea built her career by circumventing unbreachable security systems and focus on pedestrian laws, if that's all you're interested in."

"Pedestrian laws." I rubbed my jaw. "Judy, when we met, I remember thinking how amazing you were. What were you—twelve? And you already knew more about technology and hacking than most adults I knew did. You're brilliant, but you're headed down a bad path. You not only sound entitled; you've become deaf to how what you say makes others feel. It's not a good look."

"I didn't come here for you to start insulting me too." She jumped to her feet.

I stood slowly. "Judy, I love you. I want only the best for you. What I'm saying isn't an insult; it's a wake-up call. You're better than this."

The anger seemed to drain out of her, and she sank back down onto the chair. "I did nothing wrong."

I gave her the look my father had given me many times when I'd claimed the same. No matter what we'd done, he had always been there to support us, but if we'd messed up, he had always made us own up to that as well.

"Do you agree with her? Do you think without my father's money, I have nothing to bring to the table?"

As much as I wanted to reassure her, I also felt it was time for some tough love. "We all need to make our own way in life—regardless of what advantages we do or don't have. You have a tendency to believe you're invincible because you haven't put yourself in situations where

143

your capabilities have truly been tested. The most intelligent people I know don't settle for being the smartest person in the room. They seek out other rooms full of smarter people, and only then do they grow."

Judy shook her head. "I'm not the person Teagan described."

I leaned forward and gave her knee a pat. "But you could be if you aren't careful. When you're born with everything, it's easy to forget what it's like to not have been. And it's easy to forget that your father's level of success wasn't achieved alone. I hear you haven't been treating Marc well lately. You're better than that too. He would give his life to save yours. He deserves your respect."

She blinked several times in a row. "Is that why I can hear Teagan's voice in my head? Because everything she said was right?"

"I don't know everything she said, and it sounds like she crossed some lines as well. But maybe—if you practice some introspection— you'll see you brought some of that on yourself?"

Judy was quiet for several minutes; then she said, "She wasn't happy when I walked in with Riley."

Oh boy. "How did that happen?"

Judy rubbed her hand over her forehead and said, "Maybe I *should* start at the beginning."

At first when Judy began to describe her first encounter with Teagan, it sounded like a story someone had to have made up—a room with no doors? A skunk-spraying security system? Some mysterious hidden area beneath the printshop? None of it sounded realistic.

I thought back to a question Teagan had asked me: *"You don't think it's odd that all I've done with my MIT degree was open a printshop?"*

I hadn't, but now I wondered if the thing she didn't feel ready to tell me was related to whatever Judy thought Teagan was hiding below her shop. *I hope it's not something illegal.*

When Judy got to the part where she'd walked into the printshop with Riley and shared what she'd said to Teagan, I understood how it had become so heated. Judy didn't sugarcoat her part in the altercation, and I cringed as she repeated what Teagan had said to her.

We sat there in silence when she had finished as I took a few minutes to make sense of what I'd learned. Finally, I said, "You're not nothing, Judy. You are special. But you're special in the way every living creature on this planet is. I have a story to tell you, and as I do, I want you to put aside how you feel and ask yourself how the things you said might have reminded Teagan of someone we all want to forget."

In Judy's eyes I saw both the child she still partially was and the woman she was becoming. I didn't hold back what I knew about her grandfather. She was old enough to handle the truth, and it wasn't her first glimpse into his dark side.

I told her about Fara, how he'd abused her so badly she was permanently injured from it. I told her about Teagan, how protective she was of the Ragsdales, and walked Judy through how her actions could appear to mirror those of her grandfather's.

A solemn Judy sat forward and looked a bit like she felt sick. The hand she brought to her mouth shook. "He hurt my father as well."

"I know," I said gently.

"I don't want to be anything like him."

I gave one of her hands a squeeze. "Grow up, Judy. Not because your parents want you to, not because I want you to, but because you owe it to yourself to become the amazing person you were born to be. You're destined for something great; make sure you deserve it."

She sniffed, then said, "Why do I feel like you're passing on a lecture you've received?"

I chuckled. "Guilty as charged. You and I are at different crossroads, but we're both at them. You need to go to school, hang out with people your age, and challenge yourself. I have been in school too long. It's time for me to take what I've learned and do something with it."

She looked down. "Dad and I had our first real argument. I said some things I'm not proud of. Mom was pissed. She tried to ground me, but I'm a little too old for that. Dad walked away." She swallowed visibly. "I felt like I won, but I didn't, did I? Mom says Dad won't raise his voice to me because he never wants the rage his father passed down to him to touch my life." She wiped a tear from the corner of her eye. "Do you think he sees his father in *me*? Is that why he walked away?"

In a thick voice, I said, "No. Your father adores you. You do owe him, and your mother, an apology."

She stood. "And Marc. You're right—I have been thoughtless lately. He has always been there for me, and I've taken that for granted."

I surged out of my own seat. She was far from perfect, but I loved Judy. I'd been raised to appreciate that everyone's journeys held challenges. We all needed guidance now and then. "And Teagan." I hated the idea of two people I cared so much about not getting along.

A flash of resistance came and went in Judy's eyes. "She owes me one as well."

I ruffled her hair, knowing it would annoy her into swatting at me. "Then thank God we're all adults and can make something like that happen."

"Stop," she growled, then, in a calmer voice, said, "So there's obviously something going on between you and her."

"You could say that." I gave her the same G-rated version I'd given my parents. "This would all be a lot easier without the Corisi-Ragsdale connection, but I'm confident we can work through it. I'm hoping to be able to change her mind about telling the Ragsdales, but she's in a tough spot as well. Fara is afraid of your family—afraid of what they might do to her and her children."

Judy pursed her lips. "I didn't help that situation either."

"Nope."

She stuffed her hands in the front pockets of her jeans. "I didn't see the harm in getting to know Riley or going with her to meet Teagan, but I do now." She groaned. "I can't tell my parents about our bet while they're already upset with me."

146

"I agree. I'd do your apology tour first."

"I hate it when you're right." After giving me a long look, Judy said, "I used to wish I had a big brother, but with you I feel like I have one. Thanks."

"I never wished I had a pain-in-the-ass little sister, but—"

She smacked my arm, and we both laughed. Her expression turned pained. "An apology tour."

"You'll survive it, Judy. You've got this."

She made another face, then asked, "You're not concerned that Teagan might have an entire life she might be hiding from you?"

That wasn't how I saw it. "An entire life or a work project? One might be a bit much to take; the other I'd expect more time together will resolve. Not everything in life has to be immediate, Judy."

Her eyes narrowed. "You have to at least ask her about it."

"Oh, I definitely will."

That night, I hoped. Unless we spent all our time together otherwise occupied.

"You really like her." Judy searched my face.

"I do."

She squared her shoulders. "Then I'll try to as well."

CHAPTER EIGHTEEN

Teagan

I was still brainstorming for improvements for my side smoke screen project when my phone vibrated with a message. Did the world need a minirobot capable of detecting and eliminating insects in a home? Maybe. If I kept the treatment all-natural and the robot also removed the insect carcasses, people might buy that. Even if they didn't, I just had to make it creative enough to appear to be an invention I'd want to protect.

I didn't recognize the number. The text read: I will say this in person the next time I see you, but I'm sorry. I shouldn't have let myself into your shop. I shouldn't have lied to Riley to access it the second time. I understand why you were upset with me. I hope we can start over. —Judy Corisi

Holy crap.

I read the message through two more times. Was her apology sincere or a ploy to soften my defenses? Either way, I said the only thing I could. Apology accepted. I'm also sorry about the things I said. I went too far. I'd love to put it behind us.

I'd say we could forget it, but you said some things I needed to hear. So, thank you.

Now I knew her apology was bullshit. No one did an about-face that fast. Still, I didn't have much choice but to play along and shut her down when she tried for access to my research again. You're welcome.

I waited for her to ask to see me, my shop, or Riley again. She didn't. There wasn't anything more I wanted to say to her right then. The next move was hers. I hoped it was a mature, nondeadly one.

A knock on my door took me by surprise. I put my laptop on the couch and stood. "Who is it?" I called out, picking up the empty wine bottle by the neck before approaching the door. *I need to up my home security as well.*

"It's Gian."

I put the bottle down and checked my appearance in the mirror. I looked exactly the way a person would when they'd been working on a computer while day drinking on their couch. I breathed into my hand, got a good whiff of wine, and groaned. It wasn't as if I could tell him to wait while I brushed my teeth, fixed my hair, and applied makeup.

Fuck it. I opened the door. "Sorry I didn't—"

He leaned in to kiss me, and I met him halfway, completely forgetting what I had been saying. When he raised his head, he said, "I missed you."

"I missed you too," I answered in a husky tone.

His smile warmed me right to my toes. "I told myself I'd wait to hear from you, but then I got in my car and ended up here."

I wrapped my arms around his neck, sliding my body up his as I did. "I'll let that go just this once."

He kicked the door shut behind him and swung me up in his arms. "I appreciate that."

Somewhere in the back of my head, a little voice told me there were things we needed to discuss before we had sex again. I told that voice to shut the fuck up.

He carried me to my bedroom and lowered me to my feet beside the bed. Our kisses were hot as hell, but his touch was slow and sure.

We shed our clothing on the floor beside my bed, then tumbled onto the sheets.

Every time we had sex, it was different and wonderful in its own way. This was tender and felt like a declaration. Regardless of everything else going on, we wanted to be together.

We rode the waves together, each of us taking the lead at times, until we came together and lay spent in a tangle of limbs. He pulled a blanket over us and hugged me to his side. I closed my eyes and breathed him in.

He kissed my temple and asked, "What is it about you that makes conversation impossible until after we fuck?"

I tipped my head back so I could meet his gaze. "I'm irresistible?"

"You really are." He claimed my mouth with a kiss that made me want to spend the rest of my life right there in his arms. A feeling that all-consuming had to be more than a chemical reaction. Didn't it?

I traced his jaw with my fingertips. "I'm sorry I didn't answer your text."

He propped his head up on one arm and grinned back at me. "You're forgiven."

My perma-smile was back, and I liked the me I saw reflected in his eyes. I felt like I could be myself with him, and it was good enough. Before him I'd considered myself a bit of a loner, but that wasn't the life I wanted anymore. I'd always wondered what it would be like to feel this attached to someone. The speed at which he'd gone from stranger to person I didn't want to imagine my life without was frightening.

Would things take a quick turn once he found out how I'd spoken to his niece? I could have waited for a better time, but would there ever be one? "I spoke to your niece Judy today."

He didn't look surprised. "And?"

"It didn't go well."

He ran a hand through my hair. "I know."

"How?" I sat up, the blanket falling away as I did.

He cupped one of my breasts and brought it to his mouth for a kiss before saying, "She came to see me. If she took what I said to heart, you should be receiving an apology soon."

I wanted to focus on what he was saying, but his tongue began to do these tantalizing little circles around my nipple. I had to do something before my brain completely shut down again, so I pulled the blanket up between us. "Stop. This is important."

His cheeks were flushed. "Sorry. You're right."

I used the lull in our conversation to refocus and clear my head. He appeared to do the same. "Judy went to see you? What did she tell you?"

He rolled onto his back, keeping one arm behind me and holding out his other arm toward me. "Bring it in, and I just might tell you."

I didn't move at first, but when he waggled his eyebrows at me, I caved and settled myself against him, tucked along his side with my head on his shoulder. "Good?"

He slid his hand down my back until it came to rest on the curve of my ass. "Yes. Now, what were we talking about?"

Really, did anything else matter? I traced the muscles of his broad chest, slowly made my way across his stomach, then closed my hand around his already hardening cock. "Something that can wait until later."

"I like the way you think." He lifted me until I was lying on top of him.

Bracing my hands on his shoulders, I pushed myself into a seated position, then raised myself up and lowered myself onto him, taking his shaft deep inside me. I started slowly, then got wilder in my movements. His touch started gentle but became rougher as I did.

I rode him until I was calling out his name in ecstasy. He came with a powerful upward thrust soon afterward. I collapsed onto his chest, lying there with him still inside me.

It might have been the wine I'd had or the number of orgasms I'd fit into that day, but I fell asleep just like that. I dreamed I was floating on a warm, comfortable cloud. Gian was there with me, telling me he loved me.

And there was a unicorn with braces; I had no idea why.

CHAPTER NINETEEN

GIAN

I held Teagan as she fell asleep, then eased her off and tucked her against my side. I hadn't come over for sex, but I hadn't come over not to have it either. When it came to Teagan, it was proving damn near impossible to believe I was a grown man with extensive experience with women.

"Because I love her." I said the words aloud and kissed Teagan's forehead. "I love you, Teagan Becket." *Sebastian's right—when it happens, you just know.*

Teagan smiled. Was she actually asleep? I waited for her to open her eyes. When she didn't, I decided the smile must have been in response to something she was dreaming. I closed my eyes and let myself drift off as well.

It was still night when I woke with Teagan in my arms. In the dim light that shone from the open door of the bathroom, I saw her eyes flutter open. "I'd say good morning, but it's not yet midnight."

She rubbed at her eyes. "Sorry. I must have been tired."

I kissed her gently. "I slept as well. You're running me ragged."

One of her eyebrows arched. "Mm-hmm."

"I came over to talk, and you jumped me."

"That's how it happened?"

"That's the story I'm going with."

She nodded, humor in her eyes. "I see."

I wondered what she saw. Were my feelings for her obvious? If she'd heard me say I was falling for her, she gave no indication of it.

"Before I let you distract me from answering, you'd asked me about the conversation I had with Judy."

My joke missed its mark, and her expression became more guarded. "I lost it on her, and I'm not proud of that."

When her eyes fell to my chest, I gave her bare ass a light slap. "Don't feel bad about anything you said; she needed to hear it. Some of what she told me did sound harsh, but once she told me the context in which you said it, I understood."

"You did?" She didn't sound convinced, but her eyes rose to meet my gaze.

"She was an arrogant Corisi pushing for things she had no right to. She would have reminded me of her grandfather in the worst way."

"That's it—exactly."

"Don't sound so shocked. I love Judy, but I know she can be a challenge." I ran my thumb lightly over her bottom lip. "Remind me to tread carefully around your temper, though—you went for the jugular."

She took my hand in hers and lowered it from her mouth. "I don't normally, but nothing about this week has been normal."

I was in full agreement about that. "You'll see a different side of Judy the next time you meet up. She now knows the history between Fara and Antonio. She felt horrible once she saw the role she was playing in making the situation more difficult."

"She apologized via text, saying she'd apologize again in person."

"Good. I'm proud of her."

Teagan's hand tightened on mine. "I wasn't sure at first that Riley should know, but she has a right to. I'd like to be the one who tells her, though. I don't want her to find out from someone else and then discover I knew and said nothing."

"That makes sense."

"Promise me something."

"Anything."

There was an urgency in her tone that I hadn't expected; it hinted that there was a lot more going on behind her calm expression than she was letting on. "Promise me you won't let anything bad happen to the Ragsdales. They have been more of a family to me in many ways than my own. I'd give up everything I have—my freedom, even my life—to keep them safe. I don't want it to come to that."

I hugged her close. "Hey. Nothing but good things will come from this, but if a promise will put your worries to rest, I promise you that I won't let anything happen to them. You're not alone in this."

She shuddered against me. "Did Judy mention anything besides Riley?"

It didn't feel like the ideal time to layer anything else on, but I also believed in being direct. "She shared her suspicion that you are living a double life . . . working on something she felt must be incredible. Is it?"

"Not yet. It might be one day."

"So you really have a high-security room below your printshop?"

"Yes and no."

She tensed against me. I didn't want her to feel cornered, but I always wanted to understand. "Did you move its location because Judy stumbled upon it?"

She held my gaze but didn't give any indication that I might be correct. I wondered what she'd think if I told her that a little mystery only made her sexier. "You don't have to tell me. Not yet."

She let out a breath, as if she'd been holding it. "No one knows what I'm working on, but even if I wanted to tell you—which I don't, but even if I did—I couldn't. You're not a good secret keeper."

My mouth dropped open. "Hold on one second there, missy. I am Fort Knox when it's important."

"You told me all of your family's secrets on our first date—just laid them out for me."

"Because . . ."

"Because?"

It was too soon. It was too much. I said it anyway. "I knew we were meant to be."

This time it was her mouth that fell open. She blinked a few times, then just stared at me without speaking. Her mouth snapped shut.

Another man might have read her uncertainty as a cue to back off the topic, but where would the fun have been in that? I added, "When it's right, it's right." The best part? I wasn't saying anything I didn't actually feel.

Her eyes narrowed. "I'm not telling you what I'm working on."

I smiled and ran my hand through her hair. "I already said that's okay."

"Even if it wasn't, I wouldn't."

"You will, and it won't be a big deal, because we'll be together."

She gave me another assessing look that almost brought a guilty smile to my lips, but I held it back. I did believe we would end up together, but it was also fun to torture her a little with declarations. She looked as if she had no idea how to deal with them.

She remained silent. I could have stopped there. I probably should have, but I was on a roll. "It's a lot to take in, isn't it? A week ago marriage was the furthest thing from my mind. Now I imagine us in a big house, two dogs, possibly a pony for the kids."

"Kids?" Her eyes rounded.

"I'm thinking five. One would be lonely. Four and there would always be an empty seat in our passenger van."

One corner of her mouth twisted. "You're an asshole."

"Is that any way to talk to the future father of your children?"

She shook her head. "You really had me going there for a minute."

I rolled so we were face to face. "Okay, no pony. Then, Teagan Becket, tell me—what is it you do want? What's your five-year plan? Your ten year? Not with your business, whatever it is, but with your life. What do you want it to look like?"

CHAPTER TWENTY

TEAGAN

There are moments in life that shake us straight to the core and leave us forever different. Lying in bed with Gian, imagining my future both with and without him, was one of those moments.

If I could wave a wand, would I redesign my life? Was I living the one I wanted?

When it came to my research, I had concrete goals—short and long term. But for me? My personal life? I wanted more.

In five years I didn't want to be returning to my apartment alone each night. I wanted a life full of laughter and maybe a little chaos. I didn't want to spend all day working alone, sharing my achievements as well as my failures with no one.

Oh my God, I wanted the life Riley had always planned for us—the one where we raised our families together. I wanted the real deal—the happily ever after.

Panic rose within me as I stared into Gian's eyes. We hadn't known each other long enough to know if what we felt for each other would last. In bed we were compatible—combustible, really. But didn't that fade over time?

Did he really want a large family? It made sense that he would, since he was from one. But was that what I wanted?

I didn't know.

How could I not know?

His smile was reassuring. "Breathe, Teagan. This isn't a job interview. There are no wrong answers."

I nodded but still said nothing. I couldn't. I didn't have any answers. Only questions—more than I knew what to do with.

I was still freaking out in my head when he started to speak slowly and in a tone that soothed me. "One tough question, and I activated your amygdala, a little almond-shaped collection of nuclei right at the base of your temporal lobe. It sent a signal to your hypothalamus, which is usually more of a maintenance guy. He handles your blood pressure, temperature, calorie intake. But he also gets the big jobs like making us feel good after sex or telling our adrenal glands it's time to wake our bodies up with a burst of adrenaline. It's the adrenaline that has your heart thudding, but you can blame cortisol for how your mind might be racing. It increased your blood sugar in your bloodstream, which is being absorbed by your brain. Bad news? You're not actually temporarily stronger. Good news? The endorphins your body is releasing inhibit your body's ability to feel pain. So if you want to punch me, you'll probably still break your hand, but it won't hurt."

By the time he was done, I was smiling along with him. Not every woman would have enjoyed his impromptu biology lesson, but I did. It made me think that maybe we were more alike than we were different. "How do you do it? I don't want to punch you anymore."

"Whew, because I was hoping for something less painful."

Gian was the first man I felt I could really be myself with. Neither of us were what some might have called *normal*, but with him I'd found someone I didn't have to pretend with. I ran my hand over his chest and relaxed against him. "I'm amused whenever people suggest we should make computers more humanlike. Nothing you just described has a place in AI software. Why would we want a machine to be flooded with chemicals which make some of its functions less effective?"

He tipped his head to one side. "I never really thought about it, but I agree. I don't want to drive a car that's afraid."

With a cheeky smile, I said, "I don't want to use a blender that enjoys being turned on."

"I'll never look at my appliances the same way again."

We shared a laugh and a kiss that ended with me laying my head on his shoulder and savoring simply being with him. I wanted to tell him about NYD. Not only would he understand what I was working on, but I had a feeling he'd agree with the importance of it. All I had to do was let go and trust him.

I closed my eyes. I hated myself for not being able to take that final leap of faith. Did it mean that what we had wasn't meant to last?

Riley had told me I should be able to enjoy being with someone even while I kept a part of myself private. Why couldn't I?

Gian had told me some mystery was okay in a relationship. He wasn't pushing, so I couldn't understand why I was panicking.

His arms tightened around me in the most delicious, possessive way. "When will you tell Riley?"

I tensed, and my eyes flew open. *Oh, shit, and then there's that.* "Why?"

"Dominic deserves the same consideration. My schedule is likely more flexible than yours, but I could do it tomorrow if you think that's when you'll be telling Riley."

It was time. I knew that, but that didn't make it easier to commit to telling her. I kept my tone calm. "That sounds like a solid plan." I hugged him tighter. Once we opened this door, there was no going back, and we'd have little to no control over how it worked out.

"It'll be okay, Teagan. You'll see." His deep voice wrapped around me like a warm blanket.

I nodded, although I wasn't confident that it would be at all.

"Go to sleep," he said gently.

"Don't tell me what to do," I mumbled.

He chuckled.

I took a few deep breaths, did my best to calm my thoughts, and began to fall asleep—not because he'd told me to but because I was emotionally exhausted. Even as I began to fade away, I felt like that was an important distinction to make.

CHAPTER TWENTY-ONE

TEAGAN

The next morning I woke to a note placed beside me on the bed. It said: Flying down to see Dominic. I'll see you tonight. —Gian

I picked up my phone and checked my messages. There was one there from him as well. I hate that I left while you were sleeping, but I didn't want to wake you.

It was all uncharted territory for me. I had no idea what to respond, so I texted: Safe travels.

I reread the message after I sent it and groaned. *Safe travels? Who even writes that?*

Had I been brave enough to write what I was feeling, I would have said: *Always wake me before you go. I don't like waking up without you.*

I didn't send that text, though. It felt too needy. *Safe travels* would have to be good enough for now.

There was also a message from Riley saying she'd be late because she needed to run a quick errand on the way in. I sighed. It was a good thing I didn't care if we ever turned a profit on the shop. Really, this morning, Riley's chronic tardiness was the least of my concerns.

I wrote: Do you know if Kal is around today?

I can check.

If he is, could you ask him to come with you to the shop today?
There's something I need to tell both of you.

Is it bad?

Since there was no way for me to know, I wrote: No.

You freaked me out for a second there. Let me guess, Gian broke
up with you and you want to take Kal out on a date to make him
jealous.

I shook the phone, as if by doing so I might shake some sense into
her. No.

You're engaged and want us to be part of your wedding party?
Kal will balk at first, but I was just in a wedding with a male
bridesmaid. It happens.

How Riley's mind worked was often a mystery to me. Could you
just ask Kal?

A moment later she said: He has the day off so he's in. Does an hour
work for you?

Perfect.

I was showered and dressed before I returned to Gian's text and
my lame response. He must have answered while I was in the shower,
because I had a new message from him. I could get used to waking up
next to you.

My face warmed, and I held the phone to my chest. There were so
many unknowns, and I'd never done well with those—not in computer

programs and not in people. Gian was off to meet with someone who had the power to destroy everything and everyone I cared about. He'd promised me nothing bad would come from this, but could anyone follow through on a promise like that?

Are you in New York yet? When I realized I hadn't responded to his comment before asking that, I added: Will you still be saying that when there are seven of us in the bed?

He didn't answer immediately, which made me wish I hadn't tried to make a joke. I wasn't known for having a great sense of humor. It was possible he hadn't understood the reference. You know—when we're married with five kids and they all squeeze in between us.

Nothing.

Oh God, I'd taken a joke he'd made and brought it up the next day in a way that might have made him think I'd taken him seriously. Was that why he wasn't answering?

I wrote: That was a joke. Like the one you made yesterday. I know we aren't getting married.

I read the message over after I sent it and cringed. I wasn't opposed to the idea of getting serious with Gian.

When still nothing came back from him, I texted: The kid thing was a joke, too. I never slept with my parents. Not even when I had a nightmare.

I went to text something else but stopped myself and took a deep breath. *Calm down. One joke doesn't end a relationship.*

My phone rang—Gian. I answered on the first ring.

"Sorry I couldn't answer," he said. "The helicopter just landed. The pilot frowns on texting while ducking under rotor blades."

I'd never been in a helicopter, but I could imagine everyone thought that was a bad idea. "So you're there."

"I'm here."

I swallowed hard. "I'm meeting Riley and Kal at my shop."

"I didn't offer to go with you for that, but you and Riley are so close I thought you'd want to do it on your own. I should have asked, though."

I'd never dated anyone who cared so much about how I felt. Was this what having a partner was supposed to be like? Like I had someone in my corner? I could get used to that feeling. "No, your instincts were right. It would have been strange to have you there while explaining who you are. It'll be easier this way." As he offered me more, I wanted to be more for him—but it didn't come naturally. "Did you—do you wish I'd gone down to see Dominic with you? I'm sorry. I didn't even think to ask."

"Next time. He already knows about you, although not about what I've come to tell him."

"He does?" An instant battle began to rage within me. Part of me wanted to imagine him telling his brother because he wanted to talk out his feelings about me with someone—the same way I'd wanted to discuss him with Riley. The little voice in my head, the one that tended to lean toward imagining worst-case scenarios, was afraid to ask what he'd told him—in case it had anything to do with my work.

I could hear the smile in his voice when he said, "He thought I should have sent you something better than a clock. He didn't think it was romantic at all."

Perhaps because my emotions were all over the place, I blurted out, "Honestly, I thought it was a surveillance device until I disassembled it."

"A surveillance device? Oh, I get it, so I could figure out the nature of your top secret work." He laughed. "And you took it apart. Did you put it back together, or is it still a pile of pieces?"

"I put it back together—with Riley's help. She thought you sent me it that way because I like puzzles."

"Well, now I know which one of us will be building the furniture in our family. I put a dollhouse together last Christmas for my youngest niece. It took me three hours. Three hellish hours I'll never get back."

I chuckled. "You poor thing."

"It *was* rough." A voice spoke in the background; then Gian said, "I'm heading in to see Dominic. If you want to talk after you see Riley, text me. Otherwise I plan to fly back early. Have dinner at my place tonight."

I spoke the concern that came to me. "Shouldn't we see how everything goes today before we make any plans?"

"Teagan, this is complicated and potentially messy, but nothing could happen today that would make me not want to see you tonight."

His no-games approach allowed me to relax with him enough to share, "I hope I'm doing this right." I was referring to including Kal in the conversation with Riley, but as I said the words, I realized my worries encompassed more than that.

If a friend had come to me in similar circumstances, I would have told her to tap the brakes. The situation had too many moving parts for me to blindly trust a man I'd known less than a week. But if I didn't trust him, what did we have?

Just good sex?

I wanted more than that with him.

"I'm hoping the same thing. I invited Sebastian. If you think your conversation has the potential of being confusing, imagine mine: *Dominic, as a brother you never knew existed, I asked your other brother, the one we're still pretending is your cousin, to help me tell you that we've found two more of your siblings.*"

"Yeah, I can see how that might be awkward. I'm a little nervous about how I'll explain to Riley that I knew but didn't tell her at first. And that she met her niece already, and I didn't tell her who she was."

"I have two highly successful methods for situations like that."

"I need all the help I can get—so lay them on me."

"Be honest. I've never met a person who wanted a lie over the truth. And tell Riley you love her. Sometimes people need to hear that—even during an argument. In fact, during an argument is when people need to hear it most."

I loved my parents, but I couldn't remember the last time we'd said the words to each other. I was sure we had. Maybe when I was young. Had I ever said it to Riley? I didn't know. "So if we're arguing, and you start throwing the *L* word around, I'll know you're just employing a debate strategy."

"That's not what I said."

I knew it wasn't, but I felt uncomfortable with my own awkwardness with the word, and that had me feeling defensive. I took a deep breath. It wasn't Gian's fault I hadn't told Riley as soon as I'd found out about the stupid bet. It wasn't his fault I couldn't remember the last time someone had said they loved me. "Sorry, I'm just tense."

His voice softened. "You've got this, Teagan. Call me later."

"I will." I sensed he was about to end the call, so I said, "Gian."

"Yes?"

"I'll see you tonight. Thank you."

"Looking forward to it, and you're welcome. Bye."

He'd already ended the call when I replied, "Bye," and lowered the phone.

CHAPTER TWENTY-TWO

GIAN

I was returning my phone to the breast pocket of my jacket when Sebastian came into view. He wasn't alone. Mauricio and Christof flanked him.

We hugged in greeting. "What are you all doing here?"

Mauricio joked, "If you're going to have a meeting of the minds, you have to invite the minds."

Christof's expression looked more serious. "When Sebastian said he was coming to lend Dominic emotional support, I knew we had to be here as well. Brothers. Cousins. I don't care what labels we go by—we're family."

Just then Dominic stepped into view; his face was tight and guarded. "Why don't we move this out of the hallway?" With that Dominic turned on his heel and headed into his office.

Sebastian put a hand on my shoulder. "This is good, even if it starts off rocky."

I nodded. I'd promised Teagan everything would be okay; now all I had to do was make that happen. Once we were all inside Dominic's office, door closed, we stood in a loose circle.

Tension vibrated in the air.

A moment later, before any of us started to speak, the door opened, and Judy walked in and came to stand beside me. She pocketed her hands and shrugged. "Your mother told me what you were all doing, and since I started this with you, I didn't want you to have to take the heat alone."

Now that was the Judy I knew and loved. I put an arm around her shoulders and hugged her. "I should have invited you."

Dominic cut in. "As much as I appreciate all of you being here, I don't like surprises. So if someone could tell me what this is about, I'm less likely to get an ulcer."

Judy left my side to go to her father. "It's not a bad thing, Dad. Actually, once you get used to the idea, I bet it makes you really happy."

"Judy." Dominic said his daughter's name in a warning tone all children understood.

I stepped forward. "Antonio Corisi had twins with a woman in Lockton, Massachusetts. You have another brother and sister—about my age."

Dominic frowned, then turned his attention to me. "The Becket woman you were telling me about is not one of them, is she?"

"Teagan is her friend," I quickly assured him. "No, your sister's name is Riley. Her brother's—*your* brother's—name is Kal. Kal Ragsdale."

He relaxed visibly, then frowned again. "How many people knew about this? And for how long?"

Judy slipped her hand into his. "If you're going to be upset with anyone, Dad, be upset with me. Once I decided to surprise you with this, I put everyone else in a difficult spot. I didn't see that at the time, but I see it now."

"It's my fault," I interjected. "Judy and I made a bet about who could find more family for you faster. I was the one who came up with the idea. My only defense is I didn't see the harm in it at the time."

He looked around the room. "You're all here, so you all knew?"

Christof raised a hand in clarification. "Yes and no. We're here because what happens to one of us happens to all of us—and you, Dominic, are one of us."

"Stuck with us." Mauricio meshed his fingers together before him.

Sebastian nodded. "Labels don't mean anything. Right here. Right now. This is what matters."

Dominic hugged Judy to his side. "I want to be upset with you for keeping this from me, but how can I be?"

"I said it yesterday, and I'll say it again now, Dad. I'm sorry for how I've behaved lately. You'll see better from me from now on."

He kissed the side of Judy's head. "That's good to hear." Then he looked around the circle of us again. "Which one of you should I thank for my daughter's change of heart?"

I wasn't about to tell him, but Judy surprised me by saying, "You can thank Gian's girlfriend for that. I crossed a few boundaries with her, and she cut me right down to size."

Dominic didn't like that. Before he said anything, though, I added, "They've already sorted it out."

Judy nodded. "We did. She didn't say anything that I didn't need to hear. So don't be upset with her. She's the reason I apologized to you and Mom yesterday. It's because of her that I've decided to enroll in college in the fall."

"Sounds like you had quite a talk," Dominic said.

"We did." Judy met my gaze. "I can't say I handled it well at the time, but then I spoke to Gian, and that helped. I apologized to Marc as well." She looked back up at her father. "So please don't be upset with him either. I should never have put him in a position where he had something he couldn't tell you."

Dominic's expression tightened with emotion. "I'm proud of you, Judy." Then he looked my way and said, "Thank you." His gaze swept around the circle. "All of you. You have no idea what this means to me."

"Please don't build me another research facility," I joked.

Mauricio chimed in. "You can build me anything you want."

Christof rolled his eyes skyward. "Sadly, he means it. That's what happens when you're as pretty as he is—you think everything should come easy."

Mauricio leaned toward Christof. "Do you know what will come your way easy? An ass kicking."

"Bring it," Christof said, posturing as if he were about to wrestle Mauricio to the floor.

Sebastian smiled. "Judy, this is your gene pool. I'm sorry."

Her answering smile was wide. "I love them just the way they are."

"We love you too," Christof and Mauricio said almost in unison.

Circling back to the reason we were there, I said, "The Ragsdales seem like good people. Both Riley and Kal dropped out of school to help their mother pay her medical bills."

"What's wrong with her?" Dominic asked with concern.

In a tight voice, Judy was the one who answered. "Your father hurt her, Dad. She hid her pregnancy from him because she was afraid he'd hurt them as well."

"He would have," Dominic said without missing a beat, then rubbed a hand over his forehead. "Do they know about us?"

"Fara does," I said. "Riley and Kal are being told about you this morning. Fara is understandably concerned that you might—"

"Be like my father," Dominic ground out. "I get that a lot."

Judy shook his arm. "Only from people who don't know you. You're nothing like him. You can't expect Fara to know that. Not yet. She hid in fear of him for so long. But he's gone, and he shouldn't have the power to scare or hurt anyone anymore. Not her." She looked up at her father intently. "Not you. Don't give him that win."

I stepped closer. "I agree. Let that bastard rot in hell watching you restore everything he tore down."

Dominic's eyebrows rose and fell; then he nodded. After a moment, he said, "Leonardo doesn't have school today. What do you think of us flying up and having dinner with your parents tonight? All of us. I'll call to confirm with Basil and Camilla."

"All of us?" I asked. "As in the Ragsdales too?"

He shook his head. "No, but I'll organize things here so Abby and I can spend some time up there. I want to meet them in a way that doesn't overwhelm them."

I probably should have let that slide, but I wouldn't have with any of my other brothers, so I didn't. "Hold on; you're going to take things slow? Respect boundaries? Who are you?"

Dominic chuckled and hugged his daughter. "Brothers." His teeth flashed in a smile.

"So we're good?" Judy asked.

He nodded.

I let out a sigh of relief.

Judy's nose wrinkled. "Hey, Dad. When you tell Mom about this, could you leave off that finding the Ragsdales was part of a bet?"

I felt a little bad for Judy when he said, "When you tell her, and *no*."

I cut in, "Shit, I forgot I have plans tonight with Teagan." I hated to cancel with her; on the other hand I also didn't want to miss dinner with the whole family.

"Bring her," Sebastian said.

I made a face. "It's a little early to bring her home to meet Mom and Dad."

"I thought you really liked her," Judy said.

"I do."

Christof added, "In our family when you bring a woman home for the first time, it's usually because you've decided she's the one."

"I'm already there."

"No shit," Mauricio said. "Good for you. I knew right away as well."

Christof shook his head.

I let his claim slide this time. I was beginning to have real feelings for Teagan, but we were already charging ahead faster than she was comfortable with. I could only imagine what she'd think if my mother interviewed her on her feelings about having children. "We need a little more time together before I introduce her to all of you."

"Oh, hang on; it's not her you're worried about, is it?" Mauricio asked. "You're afraid we'll scare her off."

I didn't want to say *yes*, and I didn't want to lie, so I said nothing.

"Things really are okay with us now," Judy said.

Which I appreciated, but it didn't change my mind. "You will all meet her soon enough. Now, are we going to lunch or flying back?"

We decided to eat first. Rather than going to a restaurant, we ate in Dominic's boardroom and spent the time laughing and sharing stories. I also had time to tell them more about Teagan and her relationship with the Ragsdales. I didn't mention what Judy had uncovered about her.

As we were preparing to head out, Dominic took me aside. "Have dinner with Teagan tonight. We can see each other anytime."

"Thanks."

He frowned. "Teagan is the same woman Judy wanted to partner with, isn't she?"

"Yes."

"What is she working on?"

"I don't know." I felt it was important to add, "But even if I did, I couldn't tell you. If she's not ready for the world to know yet—I respect that."

"I don't like secrets."

I inhaled sharply. In the past this was where I would have shut down in frustration, but I reminded myself that we were in a better place now. "But you won't look into it, because you respect me and I'm asking you not to."

"All I'd do would be to ensure it's nothing you shouldn't have your name linked to."

"No." I stood taller and looked him in the eye and repeated myself. "No."

Christof came back down the hall to see what was holding me up and motioned that the helicopter was ready. I nodded.

I started walking away, then turned back and said, "I know you can hear me, Dominic. Don't do it."

He just gave me that look—the one I never could decipher. It could have meant he'd heard me and the subject was closed. Or it could have meant he'd heard me and was going to do exactly what he wanted to.

For good measure, even as I continued to walk backward, I called out, "Don't make me kick your ass."

He smiled and waved once.

I turned just before walking into the wall. Marc Stone was at the door to see me out. "I'll talk to him," he said.

CHAPTER TWENTY-THREE

TEAGAN

I was pacing the front section of my printshop, still trying to figure out how to tell Riley and Kal that their lives were about to change. I wasn't ready, but I didn't see how I'd ever be. I was about to have a conversation with two of the people I cared about most on the planet. A conversation that would likely alter the rest of their lives.

More unsettling? Telling them meant breaking a promise to Fara. That thought made me sick enough that I'd visited the bathroom several times already that morning. She'd survived by hiding. More than most I understood the importance of staying off the radar. Revealing my work now to the world would leave my research vulnerable. Wasn't revealing the Ragsdales about to do the same to them?

I tried to have faith that everything would work out, but faith in anything or anyone didn't come easy to me. I trusted the Ragsdales, though.

And was beginning to believe I could trust Gian as well.

I considered myself a rational person. I was methodical by nature. Careful to the point of being what some would have called *eccentric*. Everything this past week felt like car brakes letting go on the way down a steep hill. It was a wild, dangerous ride, with some thrilling parts that I would have enjoyed more if there wasn't a real possibility that we were all careening toward disaster.

There was no way to know, though, and that was the hardest part for me. Would Riley and Kal remember that day as their best ever or the day I ruined their lives?

I checked my watch. It was too late to change my mind. Gian had probably already told Dominic. Right or wrong, there was no turning back.

The front door of my shop opened. Riley walked in with Kal. She had a huge teasing smile on her face. "You have to tell Teagan, Kal. We should celebrate your good news."

"You *just* promised you wouldn't say anything to anyone."

Riley waved at me. "Teagan isn't just anyone—she's Teagan. Come on. If you won't tell her, let me. Please."

Kal folded his arms across his enormous chest. He'd always been good looking, but since he'd taken up bodybuilding, he'd morphed into a version of himself I barely recognized. I remembered the Kal who preferred books over girls, who had been athletic only to get a college scholarship. The mountain of a man before me had developed when Kal had dropped out of college to make fast cash. He'd tried all sorts of jobs, but none had brought in the kind of money required to help pay his mother's medical bills. I'd laughed the first time he'd told me he'd taken a job as an exotic dancer, but then I'd seen him onstage.

Okay, Kal and I had never had a spark—but damn, that man could move. And his body was insane.

He'd said the only thing that cheered him up now was working out, and judging by the look of him, I guessed he'd been cheering himself up a lot lately. "Riley, if Kal doesn't want me to know, that's okay."

Kal shook his head. "Never tell Riley anything. She couldn't keep a secret to save her life."

That wasn't true. She'd kept mine. I cleared my throat. "Speaking of secrets—"

Riley spoke over me. "Oh, come on. You seriously care if Teagan knows?"

"There's something I need to tell both of you," I finished.

Kal threw his hands up in the air. "Fine. Teagan, a talent scout was at my last show and offered me an international gig. Her company wants to fly me around the world. I couldn't turn down the offer—it's enough to pay off the rest of what we owe for Mom and get Riley back in school. So it looks like I'm in the big leagues now."

"A headliner," Riley said with pride. "But I'm not taking the extra money. We'll talk to the hospital and see if we can get Mom's next surgery on a payment plan." Her smile held some sadness. "I know you hate dancing, Kal, and none of this is what either of us wanted . . . but that doesn't mean you shouldn't be proud of your accomplishment. You're making more money than any of your college friends with their fancy office jobs. And we won't always be in this place. The doctor said this surgery might do the trick. We'll pay that off and then both go back to school. Who knows—maybe I'll find a job so good before that that I'll pay for you to go back before me."

He put an arm around her shoulders and hugged her briefly. "I'd never let that happen, but I love you for wanting to take care of me, Riley."

Riley smiled up at him. "I've got your back—always. After all, you're the only brother I have."

I raised my hand. "Actually, about that . . ." It must have been the high pitch of my voice that caught their attention. They both turned toward me. I let out a shaky breath. "Your biological father had five children."

We all froze, and my words hung there in the silence.

Kal was the first to speak. "What are you talking about?"

"Mom said our father was dead," Riley said in confusion.

I chose every word with care. "He is, but he was with other women before that." I groaned. Really, was that the best I could come up with? "He's been dead for about twenty years."

Kal shook his head. "From the little I know about the man, I'm glad he's dead. He's the reason for our mother's pain. No offense, but I want no part of a family reunion that revolves around him."

Riley touched his arm. "Hang on, Kal. These people aren't him." Her gaze flew to mine. "Brothers or sisters?"

I swallowed hard. "One sister, two brothers. All older with children of their own."

"That's a lot." Riley moved to sit on one of the shop's stools.

"I hear five is the perfect number." I couldn't believe I'd said that. It wasn't relevant. Nothing about this conversation was about me and Gian. I needed to get him out of my head.

"We have all the family we need," Kal said.

Riley frowned. "How long have you known?"

Here goes. "Not long, and at first I didn't know if it was true. Then I spoke to Fara, and she confirmed that it was." I clasped my hands together in front of me. "She made me promise not to tell you, but I didn't feel like it was something I could keep from you."

Nodding, Riley said, "I can see that. I've asked her about him over the years. Any hint of curiosity would upset her. She said he was a very dangerous person from a dangerous family. I always wondered if we were related to the mob or something like that."

"Something like that," I said automatically. When her eyes rounded, I rushed to correct myself. "I mean . . . nothing like that." At least, I *hoped* nothing like that, but the last thing I wanted to do was fill Riley and Kal with fear when nothing yet had happened to warrant it. There was a chance the dark web was wrong and Dominic was really a nice man living under the shadow of a horrible parent. All those people who had gone up against him and disappeared? Coincidences.

God, I hope I'm doing the right thing.

Running a hand through his hair, Kal said, "I don't want anything to do with them."

"I don't if they're dangerous," Riley said tentatively. "Are they?"

"No." I prayed I was right.

Riley turned back toward Kal. "A sister and two brothers." Her mouth rounded. "I'm an aunt. You're an uncle, Kal. Maybe we should at least meet them."

"You already have." I grimaced.

"When?" Riley stood. "How?"

I chose the information I thought was most relevant and left off what would only confuse the situation more. "Your father's name was Antonio Corisi."

Riley brought a hand up to her temple. "So Judy Corisi wasn't at the shop to design a logo for her father."

I swallowed hard. "No."

Kal's expression revealed his skepticism. "Right. Dominic Corisi is our brother, and the Queen of England is our aunt."

I understood how it could sound implausible. "You have that half-right. Antonio had two children with his wife, Rosella: Dominic and Nicole. So yes. Dominic Corisi is your brother. Half brother, if you want to be technical."

"No," Kal said firmly.

"Yes," I responded, wishing I knew a better way to tell them all this.

Riley looked lost in her thoughts, and they didn't appear to all be good ones. "That would make Judy our niece. She was there to meet me?"

"And me." When Riley looked confused, I added, "It's complicated, and not all of it matters right now."

"You said you haven't known for long, but it sounds like you know an awful lot about them."

"Gian is Judy's uncle. He and Dominic have the same mother but different fathers." I left off the murder rumor because—well, how would it have helped?

"Who's Gian?" Kal asked.

179

"Her boyfriend," Riley answered, sounding like she was still trying to process what she'd just heard.

"Yeah, leave me out of that clusterfuck," Kal said with a shake of his head.

Riley gave me a long look. "Why didn't you say something when I brought Judy in? There I was thinking I'd landed a potential client for you, excited and going on about it like an idiot, when something entirely different was going on."

I felt as wrong as she apparently thought I was. Still, I tried to justify my actions. "I'd promised Fara—"

"I would have told *you*," Riley said in an angry tone, and my stomach did a little flip. Riley didn't have a temper. She floated through life, optimistic and shining like a cotton candy rainbow. Or a unicorn with braces.

"I'm sorry." My apology sounded lame even to me.

She stepped away, waving me off.

I turned to Kal. "I thought I was doing the right thing."

He growled. "If my mother asked you not to say anything, she had good reason to. Not that it matters now, I guess. They already know about *us*."

"They didn't for a long time. Judy and Gian thought there might be a chance Antonio had more children, and their search led them here."

No one said anything for several long minutes. My heart was thudding wildly in my chest. I half expected the two of them to walk out of my shop saying they never wanted to see me again. *Thank you, brain, for always kicking out the worst-case scenario as a real possibility.*

I didn't get a full-on panic attack, though, because I imagined the physical process my body was setting into motion from my amygdala—each part of my brain a minicomputer kicking out chemicals based on the code I'd written for it. Seeing it that way, I felt empowered to rewrite some of the prompts.

Dark thoughts would no longer trigger a full system shutdown. I was bypassing the cascade effect by breathing deeply and imagining nanobots being dispersed into my bloodstream to remove the adrenaline. It was actually pretty effective.

I remembered the advice Gian had given me about how to navigate this conversation. Honesty and an *I love you*. I'd delivered the first. The second couldn't hurt. I raised my voice so I was sure they'd both hear me. "I am so sorry. I love you both and your mother. You've been my family, sometimes even more so than my own. I don't know if I did any of this the right way, but I tried to do what I thought was best."

Riley turned, and although she looked conflicted, she said, "We love you too. I know how you get tangled up in your head sometimes and can't get out of your own way." She paused. "Wait, did they know what happened to my mother?"

"They didn't, but they do now." I checked my watch. "As of about an hour or so ago. Gian flew down to tell them."

Shaking his head, Kal asked, "Why is Mom afraid of these people?"

I told them the story she'd told me about the man who'd come to see her while she'd been in the hospital. The more I said, the angrier Kal looked. "So someone knew about us all along and did nothing to help our mother. I want nothing to do with these people."

Riley looked down.

I put an arm around her. "You don't have to make any decisions today. There is more to their story. Why don't we get something to eat, and I'll tell you what I know?"

Over sandwiches and coffee we ordered and brought back into the shop, and with the help of a pen and paper, I mapped out their family—or at least as much of it as I knew. I told them about Gian's family and how intertwined the Romanos were with the Corisis and also how close they all were.

When I finally stopped to take a breath, Kal said, "The story of our family is heavy on the name Gian."

I blushed. "I learned everything about your family through him."

"And she's fucking him," Riley added with a smile.

I slugged her arm. "No, I'm—"

Kal arched an eyebrow, and I realized there was no reason to lie. "I am, and it's fantastic."

Kal chuckled. "Well, okay then."

Riley clapped her hands together. "You should see them together, Kal. Talk about sizzle. I hope I meet someone who makes me feel that way someday."

"I'm happy for you, Teagan," Kal said. "Just be careful. He's probably nothing like our father—" He made a face and continued, "I hate to even call him that."

"Just say Antonio," Riley suggested.

Kal nodded. "Gian is probably nothing like Antonio was, but people with money aren't like us. If he crosses a line, if he ever makes you feel uncomfortable—tell me. I'll handle it."

My eyes teared up. I wanted this to work out for them. For me as well. "I'm sure that won't be necessary, but thanks." After a pause, I added, "I really like him."

Riley leaned in. "Like? Or more?"

I held my breath before admitting, "More?"

She stood up, ran over, and hugged me. "I'm so proud of you, Teagan. You're finally opening up and letting someone in."

A huge smile spread across my face. "I am, and it feels pretty damn amazing."

There was a lull in the conversation. Riley returned to her stool. Kal looked distracted by his thoughts.

Flapping a french fry in her hand, Riley said, "If you marry Gian, will that make us related?"

I wrinkled my nose. "Gian is Dominic's brother through their mother. You're related to Dominic through your father. The Romanos are actually Gian's cousins, but he's adopted, so legally they are also his brothers."

Kal groaned. "My brain is melting."

"Let's just say yes," Riley said with a smile.

"Yes," I said with enthusiasm, even though I was still trying to sort it out in my head. "But we're not getting married. We just started dating."

"Sure you're not," Riley said cheerfully. "Oh my God, now I need to find someone. I thought I had more time. Do not have children without me."

"I'm pretty sure you have time," I assured her. "Although I intend to have five. So you'll have to keep up."

"The two of you are nuts," Kal said, but he was smiling as he did.

Riley and I exchanged a look only longtime best friends could. In unison, we said, "We know." Then we both laughed.

Kal left after lunch. Riley spent the day with me at the shop. We talked about the Corisis, her biological father, then Gian . . . oh, so much about Gian.

In the end we both said we felt better, even if we were still confused. She wasn't sure what she should do—especially since Kal had no interest in meeting the people he felt had failed their mother.

I told her about Haven Two and how I still had my own reservations when it came to trusting anyone besides her with that information. "I haven't even told Gian what I'm working on yet. Do you think that's bad?"

She went to the table where the clock he'd sent me still sat. "I think it means you need time to get used to the idea of having someone in your life." She traced the hands on the front of the clock. "I don't want to do anything that will potentially hurt my mother, but I would like to meet my other siblings."

"You should."

"And you should get going. Don't you have a hot date with Gian tonight?"

I checked the time. "I do. I can cancel if you need me."

Riley shook her head. "Go. But promise me something."

I grabbed my purse. "Anything."

"Let yourself enjoy Gian. Don't overthink it. You'll know when it's the right time to tell him."

"I hope so." I hugged her and darted out.

I rushed back to my apartment, showered quickly, and put on a light amount of makeup. Dinner at his place didn't require dressing up, but I slipped on my favorite little black dress. I should have been exhausted after the emotional day I'd had, but I felt invigorated and very ready to enjoy Gian.

CHAPTER TWENTY-FOUR

GIAN

A first—I was glad to not have time planned with my family. I wanted Teagan to see my apartment. This simple apartment was *me*. Over the years a few women had expressed disappointment in my lodging. When they'd heard the name Romano, they must have envisioned a staffed penthouse apartment with a Jacuzzi on the balcony.

If I wanted that lifestyle, I could have had it, but I didn't care about material things. When I'd gone to Johns Hopkins, my parents had bought an eight-bedroom house so they could all come down to visit me on a regular basis. It was still in the family, but I didn't want to live there.

I'd temporarily lived a decked-out lifestyle when I'd moved to New York to get to know the Corisis. When I looked back at that time, I realized it was no wonder I hadn't felt as if I'd fit in. Rather than staying true to what I knew about myself, I'd tried to be who I thought everyone else wanted me to be. My goals tended to be concrete and based on improving the human condition.

Still, loving Teagan made me face my lack of employment. I came from a family of hard workers, and I had more than my fair share of opportunities. Before I asked her to marry me, I needed to choose a career path. I loved that with Teagan, I had someone I could be myself with. I didn't have to be the stereotypical perfect man.

I buzzed Teagan in and waited at my apartment door for her to arrive by elevator. The craziness of the day fell away as soon as she did. I had so much to tell her, so much I wanted to know, but none of that mattered yet. "I missed you," I said.

She blushed as she walked toward me. "It hasn't been that long."

"That's not how it felt." I dug my hands into her hair and hauled her in for a kiss that I hoped expressed even a small part of how good it felt to see her again.

She threw her arms around my neck and melted against me. I spun, lifting her off her feet as I did, and closed the door behind us. When I raised my head, I was breathing raggedly. "I made eggplant parmigiana. A family recipe I learned from my grandmother in Montalcino."

"Sounds delicious." She writhed against me, bringing me damn near losing my control. I wanted to show a little restraint this time. It was important to me that she knew I wasn't with her just for the sex.

I cleared my throat. "It's better warm."

She tugged my head down and whispered in my ear, "So am I."

Who needed food? Not me. "Hang on a second," I said before sprinting off to my kitchen to turn off the stove. When I returned, she was stepping out of her shoes.

I tossed mine off.

Holding my gaze, she shed her dress.

I yanked mine over my head and threw it across the room.

Item by item, we removed our clothing until we were standing naked before each other. There was no hiding how excited I was, but she looked just as revved as I was.

She stepped forward and ran a hand across my chest. I shuddered with pleasure. "I've heard you should always thank a chef personally."

In a strangled tone, I joked, "I believe it's usually after a meal."

She sank to her knees before me, cupped my erect cock in her hands, and licked a circle around the tip of it. "Not before?"

I groaned. "Before works."

She took me deep into her mouth and gave me the kind of thank-you no chef would turn down. When I came and she swallowed, I pondered chef as a career choice.

My intention was to ask her about how her talk with Riley and Kal had gone, but when she stood up and her beautiful breasts came within reach of my mouth, I decided talking could wait.

I paused and said, "I bought you a gift on my way back."

"You did?" She didn't look interested in anything but me, and I almost changed my mind about the timing of my gift.

Naked and aroused, I sprinted to my bedroom and back with a rectangular box wrapped in white-and-gold paper. I held it out between us. "I hope you like it."

She shook the box. "It's not a diamond necklace."

"No, it's not." *Oh, shit, is that what she was wishing for?* I couldn't tell by her expression, but when she looked up and I saw laughter in her eyes, a huge grin spread across my face. "It definitely isn't."

She shook it again. "Please don't let it be a puppy—if it is, it doesn't sound like it's doing so well in there."

I laughed and stepped closer. "Nope, not a puppy."

Without making a move to open the wrapping paper, she said, "I should warn you, my parents hated my keen ability to guess my Christmas gifts."

I slid my arms around her and shuddered as fire seared through me in every place our bodies touched. "I'll make you a little bet. If you guess correctly, you get to keep it."

She moved back and forth against my hard cock, making it damn near impossible for me to concentrate on anything beyond wanting her. "And if I guess wrong?"

"I keep it, but you still get to use it."

Her free hand ran down my stomach to cup my balls before closing around my hard shaft. "So this is really a gift for you?"

I shook my head, unable to come up with a coherent response. The more her hand pumped slowly up and down my cock, the more my brain melted like butter in the sun. "Forget the gift," I said in a strangled voice.

Her hand dropped away, and I groaned. "No, I'm curious. It's a sex toy, isn't it?"

I claimed her mouth with mine and gave in to the passion rocking through me. She wrapped her arms around me, pressing the box against my back. When I raised my head, we were both breathing raggedly, and her eyes were burning with the same desire consuming me. "Open it."

She eased slightly back from me to do just that. She tore off the paper with the same abandon with which I tended to unwrap her. When she lifted the lid, she cocked her head to one side. "I expected it to look different."

I laughed and kissed the side of her head. "No need to change a design that works. All the technology is hidden. This one has an app you can use with it, but I bought the one with the screen on the end—so we can see the data, but it's kept in house."

Her lips curled in a smile. "A fully self-contained system?"

"I figured you'd prefer it that way."

Between kisses she said, "Gian Romano, you just won my heart."

My chest puffed with pride and pleasure. "You ain't seen nothing yet. In general, people focus on the rush of the orgasm. This will help you prolong the plateau phase of arousal. With practice, as you increase the time spent leading up to your release, you'll produce more oxytocin, more inflammation-reducing nitric oxide. In fact, the better you get at it, research suggests you'll improve your overall immune system, fertility, and ease any monthly symptoms."

She arched an eyebrow and withdrew the vibrator from the box. "Sounds like a miracle device . . . or a lot of hype."

I turned it on, placed my hand over hers, and slid the humming instrument between her folds. She was wet and ready, but nothing

188

about this was about rushing. She gasped as we settled it over her clitoris. "There's only one way to find out."

She parted her legs, and I eased the length of the vibrator into her, settling the second prong of it against her clit. "For the sake of research." Her head tipped back.

I sank to my knees before her, eased one of her legs onto my shoulder, and kissed her stomach while manipulating the toy. She steadied herself with her hands on my shoulders.

I worked the toy in and out gently, moving it strategically until the vibrator let out a low beep to announce her body temperature was rising along with internal contractions. I didn't require technology to tell me what the flush of her skin and her quickening breath meant. The goal was to keep her in that zone for as long as possible, so I took my time.

I lowered the vibration, kissed my way up her delicious legs. I left the toy in her capable hands and stood so I could kiss my way up her back, her neck, love on those amazing breasts of hers. There wasn't an inch of her I didn't worship with my mouth and hands.

She was in a light sweat when I eased the toy out of her and carried her to my bed. She was wild for release, but I whispered for her to be patient and started my exploration of her body all over. She was a feast I was nibbling my way through.

When I turned the toy on again, she was already writhing and wet. I could have taken her then, and she would have come, but I wanted this one to be just for her. I teased her sex with the toy, asked her to show me where it felt best. She thrust the toy deep inside her and guided my hand back to it, showing me just how she wanted it to thrust in and pull out.

The instrument beeped again just before she called out my name along with a string of profanity. I'd never seen anything more beautiful than Teagan giving herself fully over to pleasure. She withdrew the toy, tossed it aside, and reached for me.

"Fuck me," she growled. "Hard and fast, Gian."

No man needed to be asked that twice. I rolled on a condom, settled myself between her legs, and thrust deeply into her. Normally I started off slower, gentler. We were both already at the wild, primal, claiming stage. I pounded into her. She clung to me and met me thrust for thrust. It was a wild fuck, more intense than any I'd experienced before.

She was whimpering and crying out with pleasure when I gave in to my own pleasure. I rolled and pulled her with me so she was on top of me. She kissed me with postorgasm heat.

"I like it," she said in a calm voice.

I laughed. "Like? I thought that was amazing."

In a low purr she said, "I'm cautious when reviewing any new product. I really need to know if the results are reproducible before I call it *amazing*."

Her eyes were shining with laughter. My heart was thudding wildly in my chest, not with excitement but with hope that I'd found my forever after. As I strove to find the words to express how I felt, she fell asleep. I held her for a long time, simply enjoying the feel of her in my arms and the peace she brought to my soul.

Dinner was very, very cold by the time we woke and peeled ourselves off the bed. We showered together, then headed back to the kitchen naked.

After making ourselves plates of food and pouring wine, we moved to the dining room. Seated across from me, looking flushed and well loved, Teagan asked, "Do you think we'll ever eat with clothes on?"

"When we have kids, we probably should," I joked.

She didn't look as freaked by the idea as she had been the night before, when I'd teased her that we'd have five. She took a sip of wine, then said, "What is it about us? I came over with so much I wanted to say; then whoosh—it all flew out of my head when I saw you."

"I suffer from a similar condition. I think it's called *we should do this every night*."

She nodded, as if I'd said a real medical term. "Sounds serious."

"I sure hope so."

She smiled.

I smiled back.

I could have sat there all night simply enjoying the view, but I did want to know how things had gone for her as well as tell her how it had gone down in New York. The sex was great, and I wanted the rest of our relationship to be as open and solid. "Dominic took the news better than I thought he would. It probably helped that Judy was there as well as all my brothers. It was actually a really nice morning."

"Did you ask them all to be there?"

"No. No, that's how my family operates, though. We support each other by showing up whether or not an invite went out. It can be a bit much sometimes, but most of the time I find it hard to imagine a family being any other way."

"That must be wonderful," she said in a quiet voice that made me want to fix her relationship with her family, but in the end that would be her choice.

I reached across the table and took her hand in mine. "It is. My family is looking forward to meeting you, but I told them it'll happen soon enough."

Her fingers laced with mine. "Is that where you see this going?"

I could have asked, *Don't you?* But she'd already told me she needed more reassurance and patience. She'd said I'd won her heart, but I wasn't naive enough to believe it was that easy. So instead I gave her what I hoped she needed. I said, "Yes." Simple. Honest.

Her eyes lit with happiness. It would take her time to get on the same page as I was, but I was all in.

"There's something I wanted to ask you."

Her fingers tensed in mine. "Shoot."

"My father tells this story about how he bought my mother with a cow."

Her eyebrows shot up. "Really?"

I shook my head. "He didn't. I mean, yes, he bought her father a cow, but it wasn't in trade for her. My family believes that love brings out the best in a person. My father wanted to do something for my mother's family. At the time a cow was the best he could do."

"I'm not sure I understand where you're going with this."

"Giving someone a cow, in my family, is a metaphor for doing something for them purely out of love. I've fumbled around long enough trying and failing to find a job I could feel passionate about, but when I imagine the two of us together long term, I want better for you than I'm doing now. You deserve a man who knows what the hell he wants to do with the rest of his life."

"Gian, you're amazing just the way you are."

"That's kind but not true. It's time for me to choose a career and commit to it."

"Wow, that sounds . . . depressing."

I forced a smile. "Or mature. I'm fortunate in that I have many opportunities . . . it's time for me to choose one and be grateful for it."

"It's a shame you can't do what you really want to." Her smile was a little naughty. "You'd bring a lot of joy to a lot of people."

I chuckled. "Not personally, but I'd like to think my inventions could." It would never happen, though, so really there was no use talking about it. My mood sobered a bit. In every way that mattered I had an incredible life. I wasn't willing to risk it by dabbling in a career my family would never accept. "Have you told your parents about me yet?"

I regretted the spontaneous question as soon as her gaze fell to the table. "I haven't spoken to them since we met. To someone like you that probably sounds—"

I cut her off. "Teagan, every family is different. It doesn't make them better or worse."

Her eyes rose to mine again. "I envy the way you are with your family. My parents and I have never had that close bond."

No parent-child relationship was perfect. Not hers. Not mine. Still, that wasn't what I felt she needed to hear in that moment. "Want to know what my dad would probably say?"

She chuckled. "Sure."

"When I had issues with Dominic, he told me I was part of the problem. It was my perception of our relationship that shaped how I acted with him. I always thought he didn't listen to me, but my father made me see that I wasn't speaking to him as directly as I did the rest of my brothers. With my other brothers I knew that no matter what I said, they'd be there for me—so I said exactly what I was thinking. With Dominic I held back, then couldn't understand why he didn't hear me the same way my other brothers did." I tapped my temple. "Things have gotten much better between us since I've changed up here."

"I can see how they would." She nodded, then said, "So I'm part of the problem?"

"Every relationship has two sides. They're equally at fault, but you are the only part of the equation you can control."

"I wonder what would happen if I went all goofy and gushed about how much I love them. We've never done that."

"Only one way to know."

"I like that. I may just try it. You're changing the way I look at many things. In fact, Riley and Kal have begun counting how often I work your name into a conversation." She blushed. "I never thought I'd be that person."

My heart soared at the confirmation that I was affecting her as much as she was me. "How did your talk with them go?"

A smile spread across her face. "It got a little tense, especially when Riley realized she'd met Judy without knowing she was her niece and I hadn't told her. But I employed your secret weapon, and we left things on a good note."

"My secret weapon?"

"Just when the conversation took a downward turn, I reminded them both that I loved them. It brought us back to a place where we could talk the rest out."

"I'm glad. I'd like to take credit for that move, but I learned it from my parents. Being left by my bio mother could have really messed me up, but I was raised by people I knew loved me. My parents still kiss and hug all of us. They taught me the value of visible love."

We looked into each other's eyes for what seemed like a beautiful eternity. When she finally spoke, she said, "I'd like to meet your family. Not right now, but when it feels right to."

"I feel the same about your parents and the Ragsdales. When you think you're ready to introduce us, I'd love to meet them all."

"Riley already approves of you. She said it's nice to see me finally let someone in."

Whoosh—my heart took another hit, but in the most amazing way. "I'm glad. And Kal?"

"He's the closest I have to a big brother. He said if you ever mistreat me or make me uncomfortable, all I need to do is tell him, and he'll handle it."

"I like him already." My respect for Kal rose, and I was glad the Ragsdales appeared to be as loyal to Teagan as she was to them.

Teagan's smile dimmed. "Kal is a really good man who is working hard to pay off Fara's debt. When you meet him, don't ask him what he does. He doesn't like to talk about it."

"What does he do?" I had to ask.

"He's a dancer."

"Like ballet?"

"Not exactly. An exotic dancer."

"A stripper?" Okay, I knew what an exotic dancer was, but I still had to rephrase because I didn't believe I'd heard her right.

"Yes." She sounded defensive. "He needed to find something that brought in good money without a degree. It wasn't his first choice. He's too proud to admit how much he hates it, but he's too good at it to leave it for a job that pays less. I just told you so you can avoid the pitfall of asking him about it in public. That never goes well."

"Duly noted." *Don't ask Dominic's brother about being a stripper.* I was not looking forward to Dominic's reaction when he discovered Kal's profession. I figured I should probably give Dom a heads-up so he could try out all his reactions on me first before finding one that wouldn't offend Kal.

We spent the next few hours sipping wine and talking about everything and nothing. As we lay in bed later that night, I asked, "So what do you think of my place? Are you comfortable here?"

She tucked a hand beneath her head and smiled. "Was I supposed to notice something? I don't really care where we are. I just like being with you."

It was the best answer a woman had ever given me, and I knew she meant it.

I felt exactly the same way.

CHAPTER TWENTY-FIVE

TEAGAN

The following week flew by in a happy blur.

Riley met with the Corisis, and the world didn't end. Though Kal didn't meet with them, everyone seemed to understand that he wasn't ready. No one told Fara, and that was hard, but not everything needed to happen at once. I was beginning to understand that.

Gian and I spent each night at either my place or his. Each morning we had breakfast together, sometimes a shower, before each heading off to get our own stuff done. He fit so easily into my life it was difficult to remember what it had been like before him. Sometimes we used the toy. Sometimes we didn't. Being with him felt as natural as breathing.

I also found myself changing, but in ways that had me smiling more and worrying less. I called my parents and told them all about him, and it felt good. I even ended that conversation by telling them how much I loved and missed them.

When they said, "We miss you too, honey. We'd love it if you came down for a visit with your boyfriend," I nearly fell off my chair. Gian had given me that moment, and it was one I'd always be grateful for. I had been a passive observer in my relationship with my parents, as had they, but from that day on I saw myself as a force of good change.

I liked to think I was a good influence on Gian as well. His struggle with choosing a career was real. When he told me he was considering working for his family's company, I felt a real sadness for him. Although he was secure in his relationship with his parents, he struggled when it came to the idea of disappointing them.

Was it from gratitude?

Guilt?

He confided that his brothers thought he was afraid of being abandoned again. He denied that it was a concern for him, but I saw what his family did. His biological mother's desertion would always be there in the back of his mind, whether he wanted it to be or not. In some ways it made him a better person. He was attentive to how people felt, genuine in his concern for people's happiness. In some ways it held him back from standing up to his adoptive parents and being proud of who he was.

I didn't judge him for holding a part of himself back. There shouldn't be a price to simply being yourself, but there often was. Both Gian and I were optimistic but also realistic. If he tried to share his dream publicly, most people wouldn't hear anything beyond his interest in sex toys.

His research would be a joke.

He'd be a joke.

The Romanos were a proud family, as were the Corisis, and I couldn't blame him for not wanting to go down that road. Still, it made me sad that he couldn't.

Researching human pleasure? Collecting data on what brought us the most? Why wasn't the world mature enough to see how important it was?

I'd never been in love, but I could no longer envision a future without Gian in it. The kids he said we should have? I could imagine their faces. The dogs? Them too.

I hadn't yet shared my work with him, and he hadn't asked me about it again. The more he didn't push, the more I wanted to tell him, but I held back.

My reluctance frustrated me. I'd never let a man that far into my life. He'd said I'd tell him when I was ready. What if that day never came? He'd opened up to me. Why couldn't I do the same? Would my research and my inability to share it be what ended us? I hated that thought every time it popped into my head.

Bagged lunch in hand, I had just stepped out of a deli shop near my new lab when a black limo pulled up next to me. A driver sprinted around to open the door. A deep voice from inside said, "Get in."

"Thanks, but no thanks." I shook my head and began to back away. "I've watched enough stranger-danger videos to know you never allow yourself to be taken to a secondary location."

A tall man in an expensive charcoal suit unfolded from the vehicle. Dominic Corisi. I considered bolting but instead squared my shoulders and stood there with my hot coffee poised to toss in his face if this turned dangerous.

He flashed me a smile that didn't put me at ease. "I should have brought my wife, but she wouldn't approve of everything I have to say."

My eyebrows rose near my hairline. "Seems like a sign that you might not want to say it." *And that I definitely don't want to hear it.*

He frowned. "There's no reason to be afraid of me . . . yet."

I swallowed hard. Unlike the Ragsdales, I had something to hide— something this man might easily steal from me if allowed to. He hadn't gotten where he was by playing nice. In a squeaky voice, I said, "You had me until the *yet.* As a general rule I try to avoid all situations I'm afraid of."

"That's no way to live."

"*Or* it's the secret to living a long life. Whatever you're here to offer me, I'm not interested. Forget you ever heard my name. You don't have to erase me. I'm barely a blip on the screen as it is."

"Erase you?"

"I've heard how you deal with people who go up against you."

He laughed. Laughed. *That's never a good sign.* "Get in the limo."

"I've already said I'm not interested in talking to you."

"Too late for that—I'm here, and we have things to discuss."

My temper began to flare. "I see where your daughter gets her attitude."

I expected him to ramp up with me, but he didn't. His expression softened. "Speaking of Judy . . ."

Oh God.

He continued, "Thank you. She said you're the reason she's enrolling in college in the fall. I'm sure I don't want to know what you said to her, but it seemed to be what she needed to hear."

I nodded. "You're welcome. See, that's even more of a reason to not have a conversation. You and I are in a good place. Let's stay there."

He folded his arms across his chest. "We are going to be in each other's lives. You're dating my brother."

"Gian." I said his name, as if Dominic didn't know it. But there was a difference between meeting at a family barbecue and tracking me down at what was supposed to be my secret work location. I felt cornered, and someone like me didn't handle that well. I wondered what he would do if I hyperventilated into the paper bag I was holding.

"Yes, Gian." He gave me an odd look. "And Riley told me you're very close to the Ragsdales."

"I am."

Ice returned to his eyes. "You and I won't have a problem unless I discover you're into something that shouldn't be linked to my family."

"I'm sorry?"

"I promised Gian I wouldn't look into whatever your little side project is, but I'll make this as clear as I can. I don't care what it is unless it has the potential of harming my family. If you're in over your head with something that's illegal, this is your chance to tell me. I'll extricate you, and we'll move forward as if all you ever had was a printshop."

"Extricate me?" Who the hell did he think he was? No wonder Gian thought he couldn't have a life of his own.

He sighed. "I've made mistakes, gotten involved in situations I shouldn't have. If you're working for someone on something dangerous, I could free you from your obligation to them."

That gave me goose bumps. "Like kill me?"

He shook his head. "Save you." He ran his hand through his hair. "Why would I want to kill my little brother's girlfriend?"

I laughed nervously. "You're here to offer to help me?"

"Isn't that what I've been saying?"

"So this"—I waved my coffee between us—"is you being nice." I fought back another nervous laugh.

His eyes narrowed. "I don't get what's so funny."

I blurted out, "I love you."

He frowned. "Are you on drugs?"

This time I couldn't hold back the laugh. "No, I just heard saying it helps awkward conversations."

He gave me another odd look. "I can't claim to understand you, but from what I hear, we're probably going to be family, so I'm trying to keep an open mind."

"Gian told you that?" I asked, warmth spreading through me.

Looking impatient, Dominic said, "Yes. Now, I don't have all day. I want to make amends for the actions of my father, but I understand that the Ragsdales aren't ready to accept help from me yet. I intend to make it appear that a grant has paid off their debt."

I began to relax. "That's the kind of erasing I support."

"Then get in the damn limo. We don't need this meeting ending up photographed."

"Right." I slid into the back of the limo. He sat across from me.

Once the door was closed and we'd pulled out into traffic, he said, "I'll ask Abby if she and the kids can meet us for lunch."

"I'd like that." Over the next few minutes I watched an intimidating man become so much more human as he explained to his wife that he was taking me out to lunch and that this would be a great way for all of us to meet.

I heard Abby ask if Gian was joining us, and I swore Dominic flushed with guilt. "It was spur of the moment," he said.

"You promised you wouldn't get involved," Abby said.

He loosened his tie and looked out the window. "I never promised that."

"Gian will be so upset if you scare her off," Abby said.

"She's coming to lunch with us. Not scared at all." He turned the phone toward me. "Teagan, tell her. We're good, right?"

"We're good," I said in a forced cheerful tone while telling myself to relax. Sure, I was in the limo of a man who was universally feared on the dark web, a place where few feared anything, but he seemed to have good intentions. "I'm looking forward to meeting you, Mrs. Corisi."

She responded, "Call me Abby. I wish Leonardo could come as well, but he's with his tutor right now." After a pause, she said, "Teagan, don't let Dominic intimidate you. He's a big softy under all that growl."

He rolled his eyes skyward, but his smile in the moment was an entirely different one than the one he'd first shown me. I thought about what he'd said earlier about how his wife wouldn't approve of everything he wanted to say. I couldn't imagine that she would have had an issue with him helping the Ragsdales, so he must have been referring to the part where he'd offered to save me from whatever dangerous situation he thought I might have gotten involved in.

They made arrangements to meet us at an upscale restaurant outside Boston. After he ended the call, Dominic turned those intense dark eyes on me again. This time, though, I didn't teeter on hyperventilating into my bagged lunch. He said, "If I scared you, I didn't mean to."

"You didn't," I lied. Then, because I felt like we just might be in a place where I could, I joked, "Maybe just a little."

His expression remained serious. "If you're important to Gian, you're important to me. You've got nothing to worry about."

I kept my hands clasped on my lap and decided to be honest. "I have a difficult time trusting people."

"I'm the same," he said.

"But when I care about someone, I'd do anything for them. You sound like you want to take care of the Ragsdales, but I want to make myself clear as well. They may not be my family by blood, but they are in every other way that matters. I prefer to hide, but I can be a formidable opponent. Be good to them."

He cocked an eyebrow. "Did you just threaten me?"

I took a deep breath. "I did. But there's no reason to be afraid of me . . . yet."

He smiled. "I like you. You're a little weird, but I can see why Gian fell for you. You've got layers."

"Thanks. You're not as bad as I thought you'd be either."

Before he had a chance to respond to that, my phone rang. *Gian.* "Should I answer?"

Dominic shrugged.

I answered with as much confidence as I could muster. "Hey, Gian."

"What are you up to? Want to meet up for lunch?"

"I—uh—I kind of have plans."

"Oh. Okay."

He didn't ask, but I felt compelled to tell him. "I'm having lunch with your brother Dominic, his wife, and Judy."

Dominic made a walking motion with each hand and crashed them together—I believe as a suggestion I tell Gian we bumped into each other. I shook my head. I couldn't lie, and even if I could, it would never have been believable. I decided to bypass how it had happened. I said, "You should join us. Dominic, I can't believe we didn't think to invite him. Lunch was kind of a spontaneous decision that looks like it's working out perfectly."

"How are you having lunch with Dominic and Abby?"

"And Judy. We're on our way to the restaurant now. Get your butt in your car and meet us."

"Sure, but—"

I cut Gian off. "Dominic, what's the name of the restaurant again?"

Dominic relayed it, and I asked, "So you'll meet us?"

"Always," he answered.

I was still smiling after we ended our call. *Always* embodied the way Gian and I were together.

CHAPTER TWENTY-SIX

GIAN

Teagan handled lunch with the Corisis like she'd always eaten in exclusive rooms in high-priced restaurants, seeming to enjoy the experience without being awkwardly in awe of it. I hadn't expected the easy banter between Dominic and her, but I got a kick out of watching. When he nodded in Teagan's direction and smiled, it felt like another piece of a puzzle clicking into place. My relationship with Teagan had never required his approval, but it meant a lot to me that he'd given it.

It didn't surprise me that Abby got along with her. Dominic's wife had been a teacher before meeting him and had somehow remained down to earth despite their lavish lifestyle. When Teagan leaned over and whispered that she liked my family, I beamed again.

I hadn't been sure what to expect with Judy, but whatever tension had been between them wasn't there when the two of them discussed Judy going to MIT in the fall. "Under an alias, so don't tell anyone," Judy said.

"Won't that affect your ability to get a degree?" Teagan asked.

"I don't care about a piece of paper," Judy answered.

Only Judy could dismiss such an achievement as casually as she had. I didn't lecture her, though, because I was pretty sure that once she spent time surrounded with brilliant people, many of whom would be able to think circles around her, she'd discover humility. Teagan must have thought something along those lines as well, because she winked at me.

Near the end of the meal, Dominic sat back in his chair, folded his arms across his chest, and said, "Teagan, clear something up for us."

I choked on my coffee. Teagan's eyes widened, but she said, "Sure."

"Be honest. You decided to date Gian despite the clock he gave you, not because of it, correct?"

I let out a breath in relief. For a moment I'd thought Dominic was about to ask her about her work, but I hadn't given him enough credit. I'd also forgotten he was playfully competitive.

Teagan took a moment to answer, as if she, too, had been taken by surprise. She exchanged a look with me that was brimming with what looked a hell of a lot like love. "It was definitely unique, but so is Gian. I love that he isn't afraid to be himself with me." Then she turned and pinned Dominic with a question of her own. "Did you give Abby a gift when you asked her out?"

Dominic's eyes narrowed.

Judy laughed. "You don't know how they met?"

Teagan shook her head and leaned forward. "No, but I'd love to."

Abby chuckled. "I guess Judy is old enough to hear the truth."

Judy's mouth rounded. "Wait. What do you mean, the *truth*? You met in Boston and went to China with him on a business trip."

"That's all true, but where did we meet, and how did I end up flying off with him?" Abby leaned over and kissed her husband's cheek. "Your father was quite a character in the beginning."

"Do I want to know this?" Judy asked.

I gave her back a pat in support. "I'm sure even this version will be a toned-down one."

Dominic sat there shaking his head but not looking overly bothered. "Your mother was in my house."

Abby quickly interjected, "Aunt Lil was supposed to clean his brownstone, but she was sick, so I stepped in so she wouldn't lose her job."

Judy gasped. "Dad, you came on to your housekeeper?"

Dominic raised his hands in defense. "It's not like I chased her around the furniture. I ordered takeout, and we talked."

Abby put a hand on one hip. "Then he asked me how much it would cost for me to stay."

"Dad!" Judy exclaimed.

Dominic leaned down so his face was level with his wife's. There was nothing but love in either of their expressions. "And she told me where I could stick my money."

Abby raised her hand to cup one side of his face. "I wanted to punch him, but I didn't."

He took her hand and kissed it. "I wanted to make her mine, and I did."

"I wouldn't change a moment of it," Abby said in a husky voice.

"Neither would I," Dominic murmured before giving her a light kiss on the lips.

There was a drawn-out moment when they stared into each other's eyes long enough for it to become awkward for the rest of us. When Dominic raised his head, he looked over at me and said, "You still have time to up your game, Gian."

Judy covered her ears with her hands. "I know I'm old enough, but I can't hear this."

I couldn't help but add, "So you don't want to hear about the time he kidnapped her?"

Teagan laughed.

Judy lowered her hands. "That's just a running joke my parents have." She looked back and forth between them, and her mouth dropped open. "Dad!"

Dominic shrugged.

Abby turned toward Judy and put her hand over her daughter's. "He was so proud of himself, but the real challenge would have been keeping me off the plane." She sighed happily. "We should fly more."

They shared another intimate laugh that made Judy cringe.

Although I felt some sympathy for her, I loved that my brother and his wife were obviously still very happily married. I nuzzled Teagan's cheek. "Do you want to be kidnapped, Teagan? Are my gifts subpar?"

She laughed and blushed. "You're doing just fine."

Judy groaned.

I winked at Teagan. "Wouldn't want to not have a story we could embarrass our children with one day."

There was a general round of laughter. Conversation flowed easily after that. We talked about everything.

Before we left, Dominic took me aside. "I really like her, Gian."

"So do I."

He frowned. "I shouldn't have asked her to lunch without you. I—"

"You don't have to say it." He wanted to protect me. "You're not my first big brother."

He nodded. "This is good—what we're doing now. We should do this again."

I hugged him the same way I would have any of my brothers, and when I stepped back, he was smiling. "I'd really like that."

Teagan drove back to my place with me. We made love slowly, tenderly, like it was as much of a promise as an act. Afterward, cuddled to my side, she told me about how Dominic had met her on the street and shared what they'd talked about. It was amazing how unfazed I could be by news like that when it was given postorgasm. I did understand why he'd done it, but I would not accept that she'd had a moment of fear at his hands. That would never happen again.

"He wants to pay off Fara's medical bills," Teagan said.

"We all saw that coming." I kissed her forehead.

"He said he could make it look like they received a grant. The Ragsdales are too proud to take money from Dominic, but they've suffered long enough. I don't see the harm in that."

"I don't either. It'll be a win-win. The hospital will probably get a new wing." I snapped my fingers in the air. "Or a new research facility."

"Because Dominic has an extra one of those just lying around?"

"He does, actually." I told her the story of how refusing it had been the first time I'd said no clearly to him. "It changed things between us—in a good way."

She nodded. "For me I think it was when I threatened him."

My mouth dropped open. "You did?"

"I did." She grinned, and I fell even more in love with her. "No one messes with my family. Not even my potential future family."

I hugged her closer. Any worry I'd had that she couldn't hold her own with my family fell away. "I love you, Teagan Becket."

She melted against me. "I love you too, Gian Romano."

The kiss we shared was long and tender. When I raised my head, I said, "You survived meeting the Corisis . . . are you ready to meet the Romanos?"

Her eyes widened, and she blinked a few times before answering, but just when I was ready to tell her she didn't have to if she wasn't ready, she said, "Yes."

CHAPTER TWENTY-SEVEN

GIAN

The morning of the day I was set to introduce Teagan to my family, I drove to get breakfast from a local coffee shop so I could have a few minutes alone. Bringing Teagan home was a big move, and in many ways it felt right—but I'd found it difficult to sleep the night before, and I'd woken up feeling uneasy.

Thankfully there was someone who could always be counted on to help me sort through my feelings, and he was an early riser. I parked outside the coffee shop and called him. "Morning, Dad."

"Morning. Don't eat before you come; your mother has a huge meal planned. She's so excited. She wants to fly down to meet Teagan's parents. Or fly them up. If you're thinking about making some kind of announcement today, you might want them here."

Breathe. "About that. I need to talk something out with you—just to get it out of my head."

"Did you have an argument?"

"No. Nothing like that." I hesitated before sharing it. On the one hand, I didn't want my parents to have anything but a great impression of Teagan. On the other hand, I needed to talk this out with someone who wouldn't judge me or Teagan. There was something I could no longer ignore. "Dad, do you think you need to know everything about the person you marry?"

"You can never know everything. I'm still learning about your mother after all these years of marriage."

"I'm not talking about little things like favorite soap. I'm talking about big secrets."

My father was quiet for a moment. "I suppose it depends on the nature of the secret. Your mother and I have always been honest with each other, even when it was difficult. She had secrets she kept from everyone, even her parents—big secrets, like Sebastian's parentage—but she didn't keep them from me."

My gut twisted painfully. I hadn't pushed Teagan to tell me the nature of her project. I wanted her to tell me when she was ready, but could we move forward with something like that unresolved?

Could I get engaged to a woman I didn't fully know?

Marry her?

Start a family with someone who held back an entire side of herself?

"I love Teagan, Dad, but I'm wondering if it's not too early to bring her home. Mom will expect me to have a ring ready, but I don't know if that's where we are yet."

"I'll talk to your mother. The most important thing to us is that you're happy. Are things good between you and Teagan?"

"So good. I like who I am when I'm with her. We get each other, and I miss her as soon as she walks away. I've never felt that way about anyone before. This is the woman I want to spend the rest of my life with, but maybe I'm rushing things."

"Love tends to bring out the impulsive side of people. You already have all the answers you're looking for from me, but if you need to hear the words, I'll say them. Take all the time you need, Gian. Just because your brothers proposed right away doesn't mean you have to. You can bring Teagan here to meet us without it becoming a wedding-planning session. I'll tell everyone she's special to you and that you're figuring things out. That's all they need to know."

"Thanks, Dad."

"If you have reservations, Gian, it's always okay to take things slowly. I don't know if I would propose to someone if I knew they were keeping a large secret from me. Marriage is hard enough without adding an unknown like that into it."

"I could give her an ultimatum, but I don't want to. I want her to *want* to tell me."

"Because you're a good man, and you know that a lasting relationship requires trust and respect."

"Yes, but Dad—what if she never tells me?"

"She will. If she's the one for you, she will."

"Thanks. We're still coming over today, but tell Mom I'm not planning to make any kind of announcement yet."

"Will do. And Gian . . ."

"Yes, Dad?"

"Your mother didn't instantly open up to me. Lust is instant. Trust takes time."

CHAPTER TWENTY-EIGHT

TEAGAN

"You look nervous," Gian said in a tone I was sure was meant to reassure me. *Do you know what has probably never, in the entire history of humankind, helped a person calm down? Telling them they look nervous.*

I didn't say it, though, because Gian looked pretty unsettled himself. We were sitting outside his parents' home, neither of us making a move to exit the car. I knew him well enough to know his moods. "What's wrong?" I asked.

He didn't answer at first, which was not a good sign. Something was definitely wrong. "It's nothing." He undid his seat belt and went to open his car door.

I placed my hand on his arm to stop him. "Gian, look at me."

He turned and did. There was something he wanted to tell me, but he was holding back. I said, "One of the things that drew me to you in the beginning was how you didn't play games. I know when something is wrong—it's right there in your face. Whatever it is, just say it."

He cupped my cheek. "I'm glad you're here."

"But?"

He held my gaze. "I'm not sure saying it will make it any better."

I kept my breathing even and told my brain to calm the fuck down. "If it helps, I'm the kind of person who would always rather know—no matter what it is."

"I've told you how traditional my family is." He laced his hand with mine.

"You did."

"It means something when we bring someone home."

My heart was racing in my chest. If he proposed, I didn't know what I'd say. I wanted to be with him, could picture forever with him, but we hadn't even had our first fight. I didn't know what to say, so I just sat there in a mild panic waiting for him to continue.

"It's usually followed by an engagement."

Okay, now I was barely breathing.

He continued, "But we're not there yet, and I don't want you to feel pressured if people talk as if we are. We'll get there when we get there. If anyone says anything about us getting married or having children, just translate that conversation into *We like you, and we hope you become one of us.* It doesn't have to be more than that."

I released my seat belt and kissed him then. His consideration for my feelings was one of the reasons I'd fallen for him. Some people said they were there to support you, but they were serving their own agendas. With Gian I really felt like we were building something together. "Is that all you're worried about?"

He gave me another long look, then brushed his lips over mine. "Let's go in."

There wasn't much I could say except, "Okay."

I had a pretty good idea what he didn't want to bring up. I didn't want to talk about it right then either. Things had been going so well with us I'd convinced myself keeping my work a secret from him was a nonissue. It was if we were just fucking and spending time together.

That was not all we were, though.

What I couldn't understand was why I couldn't just tell him—blurt it out with the swiftness of ripping off a Band-Aid. Either I trusted him or I didn't, right? *It should be that simple.*

Why didn't it feel that way in my head?

I thought about it in circles until I started to fear I'd ruin what we had just by thinking myself right out of love. I couldn't tell anyone about NYD, but I'd told Riley.

What was the worst-case scenario? I could discover Gian never actually loved me, that he was only pretending in order to gain access to my lab. Did I really think he was capable of that? And if I did, did that mean I didn't actually love him? If I admitted my fears to him, would I become someone he couldn't love?

Gian's voice interrupted and brought me back to the moment. "If you don't get out of the car, you will never taste my mother's cooking. Plus she's watching us from the doorway."

I shook my head to clear it and got out of the car. "Sorry."

He took my hands in his. "If you're not ready to meet them, just tell me, and we'll go."

Yeah, that would be a great first impression to give his family. "How about you? Are you ready?"

He gave my hands a light squeeze. "Yes and no. I didn't realize until this morning how emotional an experience it would be for me. This will always be the first time you met my parents."

So no pressure. I decided we needed to lighten up the mood a little. "But it won't be the last, so even if we fuck it up, we'll have endless opportunities to patch things up."

A slow smile spread across his face. "You're right."

"Not that I intend to fuck it up."

His expression relaxed. "Me either, but you're right," he repeated. "We have endless opportunities to do this well."

I fought an urge to apologize to him for holding back at all. What would the day have been like had I already told him everything?

He tapped my forehead lightly. "Hey, don't overthink this. In the words of my father, lust is instant. Trust takes time."

I cocked my head to one side. "Do I want to know what you said to your father that solicited that bit of wisdom?"

He grinned. "Probably not."

I would have followed up with another question, but his father had joined his mother at the door, and they were both now waving to us. I took a fortifying breath and said, "You told me not to eat so I'd be hungry. Feed me, Gian Romano, before I get hangry."

He chuckled and gave me a quick kiss while murmuring, "Maybe I want to see you a little angry. You did promise to show me how you say *fuck you*."

I flushed as I remembered I'd made that sexy joke on our nondate that had started with us ripping each other's clothing off. "You're killing me. I can't think about this right now."

His grin only widened. "It was a poorly timed recollection. I shouldn't be sporting a boner when I introduce you to my parents."

"I can't help you there." I laughed.

He growled, "Not here, anyway." Then he straightened and made a face.

"What are you doing?" I asked.

"I'm flexing my thigh muscles and thinking about baseball." He winked. A moment later he said, "All set; let's go."

"Wow. I had no idea there was an off switch."

"It's all about directing blood flow elsewhere. Flexing a major muscle for thirty seconds or so when coupled with a nonsexual thought is anecdotally documented as an effective method. Most research is based on dealing with dysfunctions, but once you understand how your body works, you realize you have so much more control over it than most people believe. That's why meditation masturbation is so popular with some."

Although it was a fascinating subject, I shook my head and stepped back. "That's not a topic for tonight. Focus on something else."

"Always difficult to do around you," he joked. We were laughing as we walked toward his parents.

They each greeted me with a tight hug that took me by surprise. His mother stood back, holding me at arm's length, and looked me over. "Gian has told us so much about you. It's wonderful to be able to put a face to a name."

His father said, "Come in. Come in. Everyone is here and excited to meet you."

Everyone. That sounds like a lot of people. I'd never been good with crowds. I must have said it aloud, because Gian bent down and whispered in my ear, "I'll guide you through the mix. If you forget someone's name, just give my hand a double squeeze, and I'll work it into the conversation."

Gian's little show of support eased my anxiety. I wasn't walking in there alone. "Thank you," I whispered back.

We walked through a house that was surprisingly modest, especially considering Romano Superstores' success. The first room we passed had several contemporary couches set in such a way that people could gather in groups. It looked comfortable. On one side there was a large flat-screen television with children's toys scattered in front of it. His mother said, "It's a beautiful day, so everyone is outside. Teagan, would you like anything to drink before we join them?"

"Water?" I wasn't requesting anything that might relax me into saying something stupid.

"Sure, we'll cut through the kitchen on our way out." She led the way.

His father lingered beside us. "I heard you met the Corisis."

"I did. They all seem very nice."

"That's good," his father said. "Not everyone can see past the hype to the good people they are. I was guilty of that in the beginning myself. It takes time to get to know people—to trust them."

I looked from Gian to his father and back. It reminded me of the advice he'd said his father had given him about lust and trust. My heart warmed. So much of what I loved about Gian was evident in his father.

"Dad," Gian said.

His father smiled. "I'm not saying anything; I just want Teagan to know that we are happy she is here and that we don't have any expectations. She can take all the time she needs."

Gian's mother returned with a glass of water for me. She took one look at her husband and asked, "What happened in the one minute I was gone? Your father looks guilty."

His father shook his head. "I was telling Teagan she doesn't have to feel pressured just because she is the first woman Gian has brought home. These things take time."

"Basil," his mother said, "you're making her feel uncomfortable."

"No," I said in a rush, "I appreciate the sentiment."

His mother must have taken that as an open door she could walk through, because she said, "You can tell me it's none of my business—"

Gian spoke over her. "Mom, stop."

"It's okay, Gian," I assured him.

His mother continued, "Have you discussed children?"

I exchanged a look with Gian. "We have, actually. The number we tossed around was five."

I thought she started sending prayers of gratitude upward in Italian, but I wasn't sure. It sounded like she was thanking God, and she looked happy. She grabbed both of my cheeks and gave me a loud kiss on the forehead before walking away with her husband.

"Now you've done it," Gian joked while hugging me to his side as we followed behind his parents. "After you've birthed four and try to tell me we're done, I'll remind you of this conversation. The fifth child is your fault."

I laughed and kissed him on the cheek. "I believe you're the one who came up with the number."

As soon as we stepped out of the house onto the back porch, a man approached who had the same jet-black hair and dark eyes as Kal,

Dominic, and Riley. Sebastian. "As someone with four children, let me assure you five is four too many."

The woman beside him laughed. "He doesn't mean that." She held out her hand for me to shake. "Hi, Teagan. I'm Heather, and this sweet but grumpy man is Sebastian."

I shook her hand, then Sebastian's. "It's nice to meet you."

Gian stepped away from me to hug both of them, then slipped his arm back around my waist. Before we had a chance to say anything further, another couple approached. This brother was drop-dead gorgeous. I wasn't interested, but I'd have to have been dead to not have noticed him. It was fun to guess Gian's brothers' names based on what he'd told me about each of them. This one had to be Mauricio.

When he introduced himself and confirmed I was correct, I clapped my hands once in victory. He took it in stride by saying, "See, Wren, women still break into applause when they see me." He nuzzled his wife's neck. "I've still got it."

Laughing, she winked at me and said, "You've got *something*, but they sell ointments now that can clear it up quick." She was lovely—not beautiful in a flashy way but the perfect complement to him. I bet she grounded him.

Mauricio growled playfully. "If you're lucky, I'll let you apply it."

Gian chuckled. "Reel it in, guys. Teagan doesn't know you well enough to know you're not usually like this." Then he smiled down at me. "I'm just kidding; they're always like this." He hugged both of them in greeting as well. It was truly beautiful to see how easily they expressed their love for each other.

Mauricio smiled at me. "Hey, I have to get all the cuddles I can in while we're here. We have three boys. When you meet them, you'll see why we drop in bed exhausted each night."

"TMI, Mauricio. TMI," Gian joked.

"Oh, you wait," Mauricio parried back. "We'll see how tired you are once your kids come."

There was a general chuckle.

"We're hoping for five," I said, although once the words were out of my mouth, I wasn't entirely sure why I'd said them.

"Five," Sebastian said, "is for quitters. Go for a full dozen." The twinkle in his eyes invited me inside their private joke.

"See," his wife interjected. "He loves to joke that we have too many, but he wants to have one more."

"Speaking of one more," a man said as he approached and gave Gian a hug, then shook my hand. He was good looking in a quieter, slightly rounder way. Not fat, but not as cut as his brothers. "My name's Christof."

His wife hugged Gian, then gave me a bone-crushing handshake. She was stunning, but man, was she also strong. "And I'm McKenna. It's so nice to meet you."

I flexed my hand. My little keyboard-warrior fingers were no match for Gian's mechanic sister-in-law. "You too. You're the one with the racetrack, correct? That must be exciting."

"It has been a dream come true." She hugged Christof. "Christof and I have two little girls who I hope will one day take over our business."

Christof chuckled. "You should see them fly around the track already in their little battery-operated cars. I see a lot of gray hair in my future."

"What do you do?" McKenna asked me.

I froze. Gian's hand went to my lower back and gave me a reassuring rub. I didn't want to start my relationship with his family with a lie, but I also wasn't about to discuss the nature of my real work with them. "I—uh—I own a small printshop. I also have a few side projects that keep me busy."

Mauricio nodded toward Gian. "We keep trying to get Gian to come work with us. Wren designs prosthetics that integrate AI. Imagine limbs that are intuitive and natural looking but can also be adapted to

219

work as tools. You can literally make a call from your wrist, chart your blood pressure, or have medicines automatically injected on a schedule. You name it, and it's becoming possible. It's fascinating stuff. If you're ever interested in coming out to see our facility, we'd love to show you around."

"I'd like that," I said, smiling up at Gian. I'd hoped his family would accept me, but I hadn't expected to like them as much as I did. I loved not being the smartest person in the room.

As Wren described what she was designing in more detail, I wished I could do the same. There was a fine line in business between being careful and being paranoid. Designs were appropriated all the time. Still, were these the kind of people I thought would do that?

I asked myself the same question after I was introduced to the herd of children in the backyard. There was a wholesomeness about the Romanos that made me want to believe I could be myself with them.

We ate outside at two long tables, one for the adults and another for the children. It was hours of loud conversation, lots of laughter, bottles of Italian wine, and good food. Oh, so much food.

Leaving took almost as much time as arriving had, but this time I was hugged by everyone as well. And it felt right.

That night Gian made love to me with such sweet tenderness I almost burst into tears. Afterward, even while he slept, I lay awake looking at the ceiling. After getting a glimpse of what life would be like with Gian and his family, I had a clear five- and ten-year goal. I wanted to be a Romano.

I considered waking Gian up and just telling him everything. I'd let the whole thing build up so much in my head, though, that I tried and couldn't do it.

I didn't know what that said about me.

About us.

Could I be so in love with someone and also be the reason, myself, that we didn't work out?

I remembered Riley telling me, *"You get tangled up in your head sometimes and can't get out of your own way."*

That was exactly how I felt.

I sent her a quick text asking if we could meet up the next day, then closed my eyes, chased sleep, and told myself if anyone could untangle me, it was her.

CHAPTER TWENTY-NINE

TEAGAN

I met Riley at a park halfway between where we each lived. Despite the early hour there were already children on the playground and parents chasing after them. It felt like the perfect place to talk about where I wanted my life to go and figure out what was holding me back.

"I brought coffee," she said as she approached. She'd gone to my favorite coffee shop. I took a whiff of the steam coming from it. And she'd bought my favorite flavor. I wrapped my arms around her and gave her a tight hug.

"Hey, hey, easy there. I don't want to wear it." Her warning was accompanied by laughter and a warm hug from her as well.

"Sorry," I said as I stepped back.

"Don't be." We started walking side by side. "I love to see you this happy. Gian has been so good for you. How was his family?"

I had so much to tell her, but her life had also gone through some major changes recently, and that was equally important. "We can get to that. First, tell me what it's like to have the Corisis in your life."

She tipped her head to one side. "Half in. I haven't been able to convince Kal to meet them yet. He's afraid spending time with them will upset Mom. I hate having a secret from her, but she has a lot of anger toward them, and I don't want it to shape my relationship with them. Nicole is so sweet, and her husband, Stephan, obviously adores her and their children. They're so down to earth. You can tell family is what matters to them most. I'm so grateful they found us."

"And Dominic?"

Riley's eyebrows rose, but she was smiling. "He's a lot. I didn't know what to think of him at first. He calls me every day, though. Just a quick check-in to see how I'm doing. It's so sweet. Even Kal doesn't do that, and I consider us close. His wife is so easy to talk to. Even though she's older, I feel like we could be friends."

"And Judy?"

Riley paused, then said, "I'm sure she will be one hell of a woman, but she has a little growing up to do. She's a little . . ."

"Full of herself?" I supplied for her.

Riley chuckled. "I didn't want to say it. Her heart is in the right place. She really wants to have a relationship with me; I just get the feeling she doesn't think I'm as intelligent as she is. I didn't realize conversations could be minicompetitions."

"She'll grow out of that." I sipped my coffee, then said, "Some of that confidence is overcompensation for insecurities she doesn't admit to having. Imagine growing up as she did, surrounded by not only wealthy but some truly brilliant people. Dominic's business partner, Jake Walton, is the son of two of the biggest names in early computer coding and encryption. Jeremy Kater—well, everyone knows his name in the tech industry. Even Dominic's security team are top in their field. There is an unspoken expectation of excellence that must be a lot to live up to. When I heard Judy's little brother, Leonardo, was working with private tutors because he was testing out of academic grades too fast to remain in school, I felt a little bad for Judy. There's no room for mediocrity in her life."

Riley stopped walking and nodded. "I didn't see her that way, but now that I have, I bet you're right. It would explain so much. She's not trying to prove that I'm stupid; she's trying to prove that she's smart."

"That's my take on her, anyway."

Riley smiled. "I'm going to be more patient with her. She needs someone like me in her life. I embrace mediocrity."

I shook my head. "That's not how I see you."

"You know I find nothing wrong with not needing to be the first in line, the tallest, thinnest, richest, or smartest person in the room. Life is about so much more than that."

We started walking again. "Yes, but that's not the same as being mediocre. I'd call that being a balanced and mature human being. There are all different kinds of intelligence. You're good with people, and you know what you want. When it comes to relationships, you move forward with a confidence I've never had. I admire that about you. I often feel awkward around people, and when it comes to figuring out what is going on in my own head, I'm a mess."

"Are things not going well with Gian?" Her expression turned concerned.

"No, they're going so well I'm afraid I'm going to screw it up. I love him. Not just, *oh, I love this man.* I mean—I'm all in. I want to spend the rest of my life with him. I met his family and adored them. We are in such a good place . . . but I'm still holding back, and that scares me. I'm ready to go see a professional about it because my heart and my head say this is the man for me. So why can't I let go and trust him with what I'm working on? You said I'd know when the time is right. Shouldn't this be the right time?"

Riley stopped in front of a bench. "You're like a pipe that is all blocked up. You need to get some of this stuff out of your head. I don't have anywhere to be today. Talk. I'll just listen. If I think you need professional intervention, I'll tell you."

She would too. I sat beside her on the bench. "Where do I start?"

"Doesn't matter. Just let it out."

I told her how being with him was rounding me out. From the great sex to the way he inspired me, I was me—but a better version of me—when I was with him. I told her that although I trusted Gian, once I told him about NYD, everything I'd worked so hard on would be vulnerable.

"You trust me with it."

"You don't know billionaires capable of swooping in and taking it from me."

"Ha. Ha." She gave me a side-look. "And you're wrong—not only do I know them, but I'm related to them."

She was. "And that doesn't bother me."

"Because you know I'd never betray your trust. Loving anyone makes you vulnerable, and you don't handle that well. But you can't go through life trusting only me. Has Gian given you any reason to believe you can't trust him?"

"No. Not a thing." In fact, he'd always been up front with me. "He tells me everything. Sometimes too much."

"Then have some faith in him. Love requires that, Teagan—faith. Once you believe in someone, everything changes, and things you didn't think were possible suddenly are."

Of all the people I could have become friends with, I was so grateful Riley and I had found each other. "A leap of faith."

"Dare to dream. If things worked out the way you wanted them to, what would your life look like?"

"I wouldn't spend so much time alone. I'd really like to have someone I could share my work as well as my life with."

"Then make that happen."

"Just like that?"

"Just like that. Be brave enough to voice what you want, and it'll come to you."

That wasn't how things worked, or was it? The last time I'd done it, Gian had appeared. The world was full of things we had yet to understand. Sure. "Dear Universe, thank you for sending me Mr. Right. Now, if possible, let's close the deal. You know, give me the whole 'marriage, kids, happily ever after' crap. And while you're at it, I'd also like to find a way to work with him."

Riley laughed. "I love it. Now all you have to do is figure out what kind of project the two of you can work on together."

"Wait, I thought this was about the universe delivering."

"How can you be so smart and not have figured out that *you're* the universe you're asking for help from? That's why it works. Once you put it out there, it happens because you make it happen. So make it happen."

CHAPTER THIRTY

GIAN

As we approached the end of another week together, Teagan and I took a walk after dinner. "How would you feel about another dinner at my parents'?" I asked.

Her hand tightened around mine. "I'd love it."

My heart was beating fast as I added, "We could make it a regular thing."

The smile she gave me was one I was sure would always make me want to move heaven and earth for her. "I'd like that. My parents know about you now. I promised I'd ask you to fly down with me."

Her declaration rocked through me, but I didn't want to make it into a big deal. I joked, "Commercial or private plane?"

Her eyes flew to mine. "You have a private plane?"

I raised and lowered a shoulder. "You have no idea the toys I have access to." Then I winked. I didn't really care how we traveled as long as we were together.

"Speaking of toys, I have a surprise for you."

That was all it took for the majority of my blood to head on down to my cock. "Sounds like a surprise I'll enjoy."

"I'm hoping you will," she said. "I think you'll love it. Unless you don't. I know you don't like having things done for you, but this is for us. And if you hate it, I'll totally understand. No pressure."

I hugged her to me. "Hey, if you did something for us, I'm sure I'll love it."

"Would you like to see it now? I'm too excited to wait."

I pulled her into my arms and settled her against proof that I was equally excited by whatever she had planned. "Now works for me."

She flushed and writhed against me, then cupped my face in her hands. "Seriously, don't feel like you have to love it; this is just me putting what I'd like out into the universe."

"I'm sure I'll love whatever it is." I would have promised to love anything while she was rubbing herself back and forth against my hard cock.

In a flash we were driving back toward Lockton. Not toward her apartment, though. Also, not toward her shop. When we pulled up in front of what looked like a storage facility with an ample amount of graffiti on the outside of it, I was intrigued. "Interesting location choice."

She unlocked the outer door. "It doesn't look like much from the outside, but just wait until you see the inside."

I followed her down a dark hallway I wanted to tell her she would never walk down again. Too secluded. Too potentially dangerous.

"Don't touch anything," she warned as she walked. "I have all entrances booby-trapped. You don't want to trip any of them."

At first I thought she was kidding, but she sounded serious, so I kept my hands at my sides. We stopped at the end of a hallway where there were no doors, just a fire alarm box. She lifted the lever, revealing a panel. She typed in a set of numbers, then put her finger on a pad. A light flickered, and a huge section of the wall folded away, revealing another door. This one had a camera that scanned her face; then a voice began to ask her questions. She answered each one succinctly. Then another door opened. I followed her through it.

One side of the room was covered with computer screens, cameras, and a variety of T-shirts. Teagan turned and held her hand out for me to take. "This is NYD, an acronym for Now You Don't. It's an AI I've been working on since before my time at MIT. Together we are designing visual designs capable of rendering people and objects invisible to other AIs. In the world of cameras being literally everywhere and AIs taking on the role of making sense of all that footage, invisibility will be nearly impossible. Nearly. If NYD and I do this right, people could choose when and how they want AIs to recognize them."

Wow. Just wow. This was not what I'd imagined she was working on, but it was fucking amazing. "Governments would pay top dollar for something like that."

She shook her head. "It belongs in the hands of the people. How can we call ourselves the land of the free if every move we make is recorded and our location is constantly tracked? I won't sell it, but I do want to perfect it in case the world ever needs it." She placed her hand on another monitor. "This is NYSM. It's an adversarial AI. Until I'm ready to start testing NYD against real-world AIs, it's NYSM's job to challenge NYD to continue to outsmart it. NYSM learns and adapts also, though. The work I'm doing now is charting how long NYSM can be fooled by a certain visual and how much the visual needs to change for it to be fooled by an image again after it has realized it's there. The best way I can explain the process is . . . imagine I showed you a photo of an apple that had been grown to look exactly like a car. You don't associate apples with cars, so your mind would try to make sense of the visual. Most likely your mind would think it's a strange-looking red car, completely disregarding apple features that don't make sense. If you show an AI certain images, they will disregard a person's face above them because a face wouldn't make sense in their interpretation of the visual. But if I told you I had found a way to grow apples in the shape of cars, you would look for apple features on the car and would likely see them. If the AI knows it is being fooled, it learns to look for nonsense features and will recognize a face even if it doesn't make sense. However, if the image is tweaked, current AIs have to learn that lesson again. What I'm trying to create is something that evolves just ahead of what it needs to fool. To grow, NYD must always be challenged."

"Can I be your adversarial human?" I joked only because I was floored by her work as well as her passion for it.

She took the question seriously, though. "You do challenge me to be a better version of myself. However, I don't see you in an oppositional role, and I have no plans to replace you."

"That's a good thing," I said lightly. "I'd rather see us as an unbeatable team."

"A team. Yes, that's what we could be. Even here, if you'd like that. I'd love your input on ways I can improve my programs."

"I'm not sure what I could add, but you have my full support."

"Would you like to see what NYD is capable of?"

"Absolutely." Over the next half hour I asked countless questions that she answered without hesitation. I didn't want to know just about her programs but also about what had inspired them. When I realized how serious she was about keeping NYD a secret as a safeguard for humanity, I fell even harder for her. My woman was a fucking hero, and the best kind—a humble one. Eventually, I looped my arms around her waist and held her close. "Thank you for letting me in. I can see why you're protective of your work."

"I thought this was something I needed to do alone, but I see now that I don't have to. We could save the world together."

Most people would be joking when they said something like that, but she was serious, and there was nothing I could imagine wanting more than to be part of her quiet crusade to protect humanity. "I'd be honored," I murmured against her lips. "This is truly genius. What an amazing surprise."

She tipped her head back and laid her hands flat on my chest. "This isn't your surprise."

"No?"

"No, the surprise is I found a way I can share in your dream as well." She raised her voice. "NYD, open the Love Shack."

The wall on the opposite side of her computers slid away, revealing another wall of technology but also a wide variety of sex toys and even a *Kama Sutra* sex chair. My mouth dropped open. She stepped back, took me by the hand, and led me across the room to this new section.

"You built me a sex dungeon?" Now that was a thoughtful gift.

"No." She laughed. "I built you a sex *lab*. Although I'd like to make clear there are only two test subjects allowed in this lab—you and me. Before you say it, I know how you felt about Dominic buying a research facility for you. This isn't like that. I haven't done any of the work; all I've done is make space for you in my life."

Never had I thought it possible to love a person as much as I loved her in that moment. She didn't have to worry that I'd feel the same way about her gift as I had about Dominic's. A sex lab was the perfect gift. "I am *not* complaining."

She placed her hand on the top of one of the computer monitors. "This might not look like much yet, but I had an idea for your research. What if you linked AI to a biometric vibrator? Hear me out; imagine a sex toy that learns how to please a person by responding and learning from both physical and verbal feedback. You could create something that could do what you did for that woman you helped with her sexuality. Not a robot, just an intuitive instrument with information but also insight into your body's actual responses. It could guide a person toward better sex. Guide couples. Data-driven, multiorgasmic sex. A teacher and a tool. You could create it here, then either market it or open-source share the technology. No one need ever know." She searched my face so earnestly. "And we could work together—on your research as well as mine."

I loved it. Absolutely loved the idea of sharing a secret lair with her and working on both projects together. "What would I tell my family?" I asked aloud, although the question was really meant for me.

"You could open a coffee shop next to my printshop." She snapped her fingers. "No, wait, didn't you say your family in Italy makes wine? Open a shop that sells only their wine. It doesn't have to be successful, but it's a great cover."

I twirled her in my arms. "Yes. Yes to all of it. This is all mind-blowingly good."

"Are you sure? I know it's a lot." She nodded toward the sex chair. "But I thought working here might involve trying that."

All my blood headed south. "Definitely. And there is no time like the present to christen my new workplace." Out of curiosity, I asked, "Not this time, but in the future you'd really let me measure your orgasms?"

She waggled her eyebrows. "Only if you let me measure yours. Then graph them."

She knew the way to my heart. "You're on." As we held each other's gaze and began to strip off our clothing, I was shaken by how much she meant to me. She not only accepted me for who I was but had found a way to give life to a yearning in me I hadn't dared allow to become a dream. I paused after dropping my pants to the floor. "Teagan."

She shot her underwear across the room. "Yes?"

"Thank you. For all of this as well as for trusting me with your secret."

"You're welcome. When I thought about it, I realized both of our dreams were about making the world a better place. I love the idea of helping people understand their own bodies more." Buck naked before me against a backdrop of enough sex toys to open a store, she blushed.

"I don't know if my goals are as noble as yours, but there's nowhere I'd rather be than here with you—working together."

She looked relieved. "I'm glad you like your Love Shack."

I laughed. "I love it. How could I not?" I closed the distance between us and kissed her deeply. "I love you, and now I know just the surprise to plan for you."

"Do you?" Between kisses she asked, "Will it top this?"

I lifted her so her legs wound around my hips and headed toward one of her gifts for me. "Nothing could ever top this, but I hope I can still pull off something memorable."

All desire to talk faded away when I lowered her so she straddled the chair, and my mind filled with all the possibilities for how we could enjoy it. "Since I haven't yet created the tool that tells me what you want, why don't you?"

Taking my request literally, Teagan listed several things I did that she really enjoyed. I laughed, lowered myself to my knees before her, turned her, and swung her legs up over my shoulders. "I can already see that I'm going to love my new job."

CHAPTER THIRTY-ONE

TEAGAN

Each time I thought my life with Gian couldn't get better, it did. He bought the building where my printshop was and renovated the shop next to mine into a liquor store that sold only wine from Montalcino, Italy.

Riley still worked at my shop, although she was considering going back to college. Affording it was no longer an issue. Dominic was piecing together what his father had tried to destroy. What he wanted more than anything else was to just be a part of their lives.

I wished Kal could see him in that light. Kal still refused to meet with him. The last time I'd asked, Fara still hadn't known that Riley was spending time with the Corisis. It was a sore subject with Riley, so we avoided talking about it, but I hoped time would bring them all together.

I hated all the damage Antonio Corisi had inflicted on those around him, but I couldn't regret that he'd existed. Without him, so many of the people I loved wouldn't have ever been born.

"Isn't this exciting?" Judy asked beside me in a grandstand full of Corisis, Romanos, and Beckets. Judy had wanted to be closer, so we were on the bottom level, while most of the family was gathered higher, where there was shade. When I'd told my parents they were invited to watch an informal stock car race at Decker Park, they had surprised me by flying up. They'd arrived a couple of days earlier, which had given them time to get to know the Romanos first.

Maybe the change was more within me than in them, but our relationship seemed warmer. I let go of the idea I'd had of what things were like between us and just let my happiness to see them again guide me. "It really is wonderful," I said.

"I can't believe Nicole is racing as well. She doesn't have a competitive bone in her body."

"I'm surprised you're not on that racetrack."

Judy shrugged. "I wanted to be with you. Plus, Dad didn't think it was a good idea. He's probably afraid I'll beat him."

More likely it was a generational thing. The racers that day were all of Gian's brothers as well as Nicole and Riley. The only one missing was Kal. I sighed.

I didn't know who to root for. Of course, I'd have loved to see Gian win, but I was pretty sure Dominic would take the race, since I'd heard he had the most expensive car on the track. Regardless of who made it across the finish line first, the beauty of the day was that they were all together. "I wish Fara were here."

"She will be one day," Judy said. "There's the green flag. Hang on; it gets loud."

Seven cars roared by on a track that was three lanes wide. The first lap was no surprise. Dominic was in the lead, Gian behind him, the others vying for spots after them. "Do you think Gian has a chance to win?" I asked.

"I set him up with a car that could do it. The rest is up to him," Judy said.

Dominic and Gian made it a full lap ahead of the rest. "What happens now?" I asked.

"The blue flag with the yellow stripe just signaled the drivers to yield to Dad and Gian because they're a lap ahead."

"Gian pulled ahead," I exclaimed with a clap.

Judy was all smiles, watching me as much as she was watching the race. "Who knows—he just might win."

The cars behind him closed around Dominic's car, boxing him in. "Oh no. It's a coup. They aren't letting Dominic get by. Is that legal?"

Judy shrugged. "All is fair, I guess."

For the next lap, Gian held his lead. The cars behind him shifted positions, which made room for Dominic to pull ahead, but he didn't. It began to look more like they were playing at racing than actually competing.

As they approached the finish line, all the cars began to slow. "What's wrong?"

Judy leaned forward. "I don't know. I can't tell from here."

Gian got out of his car and stood beside it. A banner unrolled from a wire above. It read: I LOVE YOU, TEAGAN BECKET. MARRY ME. GIAN.

I laughed when I saw his name at the end of the proposal. Did he think I wouldn't know who was proposing?

I leaned over the railing and yelled, "Yes!"

"I can't hear you," he yelled back.

I turned to Judy. "Looks like I have to head down there." Then a thought occurred to me. "Did you know they were doing this?"

"Of course. That's why I stayed with you. We're family now."

"Yes, we are." I threw my arms around her and gave her a tight hug. "Thank you."

"I'm the one you're supposed to be hugging," Gian joked from below.

"So impatient," I said with a smile and sprinted down a couple of stairs and through a gate that let me out onto the racetrack.

He met me halfway, lifted me up into his arms, and swung me around. "So how does becoming a Romano and having more kids than we can handle sound to you?"

I threw my arms around his neck and kissed him with every bit of love in me. By the time he raised his head, he was flushed and grinning. "Should I take that as a yes?"

"Always."

ABOUT THE AUTHOR

Ruth Cardello is a *New York Times* bestselling author who loves writing about rich alpha men and the strong women who tame them. She was born the youngest of eleven children in a small city in northern Rhode Island. She's lived in Boston, Paris, Orlando, New York, and Rhode Island again before moving to Massachusetts, where she now lives with her husband and three children. Before turning her attention to writing, Ruth was an educator for two decades, including eleven years as a kindergarten teacher. Learn about Ruth's new releases by signing up for her newsletter at www.RuthCardello.com.